KT-568-747

The
Neighbour

FIONA CUMMINS

PAN BOOKS

First published 2019 by Macmillan

First published in paperback 2019 by Macmillan

This edition first published 2019 by Pan Books
an imprint of Pan Macmillan
The Smithson, 6 Briset Street, London ECIM 5NR
Associated companies throughout the world
www.panmacmillan.com

ISBN 978-1-5098-7693-8

Copyright © Fiona Cummins 2019

The right of Fiona Cummins to be identified as the
author of this work has been asserted by her in accordance
with the Copyright, Designs and Patents Act 1988.

All rights reserved. No part of this publication may be reproduced,
stored in a retrieval system, or transmitted, in any form, or by any means
(electronic, mechanical, photocopying, recording or otherwise)
without the prior written permission of the publisher.

Pan Macmillan does not have any control over, or any responsibility for,
any author or third-party websites referred to in or on this book.

1 3 5 7 9 8 6 4 2

A CIP catalogue record for this book is available from the British Library

Map artwork by Fred van Deelen

Printed and bound by CPI Group (UK) Ltd, Croydon, CRO 4YY

This book is sold subject to the condition that it shall not, by way of
trade or otherwise, be lent, hired out, or otherwise circulated without
the publisher's prior consent in any form of binding or cover other than
that in which it is published and without a similar condition including
this condition being imposed on the subsequent purchaser.

Visit www.panmacmillan.com to read more about all our books
and to buy them. You will also find features, author interviews and
news of any author events, and you can sign up for e-newsletters
so that you're always first to hear about our new releases.

For Mum and Dad, with love always

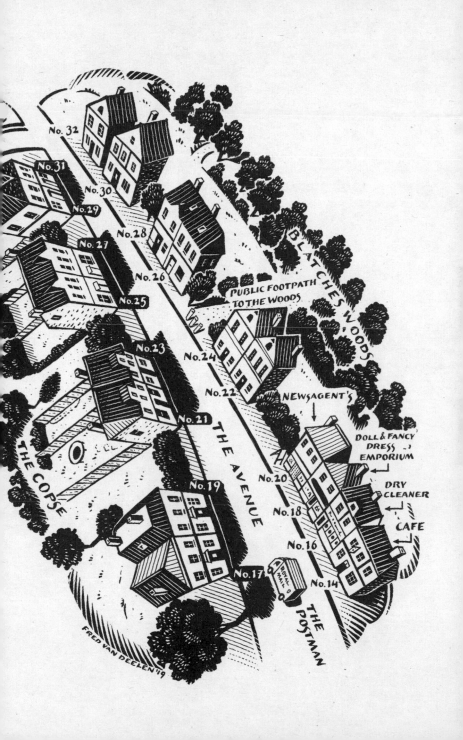

Abandon all hope, ye who enter here

— Dante

PROLOGUE

Saturday, 20 July 1985

18 The Avenue – 3 p.m.

GRAND REOPENING AND PUPPET SHOW TODAY

At first, the children were laughing.

The snap of crocodile teeth. A ballerina in a tutu tripping over her feet. The painted cheeks of a policeman blowing out a breath.

The limbs of the puppets jerked with a peculiar sort of grace, and the Doll & Fancy Dress Emporium echoed with the sound of merry voices and a promise of new beginnings.

There were two girls and two boys, dropped off by their unsuspecting parents. A handful of years between them. Gap-toothed and radiant with the possibilities of lives yet to be lived. Not knowing that in a few minutes' time a clock would be set, a countdown, their fates decided in the dark heart of a toy shop on that summer's afternoon. Four clock-work mice, whirring busily on their wheels until one day they stop moving. Run-down. Dead.

Not this week or next. Not in ten years from now. But at

a distant point in a future they could not yet imagine, when they had put away the games of childhood and were weighted down with the responsibilities of middle age. When the memory of what happened next was buried under faded fancy dress costumes and decades of dust.

In the mouth of the candy-cane-striped booth positioned at the back of the shop, the puppets swooped and whirled on their strings, and the children clapped and smiled at each other.

The show was almost at its end when the last puppet appeared. The grand finale. But there was no cheer of encouragement, no high, excited voices. Instead, the children fell silent and watchful.

This puppet was not carved from sycamore like the others. Its body was a loose formation of silk and lace scraps from a Victorian mourning costume, hemmed with black feathers, all glossy iridescence. When its strings were manipulated, it seemed to fly.

But this did not interest the children. They were staring at the puppet's head. Not a face made shiny with beeswax or carved into a leer or with ruddy cheeks, but something much darker than that.

The decapitated head of a carrion crow.

Its eyes were fixed open, two brown buttons pressed into a headdress of feathers, the tip of its beak like the curve of a hook. A glimpse of ragged edges where it had been torn from its body.

Two of the children exchanged glances. A nervous giggle slipped from another. The dolls in their boxes high up on the shelves looked on, glee in their painted faces. The tin soldiers seemed to stand up straighter. The whole shop paused to draw in breath.

And so no one noticed a small girl – the youngest of the group – back away from the puppet theatre with its dead crow's head and limp feathers, stumbling over her best shoes, finding her way to a storeroom that should have been locked.

No one saw her scramble between the old boxes and piles of dust sheets, tears wetting her face, or stopped her from squeezing through rails of fraying costumes, spider webs catching in her hair, until she found herself crouching behind a deep, wooden chest, curiosity driving her to open it.

No one noticed her at all.

Until the screaming began.

1

Now

Every killing has a taste of its own. I expect you didn't know that.

Young women are sweetened with hope, less astringent than their older selves, who reek of experience, bitter as sorrel leaves.

The boys – yes, they remain boys until they have earned the right to be called men – are seasoned with bravado, but lack piquancy. As the life ebbs from them, they taste of metal and shyness and tears.

The older generation are over-salted with loss and grief. They have absorbed the hurts of lives that have been lived, storm-battered but surviving. They do not accept death. They fight against the injustice of a thief like me.

As their airways constrict, as each pull of breath grows ragged and reluctant, their faces are sketched with panic, the dusty tapestries of their histories unfurling as the darkness takes hold. Their flavourings are persistence and regret.

I am telling you this now because I still possess the

faintest of hopes that somewhere you can hear me as I hear the police sirens lacerating the silence. The sound makes my teeth itch, like a blade being honed on a steel.

As the reckoning approaches, I suppose there is a need to unburden myself, to seek absolution for the sins I have committed. I am not sorry for what I have done. The remorse I feel is not for the lives I have taken, but for what each act of murder has cost me.

The power to take a life is a gift not many possess. I have always understood this. I do not have many talents and I am grateful for it.

But the world is not so forgiving.

Some will call me a monster, deserving of a death sentence myself. It is fair, I suppose. But I am not a monster. I have never been a monster.

I am a keeper of secrets.

And I am not alone.

The greengrocer's boy stuffing shiny apples into paper bags and pound coins into his pockets; the piano teacher who makes house calls, sneaking glimpses at his pupils' bare knees; the exhausted mother who fantasizes about shoving the pram she is pushing into oncoming traffic; the families who move in – and out of – The Avenue, as ceaseless as time.

We all hide secrets, dark and ugly.

You.

Me.

And every one of us on this dirt-filled earth.

This is the last time I will feel the sun on my face or hear the greetings of the blackbirds or inhale the scent of damask roses. Perhaps I deserve to spend the rest of my days in a cage, condemned to a life without freedom, as I have condemned others. Hush, now. Listen. Can you hear, as I do, the thunder of the funeral drums?

The police are almost upon me.

And so I'll begin. Because the time has come to finish it. Because the only way to start this story is at its end.

2

The Avenue – 3.31 p.m.

The removal van packed with the furniture and hopes of the Lockwood family brushed against the rhododendron bushes that surrounded The Avenue, breaking off one of the blooms.

That flower floated to the pavement, petals torn and mangled. The van driver, intent on finding the right house, did not notice the damage he had caused. Neither did the Lockwoods.

As heat trembled the air around them, this family had no idea of how they would come to pray that 25 The Avenue had remained a blurry photograph on the estate agent's website, or that by the end of the summer, their lives would be as ruined as the stem bleeding sap onto the concrete.

Music drifted across the sun-withered afternoon, touching leaves so dry the swell of notes might shake them free, before floating through the open windows of several nearby houses.

Those houses, grouped like guardians in this modest

street on the edge of a small town near the Essex coast, had been standing there for many years and borne witness to it all.

From behind the curtains of one of those houses, someone watched the Lockwood family crawl into the driveway behind the moving truck, snap off the radio and emerge from the silver shell of their car, unfolding legs and shaking out arms cramped by hours of travel.

An older woman, attractive, wearing crumpled linen trousers, shielded her eyes, and squeezed the hand of a man, who did not squeeze it back. A boy, eight or nine, bounced around, tugging at his mother's arm. A teenage girl, languid-limbed and insouciant, brushed her thumb across the screen of her mobile phone and did not look up at the house at all.

The someone watched this family, shiny with promise, and wondered which of them would break first. Because nobody came to The Avenue without death seeping through the gaps in their walls.

Some new families handled the proximity of murder better than others. Two or three had left within weeks, wearing the financial pain of a quick sale. But which details of the killings had the estate agent shared with the latest arrivals? How much *should* be shared, and when?

Before these questions could be answered, the decision was made.

A wail first. High-pitched. Insistent. Joined by another, and another, rising in rhythm and intensity. A concerto; the solo instruments of police sirens, a rolling bass line of distant traffic and the alto voices of the birds that nestled in this tree-lined avenue, and the woods beyond.

The woods beyond.

The neighbour glanced down the street to the archway of branches and brambles that crowned one of five public entrances to Blatches Woods. Thirty-seven acres of greenery tucked into this pocket of suburbia, criss-crossed with footpaths and bridleways. A place to get lost in. Thirty-seven acres that had come to dominate the newspaper headlines and breakfast tables; that had lowered property prices; that had cast a pall across this most ordinary of places.

The word rolled around the neighbour's mouth. *Pall.* A cloth used for spreading over a coffin.

The Avenue filled with noise and blue light as the police cars – two, three, four of them – swerved into the kerb in front of the footpath that led to the south-east corner of the woodland. A van – FORENSIC SERVICES imprinted across its side – followed a minute later.

Officers – some uniformed, some not – gathered in a knot, waiting for the white suits to ready themselves. One – his hand on the collar of a dog – was being sick. Even from behind the safety of the window, their sense of urgency was palpable. A need to cut through the decaying strings of vines that crept across the carpet moss and bracken, to trample deeper into the dense wall of trees, to interrogate the dog-walker or jogger or whoever had found it this time.

From downstairs, the click of the back door and the sounds of the kettle being filled. A dozen butterflies took flight in the neighbour's stomach. A glance at the clock. Around fifteen minutes before the door-knockings and questions would begin again.

The Lockwoods were watching this scene unfold with the frozen expressions of comic-book characters: eyes widened; mouths slack and loose; splayed fingers pressed to cheeks. Their bodies were angled towards the police cars in the way that plants are pulled towards the sun. Not a flicker of movement between them, mesmerized by the sight of Mrs Lockwood's favourite television crime dramas seemingly brought to life opposite their new home, a bruise on the surface of their fresh start.

All except the girl, who was taking photographs with her phone.

Three hours later, when the removal men had left and the sun was dipping below the horizon, but the air still ripe with heat, they brought out the body.

A single-use sheet covered the fifth victim's face, but the detective inspector on the scene – white-faced and trembling – was more concerned with accelerated decomposition in the hot weather than contaminants, and the cadaver was hurried into the mortuary van.

There was no wind to lift the sheet and expose this unfortunate soul to the journalists and photographers, the TV anchors and camera crews who filled The Avenue with their noise and coffee cups and cars that mounted the pavements at awkward angles. But there was no need.

Everybody knew what lay beneath because it was always the same.

A body, fully clothed. A painted face, subtle blush across the cheekbones; lips berry-coloured; lashes lengthened, dark and thick; a light foundation to disguise *pallor mortis*. As if the victim was not dead, but waiting to be played with, to be kissed back to life by a parent, a lover, a child.

Shoes removed. Hair brushed. Each eye gouged from its

bloodied socket with a scalpel and replaced with a miniature glass replica.

The handiwork of a killer the newspapers had named the Doll Maker.

And the face at the window knew who that killer was.

3

Now

Four little monkeys jumping on the bed, one fell off and bumped its head. Mummy called the doctor and the doctor said, 'No more monkeys jumping on the bed.'

Four of them moved into 25 The Avenue on that summer's afternoon, but when the end came, only three of them moved out. I could hear the boy crying as they loaded up the car, a knife-edge I-want-my-mother kind of cry, but I would not pry. I thought about coming out to say goodbye, to wish them well on the next chapter of life's journey, but what business of it was mine? Enough damage had been done.

Damage. When you say it aloud, there's a melody to it, a teasing introduction that finishes on a hard, aggressive note. We all damage others. A thoughtless word. A deliberate exclusion. A knife in the back. But you, of all people, understand that.

But I'm getting ahead of myself. If there's one lesson I've learned, it's that getting ahead of oneself is always a mistake.

Pride comes before a fall. Don't sell the skin until you've caught the bear.

So where were we? That's right. The Lockwoods. Garrick. Aster. And young Evan. But it was Olivia Lockwood who interested me. The mother at the heart of the family.

Except, it turns out, she wasn't its heart at all, but an ugly tumour that needed cutting out.

4

25 The Avenue – 7.36 p.m.

'I still can't believe how cheap this place was.'

Garrick Lockwood ran his hand along the oak bannister, admiring its sturdiness. His architect's eye ignored the damp patches, the hallway that felt too small, the cheap laminate floorboards that ran the length of the house. All he could see was potential.

His wife Olivia, who was in the kitchen, stopped rummaging in a cardboard box for glasses and the bottle of Prosecco she had bought for the occasion. 'Are you being serious?'

'Deadly.'

It was an unfortunate turn of phrase.

'That's not funny, Garrick.'

He chuckled, a low rumble of amusement. 'I wasn't trying to be funny. But it's true. By the time I've finished here, it's going to be stunning. They'll be queuing up to take it off our hands.'

'I hope you're right,' she said, the quiet voice of reason,

15

trying not to remember all the occasions his grand plans had come to nothing. It wasn't like they'd had a choice this time, though. This house – one of several post-war semis set on the outskirts of a nondescript Essex town – was all they could afford.

His reply was muffled, his head buried in the cupboard under the stairs. The volume lifted as he withdrew, wandered down the hallway and pulled on the iron ring of a square door embedded in the floor. 'I'd forgotten how big the cellar is. We could dig it out. Move the kitchen to the basement. Stick an extension on the side.'

Olivia placed two glasses on the worktop and closed her eyes.

The thud of a hatch shutting. Footsteps. And then Garrick was filling the kitchen doorway, head bent, already tapping numbers into the calculator function of his mobile phone.

'Sounds expensive.' Her fingers loosened the wire cage on the cork. She kept her voice light. 'Have we got enough money to do that?'

He waved an airy hand. 'We'll be fine.' Gave a sheepish grin. 'Actually, I've already submitted the plans.'

Decent of him to discuss it with her first. How typically Garrick. She breathed out her frustration. That would explain why he'd been insistent on travelling down to view the house several times while the sale was going through.

The cool box had not fulfilled its promise and she set down the tepid wine with the same controlled care she used to ask her next question. 'What about Oakhill? Have any of the flats sold yet?'

Garrick's expression folded in on itself before he shook

his head, confirming her suspicions. Money had been tight since his investment in a 'sure-fire' building development that was proving slow to shift. They'd been forced to downsize to loosen the bank's stranglehold on their finances.

Olivia had agreed to move on the understanding they would still have a garden and a minimum of three bedrooms. The Avenue had delivered that at a fraction of the price of similar properties. Both of them were banking on Garrick's skills as an architect to inflate its value and allow them to move on.

But now they were standing in this house, with its tired wallpaper lit by the flash of blue police lights, panic rose in her like the swell of the estuary they had spied in the distance on the car journey to their new life.

'Do you really think someone will buy it? Did you see the police cars? The photographers?' She resisted an urge to sweep the bottle onto the tiles, to watch the glass splinter, the liquid to froth and flatten into a puddle. The story of her life.

'*We* bought it, didn't we?'

'Yes, I know, but—'

'It's going to be fine.'

Olivia had lost count of the number of times he had promised her that. In fairness, she had moved here with her eyes open. Most of the properties had an air of neglect around them, as if they had once been loved but had been allowed to drift into a state of disrepair. And the brutal history of the place had been impossible to ignore, even if one took only a passing interest in the news. After the third murder, the TV and radio bulletins were filled with talk of serial killers for days and days. The newspapers blazed with lurid headlines. When the fourth murder happened, a few days before the Lockwoods were due to exchange contracts, she had tried to persuade him to pull out, but found herself agreeing with Garrick's insistence that some morbid individual would enjoy the cachet of owning a house on this road. The Avenue had become synonymous with Cromwell Street and Rillington Place.

But now she was here, now she had seen the police and the sheeted hump of a fifth body, she was convinced they had made a terrible mistake.

'But what if we're stuck here forever?'

'And whose fault would that be?' Garrick's tone was cool.

She drew in a breath and counted to five. 'Don't start that again.'

'I didn't. Remember?'

Olivia clenched her teeth until the outline of her jaw was visible through her skin. Her anger was like the strike of a match, poised to flare into life. She snuffed it out with the cold, hard facts of her guilt. Garrick's financial incontinence may have forced them to sell their beautiful home in Cheshire, but she was the reason they had moved down south.

Her body loosened. 'I know. It's just—'

'Look, Liv. We both had our parts to play. This is our fresh start. Let's not waste it on recriminations, eh?'

She opened her mouth to answer him, but there was nothing to say.

'Let's open the fizz, shall we?' His tone was placatory. 'We're here now, might as well celebrate.'

The pop of the cork filled the silence in the kitchen.

Olivia had already taken her first sip by the time she noticed Garrick's attempt to clink glasses, and by then it was awkward and too late. She remembered all the times she had felt the tiny bubbles burst against her lips. Weddings, christenings and lunches with friends. Birthday parties. Restaurant meals.

That last, unforgettable night.

Garrick was fiddling with some leaflets the previous owners had left in a drawer. 'Shall we order a takeaway? Indian? Chinese?'

'Sure. Whatever. I'll go and ask the children.'

As she walked towards the kitchen door, her phone, which she had left charging by the empty fridge, began to vibrate.

Garrick lowered the menu he had been scanning. A blush stained Olivia's cheeks.

'You can – I mean – I don't mind,' she said, gesturing towards the handset, its tiny blue light flashing a warning. A trickle of sweat in the hollow between her breasts.

Her husband took a step forwards. Fidgeted. Stopped.

'Actually,' he said, 'there's no need for that.' He made a performance of turning over the menu, a study in nonchalance. 'I trust you to keep your word.'

She smiled at him then, and the carousel in her stomach began to slow. In as casual a manner as she could muster, Olivia picked up her phone and slid it into her pocket.

In the shadows of the hallway, her eyes scanned the message. And deleted it.

5

Now

As each death has a taste of its own, each body reveals its peculiarities in the moment of dying.

The twitch of an eyelid; a gasp, as if surprised to be inhaling one's final breath; the futile lifting of a hand to reach out and hold onto life.

I have learned that some slip away without a struggle, but for others, fear leaves its imprint in the stretched-open mouth, the eyes which do not close. That death itself is a burden, weighting down both the human shell and my soul.

And I have learned, at great cost, that I do not enjoy blood. That spatter is like flicking a loaded paintbrush against the walls and the floor, that scrubbing with a hard brush and soap does not remove the memory of what has gone before.

Did you ever bite the inside of your lip? Place a cut finger in your mouth and suck until the bleeding stopped? Swallow down the metallic heat of a nosebleed?

Blood is rust and old pennies, copper wire and iron. The same, but different.

Like fingerprints and irises.

Like killers.

None of us are identical.

Some prefer to strangle their victims, gifting a necklace of bruises. The split-open-skin-and-bleed-out method of slashers. Stalkers with blunt-headed hammers. Wronged husbands and wives. Opportunistic killers who act in the heat of the moment.

And there is me.

I detest mess. The savagery of murder. I have witnessed it twice and I do not wish to witness it again. I crave order when I kill. Control. Social niceties. I watch, I plan and prepare.

And when it is time, I do not turn away from difficult decisions. I seek out those who can no longer be permitted to live.

Here is what else I have learned.

The past is a place I lived in once. I buried its secrets in the dirt of my memory and I left it far behind. But it always catches up with us in the end.

They say knowledge is power, but that is not true. When that little girl opened the chest in that toy shop she set off a chain of events that would echo down the years, a scream that needed to be silenced. Puppets with cut strings.

Her curiosity didn't just kill the cat, it killed everyone else.

6

25 The Avenue – 7.37 p.m.

Evan Lockwood lay on his old bed in his new bedroom. His mother had not got around to duvet covers and pillow cases yet, but he didn't much care. He was nine and didn't notice whether his bedding was fresh on, three weeks old or non-existent.

The late-evening sun was splashing golden paint onto the walls, and he was buried inside his quilt, which smelled of home and the dirty washing basket. The backs of his knees were sticky in the heat.

In his left palm was a shiny black ball the size of a cantaloupe melon. A white circle with a number eight in its middle was painted on the top. A birthday present from his cousin.

'It's a Magic 8 Ball.' The words had bubbled out of her before he'd even had the chance to tear off the wrapping paper. 'It foretells the future.'

'Cool,' he'd said, and meant it. His eyes pricked. He would miss her.

Bunching his duvet into the rough shape of a pillow, he shoved it up against the wall and leaned into it. He pursed his lips, thinking, and whispered his first question.

Will we have pizza for tea?

He tipped the ball over and the answer appeared in a triangular window.

Most likely.

Evan grinned, his stomach rumbling its approval, and chewed on his lip while he thought of another.

Is the Tooth Fairy real?

He liked to pretend he was almost grown-up, but he was still losing his milk teeth, still clinging on to childish fantasies. Two mornings ago, when he had slid a hand beneath his pillow, there had been no money, just the pearly treasure he had lost while eating an apple the day before. When he'd told his mother, who was packing books into a box, her cheeks had flamed red. But she'd insisted the Tooth Fairy hadn't forgotten and had just been busy. Evan wasn't so sure.

Ask again later.

He tutted. Those non-committal replies were the worst kind. He gazed around the bedroom. It was weird, being in this house. *A new start.* That's what his parents kept calling it. Evan didn't understand it. Like his toys and furniture and the kitchen pots and pans, surely all the shouting and crying and arguments would move with them too.

He pressed the tatty old bear he'd had since he was a baby to his chest, and whispered another question, crossing both sets of his fingers.

Will we be happy here?

He tipped the ball and it slowly revealed its answer.

My reply is no.

7

Now

My earliest memories come to me not in pictures, but sounds. The frantic pump of a spinning top. The twist of a key in a clockwork mouse. The mechanical winding of a jack-in-the-box crank.

Half a pound of tuppenny rice. Half a pound of treacle. That's the way the money goes. Pop goes the weasel.

Birdie would settle me in a corner of our shop and surround me with toys. She would pull them from the shelves, ignoring the price tags, generous with these expensive knick-knacks, if not her affections.

The floor was always cold, but it did not matter. My childish fingers would grasp for the top, a crazy, whirring riot of colour and motion. I would lurch after the mouse on unsteady legs. But it was always the jack-in-the-box that held the most fascination.

Le Diable en Boîte. A boxed devil, like me.

A prelate once saved a village from a drought by discovering a well with healing powers. He was so holy he caught the Devil in a boot. Folklore, of course, but bound in truth.

Like the Devil, I was cast out.

My mothers didn't want me. Not my birth mother, whose name I never knew. Not Bridget, my adoptive mother, besotted by the curled fists and rounded cheeks of a baby – 'Come to Birdie, come to Mama' – but who fell out of love as my views and behaviour took on a different shape to her own. Used her own fists to mould me into the type of child she could be proud of. Pinched me. Slapped me. Pressed the vicious edges of her watch's metal strap into my face whenever we were running late. *Tick-tock. Tick-tock. Tick-tock.*

Her tongue was as sharp as a shard of glass. Some days, I dreamed of cutting it out. Imagined her mouth filling with blood. Choking her. The bladed edges of her viciousness reduced to a stump, blunted and useless.

But the jack-in-the-box I loved. The surprise of it. And then, when I knew what was coming, the *anticipation* of that surprise.

Death is like that. One knows it is coming. Old age. Illness. The gradual decline of one's body. But for some, it is not like that at all. Their death is abrupt. A shock.

The five-car motorway pile-up in the early hours of the morning. A stroke in the armchair on a Sunday afternoon. An accidental drowning in a lake on a summer's evening.

A murder.

It strikes me as curious that there are millions upon millions of people in this world, but only a few will share with me this particular human experience. The deliberate taking of a life that does not belong to us. It is intoxicating, like being a god in the sky.

But it is not something one discusses in the supermarket queue or the doctor's surgery or the office. I cannot say, for example, 'Did you see the way her left hand jerked thirty-two seconds before the moment of death?' or 'Poor soul, he suffered from a terrible case of *rigor erectus.*'

The police sirens scream at me. Three minutes. Perhaps less. Time feels like it is slowing down. I am sitting in the chair and she has put on some music. I'm tapping out the beat with my fingers.

Did you know that the act of murder has a rhythm all of its own, a slowed-down version of a jack-in-the-box tune?

Sing with me.

Half a pound . . .

On that first beat of time, the victim is still breathing in air; still laughing, head thrown back with the sort of abandon that implies they have no idea of what is to come.

. . . of tuppenny rice.

By the second beat, their eyes have widened. They know something is terribly wrong.

Half a pound . . .

The third beat, and they are a jerking, skin-covered shell.

. . . of treacle.

On the fourth, a caved-in memory.

That's the way . . .

By the end of the fifth, they are nothing but an empty sack of humanity.

. . . the money goes.

On the day they moved in, I saw Olivia Lockwood sitting at the dining-room table. She was wearing a green shirt and a white skirt. Drinking a glass of wine. Eating a slice of pizza. Three weeks later, I dreamed of closing my fist around her heart until it stopped.

Pop goes the weasel.

8

4 Hillside Crescent – 9.30 p.m.

Breathe.

Breathe.

Come up for air. Inhale. Exhale. Swim through the darkness. Eyelids flicker. Open. Close. Close. Open. Shadows into shapes. A chair. The wardrobe. The thrown-down light of a lamp. Water. Take a sip. Breathe. Breathe.

Adam.

Stifling air. Breathe. Slow. Inhale. Exhale. You're OK. Another sip. Breathe. Adam. Breathe. Keep breathing. Keep breathing.

My name is Wildeve Stanton and I am in my own bed.

The sheet was tangled around the bone of her ankle, and she tried to kick it off, but her body was loose and liquid, refusing to do as she asked. She struggled to sit up but the lead in her chest pinned her to the mattress. *Don't panic. It's the sedative. Keep breathing.* Dry mouth. The taste of stale wine and despair.

Adam.

THE NEIGHBOUR

Keep breathing. Count them. One. Two. Three.

Everything was jumbled and indistinct. Flashes of memory. Voices. But it was not about words, just feelings. Not lead, but stones, piles and piles of them in the hollow of her stomach. She was walking into nothingness, surrounded by the collapsing walls of a paper house.

Again.

On my own again.

A blackened sky lit by the dull rind of the moon. Evening, but not late. The air still held the heat of the sun and it filled her lungs, stifling her. Why was the earth not breaking open and falling into the seas? How was it her heart continued to pump when everything else in her world had stopped?

Her hand touched the sheet of the too-big bed. *Remember him.* But remembering burned. *Adam.* The night stretched in front of her, hours and hours of darkness.

Her hand closed around the bottle and she swallowed down her sorrow with another mouthful of red wine. Over and over again she drank, deep and long, until the liquid spilled down her chin and bloodied her nightshirt with grief.

9

Now

If the emporium was a place of shiny toys and birthday promises, in darkness it became somewhere else.

Birdie would lock the door behind the last customer and turn over the CLOSED sign before she turned on me.

'Clean the floors,' my adoptive mother would say, and I would hide away my homework before she tore it up. She'd done that more than once, when my response had not been quick enough, so I had learned to be clever, setting up a makeshift desk behind the doll's houses and wooden baby walkers filled with alphabet blocks, knowing that by the time she had picked her way through to hand me a mop, my school books would be inside my bag.

The winter I was nine, when the air was so cold it hurt my chest and the night began when it was still afternoon, she flipped over the sign and tipped a bottle of caustic soda across the inside of my wrist.

An accident, she said. *You clumsy boo.* But I knew what it was. My punishment. Because I'd been too slow to answer her. I would not – could not – stop screaming, so she went back to the flat and left me on my own, locked inside the shop.

I lay on the stone flags, as I had done as a much younger child, the substance eating its way through my skin, fire spreading up my arm. I could not get up because even the tiniest movement fuelled the flames.

In the shadows of the shop, wracked with pain, the fumes irritating my lungs and making me cough, the horrors of my imagination came to life.

The puppets with their strings swung back and forth on their hooks, pointing their wooden hands at me. The toy monkeys jeered, chattering and baring their teeth. Clockwork mice crawled across my fevered skin.

The dolls climbed down from their exalted position high up on the shelves. They pulled at my hair and clothes, their porcelain fingernails scratching at the rawness of the open wound, their pale, enquiring faces daubed with the plasma that leaked from my chemical burns.

When Birdie came back in the morning, I was unconscious, toys strewn across the shop floor. Through fear or pain, neither of us knew.

Three skin grafts, I needed, the replacement flesh harvested from my stomach. In front of the doctors, Birdie ruffled my hair and called me a *silly boo*. When she thought I was asleep, I overheard her telling a nurse how I'd climbed on a stool to reach the caustic soda after she'd warned me not to play with it.

As soon as we were home, she handed me one of the broken puppets. A peace offering, she said. Tangled strings and chipped paintwork, its nose sheared off completely.

I could have packed my things and stolen some money from the till or Birdie's purse, and run far, far away.

But Birdie wouldn't have suffered then, and where was the fun in that?

10

25 The Avenue – 9.30 p.m.

Across the hallway from her brother, Aster Lockwood was considering the myriad ways she could run away. Hitch-hiking would be too risky, but she didn't want to spend her own money on the train fare. Perhaps she could borrow her mother's credit card. Or persuade Matthew to drive down and collect her. The lure of a semi-naked selfie never failed to surprise her.

The removal men had put together her bed, but the rest of her former life was in cardboard boxes strewn across the floor. She couldn't be bothered to unpack, especially as she wasn't planning to stay.

Two months ago, her parents had sat them down, Aster and her brother Evan, and told them they would be moving from their family home in Cheshire to a small Essex town near the sea. It would mean new schools and new friends. Evan had cried. Aster had picked up her glass of cordial and poured it over her mother's head.

'This is your fault.' The words had been a hiss. 'I hate you.'

Olivia had not shouted or even reacted. She had sat there, hair plastered to her face, the pink liquid dripping down her shirt, soaking her bra and her skin. Aster had enjoyed slamming the door, and the surge of power it gave her. If her mother thought she'd forgive her for ruining everyone's lives, she'd be waiting forever. Her mother was so old. The whole sordid mess made her feel hot and sort of dirty.

Her new room wasn't bad. Bigger than in the old house. With a sofa and TV, it might even be decent. The curtains had been taken down and packed up by the previous owners, but her father had promised her shutters. She scrolled through her phone. Matthew was already asking when he could visit. She supposed she'd have to check with her mother, which irritated her because her mother never bothered to check anything with the rest of the family.

Aster wandered over to the window and looked out on the street below. A length of police tape cordoned off the entrance to the woods where the body had been found. The trees were thick and dense, spread out so widely that she couldn't see where they ended. A couple of officers were standing on the pavement. A woman with a large bag on her shoulder and a camera in her hand was firing off shots while a man in a suit was talking on his phone and scribbling notes on a pad.

She would post the pictures she'd taken later. Her friends would lose their shit when they saw the dead body, even if it was hidden under a sheet.

Her gaze strayed to the house opposite. It was much the same as theirs. Semi-detached. Red-tiled roof. But less unkempt than many of the neighbouring properties. The walls were pale green, a much nicer shade than their own, and the front garden was filled with floral bursts of violet and yellow and orange.

Aster wondered who lived there. More importantly, whether any teenage boys did.

At the top of this house across the street was an open window. She could see curtains, drifting in the lightest of evening breezes. There was something else too. A glimpse of black and silver, sleek and elegant.

Aster pressed her palms against the glass and waited for the curtains to still. There it was again. A telescope.

Were the nights ever dark enough to pick out the stars above this unfamiliar town a million miles from the moorlands and vast, black skies of the home she had loved so much? A hotness burned behind her eyes.

She flung herself on her bed and buried her face in the pillow.

And so Aster Lockwood did not see the swivel of the telescope seeking out her bedroom or the careful adjustment of the focusing mechanism, a few turns to the right. She did not see a shadow move from behind the curtains to stand in the square of glass lit by the cool fire of moonrise.

She did not see the watcher then, or when she returned to her bedroom after an ill-tempered hour watching television with her family. She did not sense the heat of a stranger's gaze, and if she had, she would not have understood it. All thoughts of the telescope and its owner had long slipped from her mind by the time she undressed for bed, a blur of pale skin framed in the window of her new bedroom, the fall of the lamplight shading in her curves and hollows like a body in a crime scene photograph.

11

Sunday, 29 July 2018

27 The Avenue – 9.43 p.m.

In the house next door and separated only by a brick wall, Audrina Clifton had the uncomfortable sensation that she, too, was being watched.

In the stillness of that summer's evening, drawing her nightie over her grey curls and rubbing in face-cream, she became possessed by the conviction that she was not alone.

Her ears picked up the faintest drift of laughter.

Like a child playing hide-and-seek, she pressed her liver-spotted hands to her face as if that might disappear her from prying eyes, the callus on her thumb rasping against her skin.

Middle age was now a memory to Audrina, but she wasn't one to worry about her advancing years, the slackening of her skin or pouching beneath her jawline, the arthritis that swelled her joints. On the few occasions she had needed to use her wheelchair, she had found herself invisible. But while she was not embarrassed about the scars that time had left upon her, she resisted exposure to a stranger's gaze.

THE NEIGHBOUR

She had lived in this house for many years, but, in recent months, she had become increasingly convinced that someone was spying on her.

Audrina snapped shut the curtains, and in that flurry of movement, a pale pink peony petal from the vase on the windowsill floated to the floor.

The thud of a door closing.

Imaginary spiders crawled across the back of her neck. Heart pumping too hard, she groped in her bedside drawer for a knitting needle and spun around, hoping to find her husband Cooper in their bedroom, laughing at her fears, his pyjamas smelling of pipe smoke.

But he was not there.

She let out a breath.

One of her greatest fears was a home invasion. She had read in the newspaper about an elderly woman a few streets away who was beaten up and tied to her bed while her bungalow was ransacked. Thrusting the needle forward, she heard another thump behind her.

A rush of adrenaline made her feel light-headed. Her world seemed to blank into nothingness. The roar of her heart filled her ears.

Another burst of laughter, and the strains of music. A boy's voice crying out for his mother.

For a beat in time, Audrina was immobilized, and would not have been able to run even if she'd wanted to. But then, quite suddenly, she smiled out her fear. *Of course*. The new family next door. Relief made her shoulders sag.

She scanned the bedroom. All she could see was the polished oak of her chest of drawers, its bronzed handles and the willow-patterned jug and bowl atop a crocheted doily.

And a beanbag frog from Liberty that had belonged to her son a long time ago.

She took a step towards it.

Despite the stifling heat, goosebumps stippled her forearm. One hand clutched at her throat. The thunder of blood in her ears again.

The frog had been propped against a paperweight when she had come to get ready for bed, she was certain of it. She had not jogged the chest of drawers, had not even touched it.

But now the frog lay face down, its limbs splayed outwards, a split up the seam of its fabric like a knife wound.

12

18 The Avenue – 11.02 p.m.

The signage was a dusty wash of burnt orange and blue and the letters had faded, but it did not matter. Even if passers-by could not read the curling font that spelled out Doll & Fancy Dress Emporium, the window display gave the game away.

The shop stood on the corner of The Avenue, as it had done for more than sixty years, in a modest parade that boasted a newsagent's, a launderette, a cafe and a dry cleaner.

All windows were in Sunday-night darkness, but a light was just visible in the emporium, and the glow it threw down filled the dressing-up costumes with shadows that might have been people.

They were old, those costumes, but extravagantly made. A soldier's uniform with a fraying cuff and heavy medals that might pass for the real thing. A dress handed down so many times that no one could remember its original owner, but with flounces and lace that fell apart when touched. The rusted metal of an astronaut's helmet.

Some of the costumes had not been worn for years,

shoved at the back of the shop in piles that teemed with moths and spiders and their contrails of silk. The fabrics had lost their lustre. A scratched button here. A loose wisp of cotton there. If one pressed an ear to those discarded bundles, the whispers of past glories, of balls and parties, would play like a gramophone record, scratches and all.

But no one ever came to the shop to hire a fancy dress outfit.

They came for the dolls.

Because beyond the costumes, past the overfilled rails and the wigs made from human hair, the riding boots and leather crops, the buckles and belts and shoes with bows, was a room.

A man worked alone at a trestle table and he did not look up. A ceiling fan worked noisily to ease the thick heat. A lamp bent over in submission lit his way. Sixteen porcelain heads rested in neat rows of four at the far end of the bench. White and smooth. Hairless. Blank-faced.

On the paint-spattered surface in front of him, he was bringing one of those dolls to life.

For a man of his size, his brush strokes were deft and precise. A delicate sweep of black for the eyebrows. Daubs of green for the eyes. A brush so tiny it was lost in his hand, another held in his mouth. Eyelashes. A speck of white, and the suggestion of a tear.

To him, the eyes were the most important part of the face. He believed each doll should tell a story with her eyes, that to look into their depths would be to learn something new.

He wore an old pair of cargo shorts, thinning at the knee, and his ill-fitting T-shirt was full of holes. He wasn't the type to bother about haircuts or shaving or mobile phones. His house was unkempt and unloved, even though he could afford better. His interest in appearance stopped with his creations.

His dolls sold for a great deal of money.

They featured in specialist magazines and drew crowds at toy conventions. He had sold several to a very famous celebrity couple for each of their three daughters. Collectors from New Zealand to France queued up each year for a new Lovell doll, waiting patiently for photographs of his progress amid discussions of hair colour and clothing and the shade of their lips.

They were the work of a dedicated craftsman.

Each took several days to finish, their pretty heads needing firing between each application of paint, which shimmered with its own translucency. He breathed in the smell of his work, of turpentine and oil and mixing medium, and it settled him.

After an hour, Trefor Lovell flexed his fingers and put down his brushes. He placed his latest creation on a shelf to dry, opened a drawer and reached for the talking pull-string doll he'd owned since 1971. Her head was much bigger than her body and when he pulled on her string, a recorded voice played, crackly with age.

His knees creaked like an old rocking chair as he walked over to the desk telephone, which sat next to a pile of orders, printed off the internet, and a spike for the ones he'd fulfilled.

He listened to the rhythm of his call ringing out in a darkened house on The Avenue a few hundred yards away.

When the receiver was picked up and a voice, quiet and

guarded, spoke into the night, he did not reply, but placed it back in its cradle.

By the second hand on the watch on his wrist, he waited for two minutes to pass, and pressing the tip of his finger into the rotary dial, careful to withhold his own number, he dialled the same house once more.

This time the telephone rang out again and again until the sound was scratched into his mind.

Three minutes and forty-seven seconds later, it was answered.

'*Hello?*' A pause. More aggressive. '*Hello?*'

Lovell waited just long enough for the silence to fill with threat, then pulled the doll's body away from its oversized head. This action tugged on the string which was connected to a phonograph inside the toy. He had used his skills to doctor the recording and, after a moment's pause, the doll began to speak, a slow, mechanical sing-song.

'*The stains of your sins will never wash clean.*'

'*Who is this?*' Ill temper leaked its way down the line. '*What do you want?*' A gathering of strength. '*If you call again, I'll ring the police.*'

Lovell picked at a spot of dried paint with his thumbnail. He knew the voice at the end of the line would never call the police. He breathed quietly.

'*Please.*' Pleading now. '*Leave me alone.*'

He closed his fingers around the doll's body and pulled for a second time, enjoying the stretching out of the string between her head and torso.

'*The stains of your sins will never wash clean,*' the doll said again, her words rusty with menace. '*And you are going to be punished.*'

THE NEIGHBOUR

He didn't bother to ring a third time because he'd said what he'd wanted to. He had learned long ago that words were a powerful weapon, that the fear of what *might* happen, the waiting for it, was far more brutal than the clean relief of the guillotine.

The dread of discovery was something that Trefor Lovell understood.

He had lived with it for months.

He put the pull-string doll back in his drawer and withdrew the small notebook he kept in the back pocket of his trousers, scribbling the time and date next to the telephone number he had just dialled.

Next, he cleaned his brushes and rinsed the ceramic tile he used as his palette to grind and mix his paints. The porcelain doll's eyes followed him as he tidied. There was a sadness in her, exactly as he'd intended. He screwed up a stray piece of newspaper and put it in the bin, preferring to start each new day with a clear space and a clear head.

He switched off the light, locked up and headed off into the night.

Although it had just gone midnight, tipping Sunday night into Monday morning, the air was still swollen with heat. It teased the sweat from his body, from under his arms and his upper lip.

The street was in darkness but the moon was as silver and flat as a coin. He tried to recall the science behind the lunar cycle, but the knowledge drifted from him, and he realized, with a shade of regret, that he had forgotten many things with the forward march of time.

He patted his pocket. Writing things down helped him to remember.

Trefor Lovell lived at number 32 The Avenue, at the bottom end of the street. His house was less than four minutes' walk from his shop and past the public footpath that led into Blatches Woods.

A uniformed police officer stood by the entrance. Lovell's palms were damp. He nodded at the man. The man nodded back.

'Evening, sir, you're out and about late tonight.' Lovell noticed the man move his hand and rest it lightly on his radio.

'I've been working,' he said.

'Well, I hope you don't mind me saying so, but you might want to think twice about being on the streets at this time of night.' The police officer jerked his head towards the dark mass of trees. 'We found another one today.'

Lovell, who had been painting his dolls all afternoon, lost in music and the act of birth, did not know this.

'I'll be fine. I only live over there,' he said, pointing down the road to his house. 'Not far.'

'Then I'm sure someone will be round to see you in the next day or so.' The police officer laughed at Lovell's expression. 'Don't look so worried, sir. It's routine.'

Lovell cleared his throat. 'It wouldn't be the first time.'

Goodnights were exchanged. Lovell raised a hand in farewell. Jasmine, or the musk of another bloom, was heavy in the night-time air.

The police officer watched Lovell as he strolled down The Avenue, past silent houses clad in pebble-dashing, wheelie bins and the hulks of parked cars, and through his own gate. Although Lovell could no longer see him, he sensed the weight of the man's stare, the frisson of his interest.

THE NEIGHBOUR

His hand was trembling so much his key scratched the metal cover of the lock as he tried to insert it. It took every ounce of Lovell's strength not to run back to the officer, fall upon his knees and confess everything.

13

Southside Hospital, Essex – 8.59 a.m.

Monday morning. 26.3°C.

Detective Sergeant Wildeve Stanton had not warned any of her Essex Police colleagues that she was coming into work. They would have tried everything to stop her.

Simon Quick, a police dog handler and Adam's best friend, was insisting on dropping by with breakfast, but she had ignored his call. She had known what his offer had meant. But she wasn't ready to face that yet and was gone before he arrived.

She slid her car into a space in the hospital car park and removed her sunglasses. The morning sun stung her eyes. One of the capillaries had burst, and it was like a tiny red river had broken its banks. For a moment, she rested her forehead against the steering wheel and considered driving home again, to the vacuum of sleep.

Her wedding ring was loose around her finger. A month ago it had been tight. *Every cloud and all that.* A smile ghosted across her face. Adam would appreciate the sentiment. *Got to keep your sense of humour, Wild.* That's what he always said. *Had* said. She blinked twice and replaced her sunglasses with trembling hands.

Wildeve Stanton had not slept. The first day and night had passed in a blur of sedatives and cheap wine. But she had hated the fuzziness, the numbing blankness that smothered the pain. She wanted to feel the sharp edges, to cut herself on them. Because if she felt something it meant she could not forget.

A car pulled into the space next to her and a nurse in a blue uniform climbed out, catching her eye.

'Lovely day, isn't it? Wish I hadn't swapped my shift now.' The nurse hoisted her handbag strap over her shoulder and grinned through the open car window. 'Let's hope it's a quiet one.'

The corners of Wildeve's mouth twitched upwards into an approximation of a smile. Even now, in the very depths of darkness, she was a slave to social convention. But it was an odd sensation, the knowledge that for others the world continued to turn, that they were still looking forward to barbecues and holidays and trips to the beach. For her, there was a disconnect, an inhalation of disbelief every time she looked down at her feet, her legs, that even though her life had been blown apart into a thousand tiny pieces, she had still managed to pull on trousers and tie up the laces of her boots.

It was touching nine when she walked across the asphalt to the small building next to the MRI department, and the sun was burning the back of her neck.

The door to the Chapel of Rest was closed. Wildeve wondered if a family was waiting inside, and if they were finding peace. She dipped her head. Her way of showing respect. Solidarity.

She drew in a breath.

She could do this.

She was Detective Sergeant Wildeve Stanton, investigating the latest in a horrific spate of serial killings, a professional with a job to do.

She was Detective Sergeant Wildeve Stanton, hungover and cotton-wool-mouthed and full of broken bits. She covered her face with her hands. They were still shaking.

To steady herself, she began to run through procedure, as if the familiar structures of her work would hold her up and calm her.

Post-mortem examination this morning. Two hours or so. How long before the coroner agrees to release the body? How many days or weeks or months before it is taken to the funeral home, before it's prepped for the family viewing?

Her mind strayed ahead, to the heroic efforts of the embalmer, whose job it was to make the dead look more alive. Skin sliced through to raise an artery. Formaldehyde pushed through silent veins until colour seeped in and cheeks were less sunken. A mouth sewn shut. Eyes dabbed dry.

Wildeve had once asked why such care was necessary. After all, the dead could not see. But the embalmer, immune to the brutality of his job, had put down the cotton pad he was pressing gently to the tear ducts, and offered a rare smile of sadness. 'It can look as if they are crying. Heartbreaking for the family.'

Did the public have any idea of the lengths these technicians went to to preserve a body from the violence of a post-mortem? Wildeve didn't think so. But that instinct was powerful amongst her mortuary colleagues. To protect the loved ones from the savagery of murder, a car crash, the destruction of fire. To make the viewing process easier. Palatable. As in life, in death. Dressing up the truth, disguising it.

Adam's face – pale but familiar – appeared, unbidden, in her mind. Her vision blurred and she forced her shaking hands into her pockets. Pushing away that memory of him, she remembered a happier time. Knocked over, fully dressed, by a wave on a beach in Devon, the sea soaking into his shorts. She had tried to pull him out, but had slipped and followed him into the water. He'd laughed so hard he'd wept, tears rolling down his cheeks.

The coolness of the building was a relief from the sweating heat outside. She had been here too many times lately, unpicking the Doll Maker's victims for clues. But Wildeve could not look at the steel refrigerators where the bodies were stored in trays, stacked upon each other, identity tags around their toes. She did not want to think about the vanished lives inside, already waxy with death, or the leaking of gases from their bowels and intestines when the pathologist slit them open and removed the organs.

She did not want to think about any of that at all.

The door to the examination room was closed. They had started without her. But she wasn't offended. No one was expecting her and bodies were like meat. Unless they were frozen, they spoiled within hours, especially in this weather, and there was nothing worse than a rotting corpse.

Except two rotting corpses.

A bark of laughter slid from her as the low timbre of

Adam's voice filled her head. She pressed her palms to the swing doors and pushed her way in.

Six heads turned towards Wildeve, and then Detective Constable Jim Sheridan was grabbing her elbow and trying to propel her back the way she'd come.

'You don't need to be here, Wildeve,' he said. 'We've got this covered.'

She took them all in, the pathologist and her assistant, the crime scene investigators bagging and scribing exhibits, the CSI photographer, and then she was pushing back, heat behind her eyes, in the back of her throat. She did not expect them to understand. She could barely understand it herself. But she needed to be here. At work. And nothing was going to stop her.

The smell of death crept into her nostrils and filled her mouth. She swallowed, glad she had refused PC Simon Quick's offer of breakfast.

Her first post-mortem had been twelve years ago. Some of them had even wolfed down a fry-up first, filling themselves up with bacon and bravado. Three of them had been sick. Wildeve had kept down her coffee, but all these years later, she still couldn't stomach the way her senses conspired against her, how she could breathe in the essence of the deceased, could *taste* it, even. The rawness of a butcher's shop. Urine. Bleach. And that startling jaffa orange of subcutaneous fat.

She dragged her eyes from the body resting on a metal tray atop the slab, and cast around for something to lessen the tension she could feel crawling across her skin, and the weight of her colleagues' concerned stares. Music and laughter and chatter would usually lighten the grim task in hand, but this morning, there was silence.

'So, the fifth victim,' she said finally, prising Sheridan's fingers from her arm, then squeezing them to show she appreciated his concern. 'Bastard's done it again. We knew he would. What have we got so far?'

The pathologist exchanged a glance with DC Sheridan, who cleared his throat.

'I don't think now's the time—'

'Are you trying to fob me off, Jim?'

'I know you better than that. But Mac's pulling it together back at Rayleigh. There's a briefing this afternoon. At five.'

'Thank you.'

'Wildeve—'

'I'm fine,' she said. 'Let's get on with it.'

'I'm not sure – I don't know – Mac asked me to come. There's a protocol here—'

'Fuck protocol.'

The Home Office pathologist – Dr Mathilda Hudson – opened her mouth. Shut it again. Shot another glance at Sheridan, who raised his eyebrows at her, asking an unspoken question. Hudson shrugged, then nodded. The constable looked like he might cry.

'If you're sure,' he said in a voice that was anything but.

Adam always said there was something disconcerting about seeing a body in the mortuary. The skin was never as grey as expected. The dead looked like they might open their eyes and sit up.

The body lying on the tray still looked like a friend, a colleague, a lover.

Human.

Now that she was so close, Wildeve found she could not look away. Her fingers itched to touch the face, to smooth back the hair, and to cleanse from this body the violence of its death. With a painful clarity, she understood the need of some cultures to wash and purify their lost. An act of worship and love.

The forensic pathologist cleared her throat. 'We'll carry on then, shall we? But you're here to observe, Wildeve. Any attempt to interfere with this examination and you're out, and I'll have no choice but to inform the coroner. Understood?'

Hudson didn't wait for an answer, but bent over the body. A Y-shaped incision ran from each clavicle, down the abdomen and finished at the pubic bone. The ribcage had been cut open, and muscle and tissue peeled back to allow access to the internal organs, which were in the process of being removed.

Wildeve dug her nails into her palms. Tasted blood in her mouth where she'd bitten her lip. She had arrived too late to hear the tearing sound of steel cutters through bone. For that, she would always be grateful.

Experience had taught her that the organs were taken from the body in three distinct blocks. The incision at the base of the throat confirmed the windpipe and tongue had already been removed, Hudson and her technician working from inside the chest to preserve the face for the relatives' sake. They were currently cutting free the liver, stomach and pancreas.

Wildeve swallowed twice, trying to ignore the lightness in her head. She wanted to shake Hudson, to implore her to reveal the secrets of this murder, but the pathologist rarely conversed while she was working, preferring to confer her attention on the dead. Often, she left this kind of preparation to her assistant, but it seemed she had come in early to work this case.

As a detective and a wife, Wildeve appreciated the gesture.

Next to the body was a deep plastic trug with two handles, the kind her mother had filled with leaves and garden waste. It was lined with a black bin bag. Wildeve glimpsed the sheen of bodily parts. The first block of organs – heart, lungs, throat, tongue and aorta – were already inside, awaiting evaluation.

When Hudson had removed the kidneys, bowels and bladder, and all that was left was a raw cavity, the mortuary technician dipped a ladle into the abdomen and decanted the excess blood into the shallow trench that edged the dissection table. It made a wet sound as it trickled into the sump.

The pathologist, who had a reputation for showing less emotion than the bodies in her morgue, finally broke open the silence.

'Are you sure you're up to this?'

Wildeve found she could not speak at all, but Hudson read the answer in her eyes.

'All righty, then. Let's crack on for now.'

At the bench, the technician weighed the organs, and Hudson began to work through each block in turn. She used a scalpel to check for fluid in the lungs, assessed the size of the heart, and for vessels blocked by fatty deposits. She lingered here, a frown on her face.

Her voice was low and even as she recorded her findings into a small dictaphone.

'One atherosclerotic lesion in the thoracic aorta. Signs of pulmonary oedema, possible cause of cardiac failure.'

Wildeve registered the words, but she could not seem to retain them. All she could think about was how it must feel to be a killer, a thief of life, and the sheer waste of it all.

If grief created absences, was committing murder a way of filling those gaps?

Hudson murmured into the machine, deleting all emotion and replacing it with the language of science. The minutes ticked on. Wildeve was conscious of Sheridan's eyes upon her. The soft, sucking sounds of the mortuary technician at work. The detective had been too distracted to wear plastic shoe covers, and when she looked down, she noticed the pale suede of her desert boots had a tidemark of bodily fluids.

She could not tear her eyes away from the stain.

Bile burned the tender spot at the back of her throat, but she would not allow herself to be sick. She had made a pact. This was her duty.

She swallowed again.

She knew what was coming.

In a couple of minutes, Hudson would direct her assistant to slice through the scalp and open up the skull. But Wildeve did not want to hear the whine of blade against bone, the rising of the dust, and the scorched smell of Hell.

She did not want to watch Hudson bend over in observation as soon as the skull was chiselled open, seeking out signs of haemorrhaging.

She did not want to see the brain – the part of the body

that makes us all human, that lets us sing and laugh and savour and love – pulled free with forceps for analysis, reduced to a lump of meat.

Her hand gripped the edge of the table. The walls rippled, the start of an earthquake. She breathed. In. Out. In. Out. After a sort of fierce gulping, she was able to compose herself.

She had wanted to be here. This was her choice.

But it was too much.

Too soon.

In a flash, Sheridan was at her shoulder again, and she leaned into him, the solid mass of his body a comfort as her legs began to shake.

'I'm fine,' she said. Repeated it. A lifelong mantra to keep the darkness at bay.

'Let's get you some water,' he said, steering her towards the door.

She wanted to protest, to insist that she could handle it. She was one of the lead detectives on a murder case that was making national headlines, for Christ's sake. She didn't need to *lean* on anyone.

Three or four black spots in the periphery of her vision began to flash. Lightning bolts of nerve pain struck her jawline, spreading out towards her ear, the back of her head. The beginnings of an attack of trigeminal neuralgia. Extreme stress could do that. It could bring her to her knees.

Wildeve embraced the hot spikes of physical pain. It distracted from the deadness inside. She wanted to stay here until the organs were returned to the body, until the incisions were sewn closed, the body cleansed and the hair washed. To bear witness.

And she had promised. *They* had promised. Not the vows they had made amongst the rain of confetti, although she had meant every word of those too, but in the dark cloak of their honeymoon suite, a confessional for their bleakest fears.

But the room was growing smaller, the black dots running into blotches that would soon obscure her vision. And the pain was drilling its way deeper, and she needed her fix of Carbamazepine and some water, and her bed. She staggered as another blast of fire exploded in her head. She didn't want to, but it was time for her to leave.

Wildeve half turned to get a last glimpse of the eyeless body on the mortuary slab. The fifth victim of the Doll Maker.

The shock of black hair.

The birthmark on his shoulder.

Adam Stanton, police officer, husband and love of her life.

14

Now

I spy with my little eye, something beginning with A.

Did you ever learn the origins of the word 'pupil'? I know I did not teach you and it's not common knowledge, I suppose. Its roots are in Latin. *Pupilla.* Meaning 'little doll'. Because when we gaze into another's eyes, we see a tiny reflection of ourselves.

Little doll.

Birdie wanted a doll, a plaything to dress up and do her bidding. She did not want a creature with teeth and nails to scratch a way out. She wanted a dutiful child. With no man in the house, certain responsibilities fell to me. Cleaning and fixing and earning money.

When I was four and would not eat my dinner, she pressed an iron between the dip of my shoulder blades. When I was five and there was not enough money to buy food, she sent me out in the fields of the Essex edgelands to pick peas. When I was nine, she burned the skin from my wrist with caustic soda. When I was thirteen, I blinded her in one eye with a piece of broken glass. *An accident, Birdie. I'm such a clumsy boo.* Just like she said I was.

She left me alone for months after that.

I knew Adam Stanton was a police officer. I recognized his name, of course. His face. He was getting closer, and we couldn't have that, could we? Asking uncomfortable questions, grubbing around in the dirt of the past.

His skin stayed warm for four hours. Eyes the colour of estuary mud when the clouds hang low and heavy. No fanfare. No tolling of the bells. No farewell. His final word was . . . there wasn't one. A grunt. That was all.

Killing him was a risk. Order. Control. They are my watchwords, but I broke my own rules.

I do not blame him, though. He was doing his job. Too well, as it turned out.

No, the fault lies with her. Olivia Lockwood. Because without her, the murders would have been impossible to prove. But she brought down this house of cards upon us all.

15

The Avenue – 9.17 a.m.

The postman parked his van at the top of The Avenue and switched off the radio. The breakfast news bulletins were full of the latest killing. The murder of a senior police officer involved in the case had raised the stakes and a knot of journalists had already gathered at the cordon blocking the entrance to the woods.

The man, solidly built and muscular, opened one of the double doors at the back and pulled free a modest-sized bag of mail, hoisting it over his shoulder. Breathing the air was like inhaling tepid water. Even the trees seemed defeated by the heat, their leaves dry and brittle. His shirt stuck to his back despite the early hour, and he prayed for kinder weather.

The postman's fingers were pressed against the hot metal of the door, preparing to shut it and begin his round, but something made him hesitate. He glanced down the empty street. After a few seconds of indecision, he sidled

59

closer to the door and peered through the gap to the interior of the van.

The woman was lying there, rough strips of duct tape silencing her mouth and binding her ankles, her eyes wide and terrified. They spoke to him, those eyes. Pleading, asking for his help.

He stared at her, willing himself to lock the door and make a start on delivering his letters, but his trainers were stuck to the road, as if the asphalt had melted and was holding him hostage.

The woman's eyes were brown and ordinary, and they were fixed on him.

He shut his own, squeezing out the glare of the daylight and the weight of her accusation. When he opened them again, she was gone, and all that remained was a stain on the floor of the van.

The postman hadn't seen them bring out Adam Stanton's body. Sunday was supposed to be his day off and it would have looked weird – suspicious, even – if he'd been hanging around. But he had heard about it. Everyone had. What a grade-A fuck-up.

Now he wasn't sure how to feel. A seagull shrieked overhead, bringing with it a flavour of the coast. Southend-on-Sea was eight miles away. On a morning like this, it would quickly fill with day trippers, sunlight scattering glitter across the waves, the smells of hot fat and Hawaiian Tropic. But this street, with its squashed-up houses and barely-room-to-pass pavements, dog dirt and prison-gate walls of laurel and yew, was a world away, and beginning to give him the creeps. He examined this unfamiliar sensation. He wasn't one to scare easily.

This was a new job for him. Only a few weeks old and he'd given it everything so far, but it wasn't working out in the way he had hoped. Still, the residents were friendly enough and that had made it easier.

He pushed the earlier unpleasantness to the back of his mind and began to walk, his trainers playing a rhythm on the heat-baked pavement, light dripping through the gaps in the leaves.

Shifting his mail pouch into a more comfortable position, he lifted a hand to the mother from number thirty, who was struggling down her path with a double buggy. Grinned and raised his eyebrows at the suit running to the station. Offered up a good morning to Mrs Clifton from number twenty-seven, who was putting out her rubbish.

'Any chance of a cuppa?' he said, a grin on his face, one of the lads.

It had become a standing joke. He said it every time he saw her, and every few days she relented and went inside to boil the kettle. Then they'd stand at the top of her drive and chat for ten minutes or so.

She smiled at him, an indulgent, motherly look. 'Go on, then, you cheeky beggar.'

The tea was stewed – too bitter for his taste – but she'd brought him a slice of home-made ginger cake, and he nibbled its edges.

'How have you been, Mrs C?'

'Mustn't grumble.' She sipped her own tea, hands trembling slightly. *The beginnings of Parkinson's,* he wondered. *Or just old age.* Her front door was half open, and he glimpsed the shadow of her wheelchair in the hallway.

'Terrible business, isn't it?' He tipped his head in the

direction of the woods before taking another mouthful, crumbs spilling down his shirt.

She nodded, but her grey curls did not move, set solidly in place with hairspray. The spider-web cracks on her face deepened. 'Awful.'

'Do you think they'll catch him?'

'They're taking their time about it.' She glanced across the street to the officer standing by the police cordon. 'Look at him, poor devil. He must be parched. I think I'll make him a cup of tea too.'

When the postman had finished his cake, he tipped his too-strong tea into the bushes and watched her limp across the road with a tray of hot drinks for them all. Such decency was a breath of fresh air. It cost nothing to be kind.

Plenty weren't. He'd seen it all over the years. And, even in the short time he had worked here, he'd become far more intimate with the residents of The Avenue than they might have been comfortable with.

He knew who had received a court summons, who paid child maintenance and who was in trouble with the bank.

He knew who got up early and who slept in late, who had children and who did not. He knew one householder had moved in his girlfriend while his wife was overseas, tending to her sick mother.

He knew that new people had moved into number twenty-five.

He knew all their secrets.

And like so many of the residents of The Avenue, he had one of his own.

16

Now

On the day we moved into The Avenue, we celebrated with cherryade from the Corona man and gammon and pineapple with boiled potatoes.

Birdie was giddy with excitement. The flat had been cramped and the smell of dirty knickers had seeped up through the floorboards from the fishmongers below.

But the house represented the pinnacle of every one of Birdie's dreams of success – three bedrooms, two toilets and a patio. Even the rats that migrated from the copse that ran along the bottom of the garden were only a minor irritation, exterminated with pellets of Rodine that came in a red box Birdie kept in the pantry. All life sucked from their stiff little bodies.

The shop was doing well and our circumstances had changed. Lots to eat. A lady who came in to clean. But Birdie still made me earn my keep by working the till at the weekends and after school.

'I don't want any Tom, Dick or Harry robbing me blind,' she said. 'Let's keep it in the family.'

But I missed the flat.

The house was too big. A place to lose oneself, to lose sight of oneself. Just Birdie and me. I was the only child on the street and had no one to play with. My bike was new but it wasn't the same on my own. I wanted a rope swing or a treehouse, but Birdie said no. It didn't take me long to find my way to Blatches Woods.

In amongst the trees, I could hide, pressing myself against the bark, enclosed in the embrace of the branches, no gaps to fill, no empty spaces, squeezed in, safe and protected.

As soon as the shop shut, I ran straight there, building insect houses and a den for myself, listening to the songbirds and scattering seeds for them, feeling the sun and the wind and the rain.

The first one was the starling. Autumn, when the leaves had started to turn. Its beak was wide open, claws curled into its breast. I dug a hole in the earth with a stick and covered it in dirt.

The next afternoon, I found two more of them. A magpie on the footpath into the woods and, next to the rotted tree stump, a bird with pink and blue feathers my book told me was a jay.

The jay's eyes were open, a black hole set in a circle of brown.

I climbed up two or three branches, to survey a wider distance. I saw another jay, two speckled thrushes and a robin with its distinctive orange-red breast lying on the ground. By the fallen trunk of the oak, I saw the mottled markings and curved beak of a tawny owl. I collected them up and laid them in a row, a rushing sound in my ears.

You were always the animal lover, not me.

I was eleven then. I did not think of myself as cruel, merely curious. An experiment, of sorts. I had mixed Birdie's rat poison with their seeds and carried it in a margarine tub to the woods because I wanted to see what would happen.

That day was hazy-gold, a late September heatwave lighting the country, our town, this street, my own patch of shadow amongst the trees.

I sat on a log, listening to the rustle of the leaves and licking sherbet from my fingers, and thought about what I had discovered.

The glory of power over living things.

17

25 The Avenue – 9.21 a.m.

Evan Lockwood wore his football kit every day even when he wasn't playing football.

The sun seeping through the window was already heating up his bedroom, making it impossible for him to sleep. He pulled on yesterday's socks and flicked through his collection of Panini stickers. Tried a couple of tricks with his diabolo. Cocked his head and listened.

The house was quiet. He guessed his father had left for his meeting at the bank and his mother was working in the study. His dumb idiot of a sister would still be in bed.

He picked up his Magic 8 Ball and gave it a shake. *Do my parents love me?* He peered at the answer, which appeared faintly in the window. *Don't count on it.* He threw it across the room.

Evan's bedroom was at the back of the house, overlooking the garden. Aster was angry with their mother for forcing them to move, but he didn't feel the same way. It meant he never had to see Lucas Naylor again, who was

66

twice his size with a mouth to match, or worry about who to play with at lunchtime. Yes, he'd be on his own when he started at his new school, but he could handle that. Much worse to have had a gang of friends who, thanks to Lucas, were too scared to play with him than to have none at all.

The early-morning sun was chasing shadows from the grass. When he was younger, Evan had believed his shadow was his soul, and the darker it was, the naughtier he'd been. Now he was nine, he knew better. Although sometimes he checked, just to be sure.

Birdsong drifted in through the open window. A bank of roses, all pale yellows and pinks, edged the lawn, which was narrow but long. At the far end of the garden, leaning against the plums and polished leaves, was a treehouse, windows black with shadow, wood bleached and cracked by the sun.

It looked old and rickety and full of secrets.

Evan itched to scramble up the ladder and explore, but his mother had forbidden him. His thoughts strayed back to last night's conversation, as he'd got himself ready for bed.

'Can I climb the treehouse, Mum?'

'Not now, love. It's bedtime.'

Evan had stopped brushing, his mouth full of toothpaste. 'Tomorrow?'

'Dad's worried about the ladder being rotten. And the rope. We'll sort it out at the weekend.'

Evan had rinsed out his mouth and laid his toothbrush carefully on the enamel sink. In their old house, they'd had a toothbrush holder. It was a small thing, but he'd felt a longing for the familiar.

'Maybe I could climb the tree instead. I'm good at climbing trees.'

'I don't think so, love. It's pretty high. And a heck of a way to fall.'

'Can you lift me up then?' He'd shrugged on his vest, too hot for pyjamas. 'You could watch me.'

'Not now, Evan,' she'd said, drawing the sheet over him, impatience colouring her tone. 'Let's leave it until the weekend, OK?'

And then she had kissed his forehead and gone downstairs.

She was always looking for excuses, his mother. Excuses not to play football or cards or climb a plum tree. But that was last night. And this was a new day.

Evan leaned his forehead against the glass, his eyes fixed on the treehouse at the end of the garden, bracketed by bushes and overlooking the murk of a copse.

The ladder didn't *look* rotten, just old.

In truth, the whole structure looked old. A crooked roof, four windows smudged with dirt, a door that didn't fit and a rope that hung down like a snake.

But Evan didn't care. It was the best treehouse he had ever seen.

The desire to explore edged out the instinct to obey his mother.

He crept down the stairs, wincing at the yelp from a floorboard he would have to figure out how to avoid. He held himself still, half expecting his mother to appear in the door of the study, his opportunity lost. But the house stayed hushed. He unlocked the back door and stepped into paradise.

THE NEIGHBOUR

The morning sun warmed his face, the fresh-grass smell of summer as powerful as his mother's perfume. A bee drunk on pollen bumped into his arm and righted itself, droning drowsily. A bird, startled by Evan's appearance on the patio, darted across the lawn. The sky was holiday-blue.

The kind of day where nothing goes wrong.

Evan pelted down the garden, a smile splitting open his face, the untasted joy of defiance on his lips.

Up close, the treehouse was much bigger than it seemed from his bedroom window, the copse rising behind it like a sinister presence.

A gate was set into the fence at the bottom of the garden, allowing access to the thicket and the playground of trees beyond. It was much smaller than Blatches Woods, but this tangle of woodland was still big enough to get lost in.

A few metres beyond that was a narrow but deep ditch, filled with dead leaves, sticks and the memory of water. It was overgrown with weeds and long grasses, and its high bank and the fence disguised it from the house, but Evan barely gave it a second glance. His interests lay elsewhere.

The trunk of the plum tree was like a ship's mast, pushing up through the centre of the treehouse walls, which were haphazard but sturdy. The floor was made from imperfect wooden boards with a hole cut in the middle to allow for the trunk. Nailed into its bark was a rope that dangled below, an invitation. Evan tugged on it and several strands of nylon fibre came off in his hands. He turned to the ladder, which rested against the bottom of the tree, and pressed one foot on the first rung. It wobbled, but held.

The boy, who was light and fleet, scrambled up. He was an adventurer. An explorer. Climbing into a new world.

Leaves tickled his face. The sweet scent of ripening fruit filled his nose and mouth. Excitement filled him up. He did not notice the wasps crawling over the skin of the plums, or the indignant croak of a crow as it flapped its wings on a branch and lifted skywards.

The door, it turned out, wasn't functional, but nailed into place. Entry was by pulling himself up onto the floorboards through a narrow gap by the trunk. Not safe. But fun.

The roof was high enough for him to stand up, so Evan, brave but wary, leaned against the trunk and drank in his surroundings.

Despite the rising heat of the morning, the treehouse was cool and shadowed, protected by the shallow coppice beyond the garden fence. A couple of cushions filled with dust and memories lay on the floor, their covers the vivid, geometric designs from a time long before Evan. One had a faded, rusty patch.

And it was dry. No damp wood, just a smell like the banned creosote his father kept in the garage.

The second thing he noticed was the dead bugs. Everywhere. Dried husks of flies and woodlice wrapped in the sticky strings of the thick webs that decorated every corner.

He wondered which children had played here before him and where they were now.

A long, low call disturbed the peace. The boy started. His mother's voice sounded far away, but he could still detect her irritated tone as she shouted his name.

He peered out of one of the windows. It was smeared with dust and dirt, but he could see enough to know that she was standing by the back door, calling for him. 'Evan. *Evan.*' Sharper that time. She looked straight at the treehouse.

He crouched down, biting his lip and stifling an urge to giggle. Grabbing one of the cushions, he lay down on the filthy floor, staring up at the corrugated iron roof and marvelling at the way the metal moved in waves.

In the distance, the back door slammed. He wondered if his mother was right that minute making her way down the garden, readying herself to shout at him. He hated it when she did that, twisting her face into someone he didn't recognize.

He listened to the sounds of the garden waking up. The rustle of an animal in the undergrowth. A chorus of crickets. The low thrum of a plane far above, packed with holiday-makers.

He stretched out his legs and buried the back of his head more comfortably into the cushion. A spark of pain made him sit up again.

Evan ran his fingers along the faded fabric. There it was. Something hard and square inside the lining, its sharp corner had poked him in the neck. He undid the zip and felt around.

His fingers closed on a box.

Evan pulled it free and stared at it. He had no idea what it was. He had never seen anything like it before.

It was transparent, smaller and flatter than one of those boxes of cereal from a variety pack, and lined with a cardboard insert marked by a reddish-brown thumbprint. He fiddled with it until it opened.

Inside was a black rectangle with two holes in the middle and a spool of what looked like dark, thin Sellotape. The words 'TDK' and 'D-60' were printed on it. On one side was the letter A. He flipped it over to find a B on the other side.

Evan held it up to his eyes and peered through the holes

like they were binoculars. He tapped the plastic casing. His finger stroked the shiny blackness of the – what? To him, it looked like ribbon or the decorative trimmings his mother sometimes wrapped around presents. He wanted to slip his nail under it and pull it free, but some instinct stopped him.

Evan examined it again. Across the top of the flat rectangle was a yellowing sticker. He peered closer. Words in pencil. The handwriting was oversized, a little clunky. Much like his own.

Play Me.

He turned it over and over in his hands, wondering what it meant. Should he play *with* it? But it didn't say that, and anyway, he didn't know how to. In his head, he drew up a list of things that could be played. *DVDs. Instruments. Music.* He picked at the graze on his elbow. That thought wouldn't go away. *Music.*

He knew it wasn't a CD because he'd got his own player for Christmas when he was seven, and he knew it wasn't a record because it was nothing like the round, crackling discs his father played on his turntable.

He flipped it over and inspected the other side. Another yellowing sticker. And the faint remnants of the same childish handwriting, although smaller this time, more cramped.

The boy could just about make out half a sentence.

Don't ever

Frustratingly, the rest of the words were too faded to read, as if the graphite had been smudged in haste or rubbed out.

THE NEIGHBOUR

'I knew you couldn't keep away, you naughty boy.'

Evan's mother's voice drifted up into the treehouse. He leaned over the hole where the trunk stood, and looked down. She was gazing up at him, hands on her hips, and she wasn't smiling. 'Get down now.'

Evan slipped his find down the elastic of his football shorts. He didn't know what he'd discovered and why it had been hidden, but he was going to find out.

18

32 The Avenue – 11.37 a.m.

They were outside his house.

Trefor Lovell could hear them, catcalling and whispering. Experience warned him that soon they would be at his door, ringing the bell and running off. Laughing. Loud. High on the adrenaline of a dare.

If only they would leave him alone. What exactly had he done to them? Nothing, except mind his own damn business.

He imagined a rubbish truck rolling up the road, tipping over on its side and crushing them to death, their arms and legs as mangled as the spokes of their bicycle wheels. Or looping rope around their scrawny little necks and letting them swing from the branches of the hornbeam. Death by long drop or suspension? A severed spinal column or slow strangulation? Slow would be better, he decided. More time for regrets.

He finished making the bed and hovered at the top of the landing. Someone laughed again, boyish with a hint of cruelty. He was looking straight down the valley of the stair-well when the letterbox opened.

'Hey Ol' Man Lovell. You killed your wife yet? Did you bury her in the garden?'

The flap shut, and he trapped and held his next breath. There would be more. And so there was.

'It's you, isn't it? You're the Doll Maker. Are you going to give us some ickle-wickle dolly-wollies, you fucking sicko? Or are you going to murder us?' It was a teenage boy's voice. He laughed again, and Lovell recognized in it a kind of shocked delight.

Trefor freed the air from his lungs, and contemplated his next move. He needed to leave for work. He had orders to fulfil, and he was behind. Perhaps he should chase them up The Avenue. Give *them* a scare. But the last time he'd done that, they'd stuck soiled sanitary towels to his windows. After a day in the sun, the odour had made him gag as he'd cleaned up the mess.

The tips of the boy's fingers appeared in the mouth of his front door. Trefor frowned. What were they up to? Muf-fled conversation, and an exclamation of disgust. A giggle, but stifled, as if Trefor would hear, open up and demand to be in on the joke.

He took a step down the stairs, intending to confront them.

Bunches of dried lavender that hung from the bannister brushed against him, sending tiny, fragrant flowers tum-bling over his shoulders. His wife Annie had loved these vibrant blooms before she'd left him, and so he'd placed them in every room.

A small envelope – the padded type, thick with bubble

wrap and about the size of a birthday card – dropped through the letterbox, the sound breaking open the silence of the house.

'WIFE KILLER' was scrawled across the front.

Fire burned in him. He had never done anything to hurt his wife. It wasn't his fault she'd gone, he'd begged her not to leave him. It wasn't his fault that he could not bring himself to talk about it, could not face the onslaught of his neighbours, raking over the memories of his marriage, sticking their noses in. It wasn't his fault that because the gossips hadn't seen her for a few months, conveniently forgetting she'd been housebound and rarely went out, and because he was a closed and private man, they'd drawn their own conclusions, laced with a cruelty borne of ignorance.

It wasn't his fault that in the end he'd been forced to lie, to pretend she was staying with her goddaughter to satisfy the busybodies who might feel inclined to voice their suspicions to the police.

The sensible course of action would be to ignore the envelope and dump it in the bin. But a part of him was wounded by these accusations. It fed his masochistic need to pick at the scab of this injustice.

It was as light as a feather.

He shook it, but could feel nothing inside, no shift of weight, no displacement of contents. He frowned. Perhaps it was a note. Well, damn them all. He could handle that. He ran a finger along the seal and peeled back the flap.

In that split second, when he first looked inside, he believed it full of grains of rice. And that puzzled him because why would those shit-for-brains kids send him rice? There were hundreds and hundreds of these pale brownish grains, filling the envelope right to the brim, and when he looked again they were moving. *They were moving.*

Maggots.

He gagged. Dropped the envelope. And then they were everywhere, squirming across the carpet and moving over his slippers in their seemingly directionless quest for dying flesh.

Retching, Trefor lunged for the envelope while trying to sweep up a handful of the tiny, wriggling larvae, but he fumbled with it and lost his grip, tipping it over on its side. Now there were many more of them, spilling out of the bubble wrap, corkscrewing across each other, burrowing into the polyester fibres, seeking out dark places. Disappearing.

Sweet Jesus, those fucking kids. Did they have any idea what they had done?

Trefor kicked his feet, his movements wild and uncontrolled, trying to dislodge the maggots. He ran to the cupboard underneath the stairs and pulled out a vacuum cleaner, ancient and bulky. Hands shaking, he plugged it in and shoved it across the floor, hitting the skirting boards and the radiator pipes in his panic to contain the infestation defiling his home. He needed them gone. Every last one.

But it was impossible to be certain.

When he had finished cleaning up, he opened his front door and scanned the street. It was empty. But he knew who they were. He recognized their voices.

And those little fuckers were going to pay.

19

The Avenue – 12.01 p.m.

The kids on their bikes almost knocked into him as they flew up the street, their whooping laughter as cruel as the midday sun.

The postman shielded his eyes with his hand and watched them go. He thought about checking on the old guy – he'd seen them congregating outside his house earlier that morning – but decided it was none of his business.

Instead he walked up the path to number twenty-seven, more certain of his welcome there. He was thirsty, a fresh sheen of sweat coating his forehead. A couple of dried leaves clung to the cotton fibres of his shirt. Needing to kill some time, he had driven his van around to the north-west entrance of Blatches Woods, where he had sat on a bench amongst the quiet company of the trees and contemplated his next move. But now he was back in The Avenue, magnetized to this place.

As he bent to post the letter he had deliberately withheld, Audrina Clifton opened the door, floral pinny tied around her waist, lambswool slippers on her feet. 'You again?' There was a teasing note to her voice. 'I thought you'd be long gone by now.'

'Missed this one.' He waggled it. 'Looks like a bill, I'm afraid, Mrs C,' he said, straightening up and handing it to her.

She tutted good-naturedly. 'The dreaded brown envelope.'

'Bane of my life.' As she shifted on the doorstep, transferring her weight from one leg to the other, he noticed her wince. 'How's your arthritis?'

A rueful shrug. 'Comes and goes. Not too bad today.'

'And what's Mr Clifton doing on this fine afternoon? Still suffering with his back?'

Her smile disappeared, the sun behind a cloud. 'In the garden, as usual. Fretting about his plants.' She peered skywards. 'I hope the weather breaks soon. We're in need of some rain.' Her eyes met his, and she said, surprised, as if seeing him properly for the first time, 'Goodness, you look hot.'

'I'm slowly roasting to death out here. Still, it could be worse. I could be stuck in an office.' He grinned at her, his teeth bright against his sun-tanned skin.

'I expect you'd like a glass of something cold.'

'I hate to put you out.'

'It's no bother. Iced water? Or I've got some orange juice.'

'Juice would be lovely.'

He loitered on the step. She didn't invite him in. She never did. But it didn't matter. He was happy to stand and chat in the sunshine. Inside or out, it made no difference.

They stood side by side, surveying the street, watching a cat on a wall stretch in the heat. He lifted his glass. 'Never had this as a kid. But my niece loves it.'

A chuckle laced with sympathy. 'Too expensive, I expect. We used to buy those little cartons for my son. He liked them in his lunchbox.'

'And now you do the same for the grandkids, I expect?' He nudged her gently to show that he was teasing.

Her face crumpled, reminding him of a used tissue. 'We don't have grandchildren.'

The postman flushed. He patted her arm, a gesture clunky with embarrassment. 'Forgive me. Me and my big mouth.'

'Please, don't worry.' She took another sip of her drink and watched a butterfly land on the buddleia. 'Perhaps I should have worded it more carefully. We *don't know* if we have grandchildren. We haven't seen our son for a very long time.'

'I'm sorry to hear that.' The postman was used to hearing confidences. And opening up to a stranger was easier for some. 'That must be difficult.' He pulled at a loose thread on the strap of his postbag, careful to avoid eye contact in case she clammed up. 'If you don't mind – I mean, feel free to tell me to shut up – but what happened?'

A sigh so filled with regret it almost hurt to listen.

'He ran away a long time ago. A family argument and that was it. Last time we saw him.'

The postman whistled. 'Sounds tough. Have you tried to find him?'

She didn't answer straight away and he suspected she wasn't going to. But then she took his empty glass, sadness threading its way through her words. 'We're still here. We haven't gone anywhere.'

A shadow crossed the sun, and the postman remembered his own secret. 'Do you *want* to see him?'

She turned to him, and he was floored by the bleakness in her eyes.

'Wanting something won't make it happen,' she said.

Then she went inside and shut the door.

20

Now

Love has many guises.

The electrical arc of physical attraction. The comfortable slippers of a long marriage. Flip a coin, though, and it becomes the burn of unrequited desire, the tunnel-vision darkness of an obsessive. Love is the balancing act of friendship and the willing handcuffs of parenthood. The secrets we keep to protect those we should trust.

But nothing prepared me for you.

I had loved before, of course. Not often. But enough. This was different, though. Deeper. Unexpected. You taught me things I hadn't realized I needed to learn. The way your eyes looked into my hidden self. The feel of your hand against mine. Your breath on my cheek.

But as I grew older, I discovered what Birdie had known all along.

Love does not always stay the same. It congeals into something unpleasant and ugly.

THE NEIGHBOUR

For a long time, you mended something inside me I believed to be broken. But, as we both discovered to our cost, that repair was only temporary.

21

4 Hillside Crescent – 12.04 p.m.

The back of the house was cool in the heat. Wildeve Stanton had been resistant to buying it, bemoaning the shadows that lay across the garden and the sun-baked driveway with its cracked paving stones. But now, in the cave of their kitchen, she was grateful to escape the eye-screwing light.

'Here, drink this.' DC Jim Sheridan, who had driven her car home and steered her through the pack of journalists waiting on the pavement for a statement about her husband's death, handed her a glass.

She swallowed down her tablets with lukewarm tap water, ignoring the taste of chlorine. The pain in her head was like the turn of a screwdriver.

She mumbled her thanks, but the only way back was to try and sleep it off. With her eyes closed, she pointed to the ceiling, trying to convey to Jim Sheridan that she needed to go to bed.

He gave her arm a squeeze. 'I'll see myself out,' he said.

She dragged herself upstairs, aware in the vaguest of senses that Sheridan was lingering in the hallway.

When she reached the third stair from the top, she heard the familiar click of the front door opening.

'We're all with you, Wild,' he called softly. 'I hope you know that.'

And then he was gone.

The shape of the shadows in her bedroom was enough to tell her that a significant part of the day had passed while she was lost in sleep.

Wildeve stayed still, braced for a drill-burst of pain. When it came, she let out a low groan, but the drugs had begun to do their job. She rolled onto her side, stretching out an arm to draw Adam towards her, but the place where he should have been was empty.

The tragedy of sleep was waking up. Turning a new page of sorrow and awareness. A second, perhaps two, of forgetting before the memory of his murder sliced through her with its rusty and serrated blade, designed to cause maximum damage.

She lay still, eyes closed, residual sparks of pain in her head, replaying the sequence of events that had led her to this dark hollow.

Less than twenty-four hours ago, Detective Sergeant Wildeve Stanton had been in the Major Incident Room at Rayleigh Police Station in Essex, rereading the case files of Esther Farnworth, the second victim of the Doll Maker. Esther was a single mother, forty years old, white, working at the local school. In an investigation as large-scale as this, there were thousands of leads to explore. Most led to dead ends. But a handful, those hidden pathways, marked out a map to follow. She just had to find them.

Wildeve had written notes on a pad she kept in her pocket.

Motive? Opportunistic? No link established to previous or subsequent victims except locality. Why choose EF? WHY?

Every minute of what had followed was time-stamped into the neurons of her brain, and they fired together again and again, replaying the memory until her eyes burned and her throat was dry and sore.

A ribbon of steam had been curling its way upwards from her coffee cup. In the well between her breasts, sweat was clinging to her skin. The office was too hot, even with the fans on. The sound of heavy footsteps and the weight of a hand on her shoulder.

She had turned around, mouth kinked by a smile, expecting to see Adam, but it was his friend, PC Simon Quick. Despite the heat, his face was the colour of a winter sky. Wildeve had half risen from her chair.

'God, Si, are you OK?'

A hush had settled over the room, a collective intake of breath. On the periphery of her vision, she was aware of her colleagues huddling in twos and threes by their desks, and then the whispering had begun, like the muttering of leaves on the trees. A thought, as clear as the pealing of the bell from the church near her childhood home, popped into her head.

Something has happened.

She became aware of the knock of her heart in her chest,

the flecks of grey in Simon's beard, the grass stains on his knees, the pinch of her new suede boots. And in that slowing down of time, her subconscious, making connections for her at dizzying speed, offered up her next question.

'It's not Adam, is it?'

The words broke open the silence. Even if she lived for a hundred years, she would never forget the way that Simon's mask cracked and fell away.

'Wild, it's bad,' he said.

'How bad?'

Simon pressed his palms together in prayer, cupped them around his mouth and nose, and blew into the dark space.

'Si?' Her voice lifted in panic, that last vowel stretching into a plea, although she would not have been able to say whether she was desperate for information or the bliss of ignorance, to *never* know the truth of what he was about to tell her.

'There's been a . . .' Simon pushed a hand through his hair, and she was struck by how much he looked like a boy and not a man, and how strange it was that the mind filled up with random thoughts, as if they might cushion the blow of his words. 'Someone called in a . . .' His lip trembled. 'I got there first. Well, me and Theo did.'

His eyes would not meet hers, and so she watched his mouth move, trying to catch each of the words as they tumbled out. She wondered where his police dog was, but mostly she wanted him to get to the point. This preamble frightened her, as if the delay meant it was already too late.

'Adam had taken himself on a job, but none of us knew where he'd gone, and –' it was curious, the shapes that lips formed during speech – 'he was late for the briefing but no one had heard from him and then a member of the public found him, and he wasn't breathing.'

Her head had snapped up then, and she stopped watching Simon's mouth and searched again for his eyes, and when her husband's friend found the courage to look at her, the landscape was so bleak that she had to turn away.

'I'll drive you to the hospital,' he had said.

She had known then that Adam was dead. Because Simon would have told her if he was alive, however badly injured. Because she had used those words herself when she had knocked at the home of a teenage boy who had borrowed the family car, or a sister who had slipped out to meet a stranger off the internet, or an uncle who had got into a fight outside the pub.

She could not bring herself to burden their families with the truth, not all at once. The car journey to the hospital was to prepare them for what they would find there.

Wildeve had staggered against the desk, bruising the back of her thighs, a dark smudge of pain. Simon had caught her wrist and kept her upright, but the shock, the grief, was not how she expected it at all.

Her heart was not collapsing in on itself or breaking into pieces. She was not a reduced husk of herself. Instead, she walked the wide, empty spaces of pain. She felt herself opening up, like a house with a dozen empty rooms. So much nothingness to fill.

One day ago, she had been a wife. Now she was a widow.

Wildeve touched her temples. The pain was still sparking, like an ignition that would not catch, but it was dulled for now. She forced herself to get up. She needed water. Something to eat.

As she stumbled down the stairs, gripping the bannister to anchor herself against her blurred vision, she became aware of a shadow behind the front door.

Adam.

Her heart stuttered, as if he had somehow found his way home, and the past twenty-four hours had been nothing more than a terrible dream.

But the doorbell was ringing and Adam had his own key, and when she looked again, the shadow was taller and broader than her husband had been. She was about to shout, to tell the journalist to leave her alone, when a familiar voice spoke.

'C'mon, Wild, open up. It's me.'

She had been avoiding him, but now he had seen her, moving around the hallway. Damn Jim Sheridan for giving her away.

PC Simon Quick was standing in an awkward manner that suggested he was not sure of his welcome. Well, he *wasn't* welcome. Wildeve did not want this. She did not have the strength to cope with it. But it seemed she had no choice.

PC Quick made tea and carried it through to the sitting room. Wildeve could not think of anyone less suited to their name. He moved through life as if his batteries were running down, was often late and needed a decent haircut. But in the twelve months he'd been paired with his dog, Theo, they'd made a formidable team, their results earning the attention of the Chief Constable.

Simon perched on the edge of the armchair, his rucksack by his feet. Wildeve's eyes stung with the salt of unshed tears. So much to say. She had tried to keep it together at work, but here, memories in every corner, she could feel the tiny threads of herself unravel.

'Do you think you should see a doctor?'

'I'm fine.'

She wasn't. What a ludicrous thing to say. Wildeve imagined her words growing smaller, like a fading echo. *Fine, fine, fine, fine, fine.* She imagined herself growing smaller too, until she no longer existed. Simon glanced across the room at the wedding photograph on the mantelpiece.

'Bloody brilliant day.' A rueful smile. 'Had to iron his shirt for him, didn't I? Right mess he'd made of it.' He tried to chuckle, but the sound died in his throat. 'Didn't realize my best-man duties would extend to that. Bloody hate ironing.' His eyes filled with tears. 'I'm going to miss him.'

She willed him not to fall apart. She could not deal with the onslaught of his pain as well as her own. All she had to offer him was a tight nod.

'I'm worried about you. Emily, too. She sends you her love. Told me to invite you for dinner.'

'I'm fine, Simon,' she said again, the lie falling from her lips as naturally as rain. Her husband had been murdered. She would never be *fine* again. But she did not want to open up her pain in front of him because she understood the wound would never close. He had loved Adam as much as she had. It would swallow him too.

'You can come to us anytime you need to,' he said. 'I mean it, Wild.'

This time, her tone was softer, genuine. 'I know that. And thank you.'

Simon leaned back into the cushions, took a sip of his

drink, stretched out his long legs. 'I heard you went into work today.'

'Yes.'

'Are you going to the briefing this afternoon?'

She shrugged, even though she knew the answer. She just couldn't face a lecture.

'I don't think you should. It's not right. I'll stay with you, if you like.'

'It's not up to you.' A flare of anger ambushed her. 'And I prefer to be on my own.' It sounded harsher than she meant.

PC Quick's face fell. He put down his mug with care, and reached for his bag. Wildeve's hands began to shake, spilling tea onto her thighs. The stain spread across her pyjama bottoms, darkening the cotton, scalding her skin, but she didn't move. Couldn't speak.

He held an envelope in his hand.

Wildeve closed her eyes, the reservoir behind them as dry as sand. She ought to say something, a thank you, if nothing else. But how could she bring herself to do that when she felt no gratitude?

Pain began to rake its nails across her jaw, clawing at the back of her head. The drugs were wearing off. For two or three minutes, she gave herself over to it, allowing the firework bursts of agony to crowd out everything except the clarity of sensation. She screwed up her eyes, dug white-knuckled fingers into the sofa and rode the storm.

When the hurt had retreated and she managed to wrench apart her eyelids, Simon was gone and all that remained was a mug of cold tea and a letter that held the words of a ghost.

22

Now

Step on a crack, you'll break your mother's back.

Birdie disappeared when I was eighteen. It was a relief for both of us.

One day she was there, making bitter coffee and comments, the next she had gone, her cup still on the counter, a ring of scum imprinted on its inside.

She had not made a will, but as her only surviving next of kin, the shop and the house became mine.

No one knew what had happened to her. Not the couple of friends she had failed to alienate. Or the neighbours wrapped up in the cloth of their own lives. Not her new lover who insisted it was 'completely out of character' for her to up and leave without saying goodbye. He made a bit of a fuss. But, as I explained to the police, she had threatened to walk out before. That was the God's honest truth.

On that first night without her – *my* first night without her – I could breathe again. She had always kept a thick roll of cash in a tin in her wardrobe and I was used to a frugal life.

In any case, I had fallen in love. We lived in Birdie's house together, pooling our resources, creating our own happy home. I closed the shop as a mark of respect.

And so the waiting began. Seven years until her death became official. But I was in no hurry. What was seven years with a lifetime ahead of me?

The years rolled around and we could not stop them. When Birdie had still not returned, as I knew she would not, I applied for – and was awarded – a Declaration of Presumed Death. At the age of twenty-five, I had my own home and business.

In the beginning, you asked questions about my 'mother'. I drip-fed you snippets. About the hand-painted watch with the sharp-edged face she was wearing when she vanished. *Tick-tock, tick-tock.* Her love of violet creams.

But I did not tell you about the scars between my shoulder blades and on the inside of my wrist. I would not lie, but it would have been unfair to clog your feelings with undeserved sorrow for me. I have always despised pity. Those who seek it. And those who confer it upon the shoulders of others.

Even now, with the wail of the sirens, I do not require pity. My decisions have always been clear-headed and I make them with my eyes open. Parental relationships are complex. Imperfect. Filled with love and hate and duty and guilt.

Two people remembered the truth about Birdie, and neither of us was telling.

Until that telephone call eight months ago. It signed the death warrants of us all.

23

25 The Avenue – 2.13 p.m.

As soon as Evan Lockwood had scrambled down the tree-house ladder, his mother had grabbed his arm and hauled him up the garden. As she'd marched him into the kitchen, the boy had stumbled over the lip of the back door and grazed his shin.

He'd cried out, but she'd suspected it was from humiliation rather than pain. She had snapped her standard response. Same as her mother's. 'If you'd done as I asked in the first place, you wouldn't have got hurt.'

Sometimes she despised herself.

Evan was now sitting on the sofa, knees pulled up to his chin, socks down to his ankles, playing his Nintendo Switch. He'd forgotten all about it, his attention focused on his game.

In a concession to 'spending time' with her family, Olivia had carried her laptop from the study to the sitting room. She was supposed to be concentrating on a press release she was drafting for a client but she couldn't stop looking at

94

that graze, the way his skin had broken open in a dozen rubied wounds.

Sometimes her anger scared her.

When she had found Evan in that treehouse, she had wanted to strike him, to make his disobedience sting. To reduce him and see him *cower*. She had never smacked her children, but that didn't mean the impulse was not there. The red marks on his arm were testament to that.

And she wasn't naive enough to believe that violence was always physical. Words could bruise. Contempt could crush. Amplifying her voice until it drowned out all others was a type of brutality of its own.

She accepted this did not make her a Good Mother.

She loved him painfully – she loved both of her children – and she tried so hard to be gentle and calm and measured, but her reserves of patience had always been low. She wanted their childhood to be filled with sunshine, but clouds were a constant threat.

Evan could be exhausting, a bouncing puppy, already beginning to challenge her carefully constructed boundaries, but he was not cruel. Aster, on the other hand, was so distant, so contemptuous since Olivia's affair had come to light, she did not know how to reach her.

The house move and financial difficulties had ramped up the pressure even more. Necessity had brought them here, but she hated this street with its brutal history, its boxy houses and lack of character. When their last home, their *forever* home – a rambling former vicarage furnished with beautiful things and twelve years of memories – had sold after a week on the market, she had wept for days. And although 25 The Avenue was supposed to represent their fresh start, a treacherous part of her longed for the pulsing beauty of the Peak District and her old life.

Her job at the advertising agency in Manchester. Her expensive car and the cachet of long lunches and lucrative deals. A decent salary. Independence from the drudgery of cooking and cleaning and washing. Status. Respect. Him.

She looked around her new sitting room with its low ceilings, its old-fashioned wallpaper and chipped paintwork, and homesickness engulfed her.

Evan had now discarded his game and was fiddling with his shorts, hands down the front in the way that boys do. Men too. His actions reminded her of Garrick, all pleasure and none of the pain. Her husband was full of grand schemes, but refused to shoulder any of the responsibility. She had recently taken over the family finances and was shocked by his wastefulness, his disregard for money. Stupidly, she had assumed their future was promised, that early retirement beckoned to them both. But a period of unemployment for Garrick, and his hefty investment in the Oakhill flats, had broken them.

Evan was still fiddling with his shorts, and the movement irritated her.

'Stop it,' she said. 'It's not polite.'

A blush stained his cheeks. He withdrew his hand. 'Mum,' he said. 'Can I show you something? I think it might be important.'

'Just a minute, Evan. Let me finish this press release.'

He sprawled across the sofa, legs dangling over the armrest, drumming his heels against the leather.

Thump. *Thump.*

Thump. *Thump.*

Thump. *Thump.*

A muscle in Olivia's cheek twitched, but she did not speak. Her fingers plodded across the keyboard.

Thump. *Thump.*

Thump. *Thump.*

Thump. *Thump.*

She reached for the words, but they teased her, fluttering away. She tried to pin them down, but she was too slow. Flicked a glance at her watch. An hour until she had to deliver. She swore. This was her most important client since turning freelance. But she couldn't concentrate.

Thump. *Thump.*

Thump. *Thump.*

Thump. *Thump.*

C'mon, Olivia, focus. Now what was she trying to say? The subject matter *was* boring. As dry as dust. But they were paying her to make it sing, and she needed the money. But still Evan kept kicking . . .

Thump. *Thump.*

. . . and . . .

Thump. *Thump.*

. . . she could not . . .

Thump. *Thump.*

. . . think straight.

'Stop it!' Her shout made him jump. 'Just. Stop. It. I can't concentrate while you're making that noise.' She should have ended it there. Evan had stopped kicking and was struggling to sit up. But frustration with her work, the move and the long summer holidays was spilling over, and she could not prevent the despair from leaking out.

'It's always the same, isn't it? You're nine now. Old enough to have a bit of consideration for others. But, no. It's all about you, isn't it? It's all about *your* needs.'

She knew this was terrible, unkind, untrue, even, but there was a freedom in letting her fury fly, even at such a vulnerable target.

'Do you have any idea how much I do for you? And the rest of this family? I cook. I clean. I wash your clothes. So don't sit there, thumping your feet against the sofa, while I'm trying to earn enough money to feed us all and pay the bills, to buy birthday presents and ice creams.'

And just as quickly as her anger had submerged her, it was gone, carried away on a receding tide.

'I'm sorry,' she said, reaching for her son, to draw him to her. To apologize. 'I didn't mean it.'

But he backed away, tears swimming in his eyes, his face pale and shocked. 'Why are you always so mean?' He was shouting. 'I wish I had a different mum.'

'You're right. I'm sorry,' she said again. 'I'm tired and worried, and sometimes adults shout at children for one thing when they're angry about something else.'

But Evan shook his head.

'You're always angry. You always shout. I think it's because you hate me. And I hate you too.'

Then he was gone, door slamming, his feet thumping his anger into every step. Upstairs, the floorboards creaked and she could tell he'd taken refuge in his room.

She meant to go up to him, to comfort him, to glue together the tear. But she had a deadline, a million other thoughts in her head, and soon she was lost in her work.

It was only a few hours later, when she had finished her

press release and was thinking about what to cook for dinner, that she realized she had forgotten to ask Evan what he had wanted to show her.

24

Now

The summer that started it all was as tar-stickingly hot as this one. The kind of summer you could taste in hot metal air and drifting spores of pollen.

The shop front had been painted for the occasion, posters stuck about the town. A shrewd idea, that's what it had seemed like. To attract customers to our toys like butterflies to flowers. The shop had been haemorrhaging money for years, but now it was in intensive care. It seemed I lacked Birdie's flair for business.

The old fancy dress costumes had been bundled into the back room in loose, careless piles together with old bits of furniture and ancient stock. Everything out of sight.

But the shop itself gleamed with the kind of sheen that can't be bought: hope.

I can still see the wooden stacks of dominoes, the bold beauty of the jack-in-the-boxes, the perfect porcelain faces of the dolls and the stuffed monkeys with their orange and brown fur. The boxes of miniature cars and the bouncing balls and jacks and a dozen different toys we had spent the last of our money on.

I can still hear the sound the banner made as we unfurled it, the jaunty lettering an invitation to all.

GRAND REOPENING AND PUPPET SHOW TODAY

This glorious day was going to change our fortunes. It was going to change everything.

And it did.

25

4 Hillside Crescent – 3.04 p.m.

The envelope was long and white, and it had her name written across it in a hand she knew as well as her own.

Wildeve lifted it to her nose, hoping for a memory of him, but all she could smell was the chemical tinge of new paper.

She slid her finger beneath the seal and eased it open, pressing the sticky residue of glue and saliva to her lips, knowing his mouth had once been there.

Every serving police officer wrote one.

Every serving police officer hid it at the bottom of their locker and tried to forget it existed.

Every serving police officer – religious or not – prayed that it would never find its way into the hands of their family.

Wildeve tensed her jaw and a bolt of electricity streaked across her face. She needed more medication, but it affected her ability to drive, the combination of pain relief and anti-convulsants slurring her voice and her vision.

With a fingertip, she traced the outline of her name. The

truth she couldn't bear to share with Simon nudged at her: she didn't *want* to read it. This was a love letter that should remain unsent. A poor substitute for a mouth and hands, the warmth and solidity of a body. Scant comfort for when the worst happened.

Killed in the line of duty.

The paper was shaking so much that all the letters seemed to run into one another, and she tried to compose herself, to steady her heart and her hand.

As she began to read, the first lines took her breath away because there he was again, so utterly Adam-like he could have been standing next to her, murmuring in her ear.

Well, this is the ultimate fucker, isn't it? Let's hope I didn't make some stupid mistake, and instead, right this minute I'm being lauded a hero and the Chief Constable is showering you with medals for my outstanding bravery.

If that's not the case, if I messed up somehow, I'm so sorry. There's nothing in this world that makes me want to stay in it more than you.

But we both know if you're reading this, I've already gone.

My love, don't be torturing yourself about whatever it is that's happened. I hope it was quick but even if it wasn't, it's over now. No more pain. I know that won't be the same for you and I wish, more than anything, I was there to comfort you. But I know my girl is strong. You can – you will – get through this.

Do you remember that night we met? You were shouting at that guy in the bar with the octopus hands. I was off duty, elbowing my way through the crowds to check you were OK, but you didn't need me. You flashed your warrant card and

Fiona Cummins

all that bravado deflated like a popped balloon. He offered to buy you a drink, and that look of scorn on your face – I think I fell in love with you right in that moment.

Never stop being afraid to stand up for yourself. Christ knows, there are still some dinosaurs in the Force.

You are the best person I know, Wild. You're smart. You're kind. You're so damn beautiful. Persuading you to marry me has got to be one of the greatest triumphs of my life.

I'm not ready to go. I want to see the lines settle into your face. I want to share in the shining moments of your life, and be there for you when the lights dim.

But I've got to step away for now. Never – not even for a moment – imagine that I wanted to leave.

And you deserve to be loved, darling girl. So don't be afraid to let that happen.

There are people in our lives who brush past us, who bump shoulders and are gone. There are those who take our hands, who hold them and linger a while longer, who touch us and don't let go.

And there are people like you. The ones who fold their hands around our hearts, and keep us safe.

I never thought it would happen for me until you.

Even though it's over, I have lived my very best life. Because of you.

Do what you need to do, Wild. Remember to eat, to take care of yourself. If you want to hide away, that's OK. If you want to work, don't let them stop you.

And know that whatever you're doing, however bad it gets, I'm with you. I will always be with you.

I love you.

Adam

THE NEIGHBOUR

And so the tears came, grief laying its claim on Wildeve, wrenching its debt from the well inside. She cried rarely. A handful of times in her thirty-six years. She buried her face in the cushion, the fabric growing damp against her skin.

When she had composed herself, when the tears were drying to salt on her cheeks and she had splashed them away with cold water, when she had dressed in clean clothes and found her keys, the questions she had been trying to ignore elbowed their way to the front.

She and Adam had never kept secrets.

They had lived and breathed the Doll Maker case, discussing it over breakfast, in the car, the bath, in bed, in those gaps between sex and a few snatched hours of sleep.

So what was he doing when he died?

And why hadn't he told her?

26

Major Incident Room, Rayleigh Police Station – 5 p.m.

Five faces pinned to the wall of the Major Incident Room. Five bodies photographed in situ.

Ordinary men and women. All with lives. All with hopes and secrets. All with families and friends, ex-lovers and enemies. Some with money worries, struggling to get by, some with thriving businesses and pensions, a gilded future ahead. Illnesses. Scars. Histories. Full of the joys and tragedies that make us human.

All dead.

Even though DS Wildeve Stanton had seen hundreds like them before, the contrast between the photographs of the victims before they were killed and the images taken at the crime scene was a repeated kick in the gut.

Grinning. Natural. Hair mussed by the wind. Celebrating a family occasion. A pint down the pub. Tanned and on holiday. Versus the vacant stare of victimhood.

Seventeen years ago, Wildeve had stood in a bedroom in a house with her first dead body. It had belonged to her grandfather, the joker who had produced coins from behind her ear, the friendly bear who slipped her chocolate limes, the war veteran who went to bed early on Bonfire Night because the crack of fireworks terrified him. Except it *wasn't* her grandfather. His face, yes, but a mask carved from wax. His body, but an empty sack. Nothing more, nothing less.

Her grandfather had left with his last breath.

And these bodies found amongst the branches and dried leaves and insects carried the same aura of absence. Abandoned husks. But they had all been somebody once, two or three burning brighter than the others, perhaps, but all ablaze with individuality.

One of them had been her husband.

She pressed her finger to the crime scene photograph. Although she had been at his post-mortem, this was the first time she had seen him lying in the woods, reduced to nothing by a faceless killer. Eyes gouged from his face. A violent stripping of life.

Her legs began to shake. Stale, warm air filled her nose. She was shrinking, sucked into her shock. The rumble of voices sounded far away. She shouldn't have come. She couldn't bear it.

You've got this, Wild. Take your time. The patience in Adam's voice calmed her.

Wildeve drew in another lungful of recycled air, and waited for the trembling in her legs to subside.

In every murder investigation she had worked on, the killer had left a trace, his or her mark. But the Doll Maker was not like other killers.

No stab wounds. No ligatures or signs of strangulation. No bruising or bullet holes, no shattered and splintered bones. No bite marks. No bleeding out. No suffocation or sexual assault or evidence of torture.

No visible signs of injury at all.

Except the eyes.

She turned her back to the photographs and tuned in.

Detective Chief Inspector Clive 'Mac' Mackie, the senior investigating officer in this multiple murder investigation, had gathered his officers for the afternoon briefing. The post-mortem of Victim Five – formally identified by his wife as Detective Inspector Adam Stanton – had, he informed them, taken place that morning.

Mac's bloodshot eyes met hers, the strain of the last twenty-four hours written in the lines of his face. Lack of sleep and relentless pressure from the public and the media to catch a killer had aged him by fifteen years. He acknowledged her with a nod, and she nodded back, hoping that he wouldn't offer his condolences in front of the large team scattered across chairs and perched on desks. Thirty years in the police had taught him some compassion, because his next words were these.

'We all know his name. He was one of our own.' Mac rubbed the stubble on his chin. 'Forty-two years old. Working this investigation. Found at fifteen hundred hours and sixteen minutes on Sunday in a sheltered copse in the south-east corner of Blatches Woods, sixteen acres east from where Victim One – Natalie Tiernan – was discovered, three acres north-west of Victim Two, Esther Farnworth, eleven acres east of our third victim, Will Proudfoot, and an acre south of where the fourth body– Elijah Outhwaite – was dumped. Adam was off the beaten path. A father and son came across him when their dog ran after a squirrel.

'He had been due to attend a church service with Elijah's family yesterday morning, but he didn't turn up. A resident of The Avenue has contacted the helpline and confirmed that she spoke to him at around 9 a.m. We're trying to establish his movements after that. Where was he? Who was he with? Did anyone see or speak to him? Did he let anything slip to any of you? You know the drill, folks. We all want to find this bastard. Let's do it for Adam.'

His voice wavered on that final consonant. For a moment, the briefing room was silent except for a quiet sobbing from near the front. Due to the high level of media interest, an Essex Police press officer was taking notes. Mac cleared his throat of emotion. 'Right, any questions?'

Clipped, no-nonsense, his tone did not invite questions at all. But Wildeve knew that Mac didn't mean to sound so *hard*. Four years of working with him and she had learned to read his moods. This afternoon's was textbook defensiveness.

An officer down on his watch. That would break him if this case didn't. And she knew he was starting to panic. Because they had nothing of material use. Because the buck stopped with him. Because he wanted justice for the families and could have retired years ago if he wasn't so committed to the job. Because there were journalists camped out on his doorstep, questioning his abilities, demanding answers from the Home Secretary and those at the top of the government tree. Because the public were becoming too frightened to venture out of their homes at night. Because newspapers and television shows and radio hosts were baying for blood, calling for Mac's resignation, and he had a wife and kids and bills to pay, just like the rest of them.

Except her.

She didn't have a family anymore. No parents. No siblings. No husband.

'Right. Good. We're still waiting on some results from forensics. We're hopeful he's slipped up this time and left a workable DNA trace. But again, as in the other cases, there are no signs of a struggle. We're still working on the theory the victims were killed elsewhere and moved. But stay open-minded, folks. It's only a theory.'

The heat in the room was sauna-like. Wildeve's head swam. Mac was speaking, but she was not listening. A couple of fans were running but it was not enough to stop the beads of sweat rolling down the sides of his face.

As if he could hear her thoughts, Mac dragged the back of his hand across his forehead and wiped away its clamminess on his trousers. She tuned back in.

'And I want you all to stay calm. There is absolutely no evidence that the killer is targeting police officers. But the obvious question to answer is did Adam stumble across something that could lead us to the individual who is behind these multiple killings?'

The knot in Wildeve's stomach tightened. She was his wife. Why didn't she know this?

'As you'll be aware, we've carried out post-mortems on each of the victims. Three have died from cardiac arrest and two from respiratory distress. Traces of vomit in some cases. Clearly, it's more complicated than that. These were individuals, of course. With varying degrees of health. It would seem –' he cleared his throat again – 'that the eyes were removed after death. But Mathilda Hudson, the pathologist, is confident that she has now identified what caused loss of life.

'What she – and we – have not been able to do – and what we *must* do as a matter of extreme urgency – is to discover what triggered the cardiac arrests, the respiratory failure. *Why* did they die in this way? And—'

'What about gassing, guv?'

A detective constable seconded from the homicide team in neighbouring Brentwood interrupted Mac. He was loud, overconfident, speaking over the DCI. Wildeve did not know him, but she disliked him and the image he'd created in her mind.

Adam. Struggling for breath. Enough time to know he was dying. She blinked, dug her nails into her palms. Found herself back in her past.

A flat. A broken window. A 'Do Not Enter' note pinned to the bedroom door. As a younger officer, she had spent time with the Met's dedicated chemical unit in London. 'Carbon monoxide suicide,' the DC had explained when they'd forced their way in. The poor bastard had used a gas canister and was still wearing his mask.

Because his mouth and nose had been covered, there was none of the telltale smell of death. He had looked alive, healthy, almost radiant, the haemoglobin absorbing the carbon monoxide and pinking his skin. Was it possible that Adam had died this way?

'None that we can determine so far,' said Mac. 'Two of the victims had dangerously low oxygen levels in their blood, as you'd expect with respiratory failure. But the pathologist could find no traces of gases that might have killed them.'

'But it's true that a post-mortem can't pick up everything, right?' A senior female officer – Antonia Storm – spoke with calm authority. 'I mean, isn't it impossible to identify some poisons, for example?'

An awkward quiet settled onto the room. Everyone knew that Storm had been working with the Met five years ago when notorious serial killer Brian Howley had ambushed and almost killed her and another officer with a banned pesticide. Old-timer DI Alastair Thornberry had persuaded her to transfer permanently to Essex. A long time ago, but her history still cast a shadow.

Mac nodded. 'Yep. Hudson has state-of-the-art technology. She always runs a thorough and extremely comprehensive analysis. But none of that will be enough if it's a substance that's so rare we don't have a clue what we're looking for.'

A young PC that Stanton didn't recognize raised his hand.

'Taylor?'

The officer stumbled over his words, as if he couldn't find the right way to frame them. 'Is it – could it be – possible they died from fright?'

A titter slithered around the room. The police constable blushed. One or two colleagues flashed a worried glance at Wildeve. Mac held up a hand to silence the detractors.

'That's not as daft as it sounds. It's something we've discussed. We haven't ruled it out, put it that way.'

A spike was drilling its way across Wildeve's jaw. She gritted her teeth, an instinctive act, even though it worsened the sensation. She forced herself to concentrate on Mac, to focus on him instead of the revolving bursts of pain.

An image of Adam's pale face appeared on the interactive SMART whiteboard. Acid rose at the back of her throat. She put her hand across her mouth. Reached for the waste-paper basket.

Mac zoomed in. In the place where Adam's eyes should have been, something glinted in the camera flash. He clicked another button and a video began to play. A gloved Scenes of Crime Officer was filmed removing a piece of evidence from his bloodied sockets.

Mac hit pause. Zoomed in again. Lying on the SOCO's palm was a miniature glass eye, muddy-brown in colour, distinctive yellow flecks across the iris.

Although news of the eyes had leaked, the details of their colouring had not. Each glass eye matched the original eye colour of its victim. 'Highly unlikely to be a copycat,' said Mac. 'So anyone got any bright ideas?'

The officers assigned to the case – pooled from the four homicide teams across the county because of the large-scale nature of the investigation – had circled this cul-de-sac a thousand times. They had argued amongst themselves about what – or who – it might mean.

Wildeve glanced down at the notes she had scribbled on this part of the investigation before Adam had died, her stream-of-consciousness musings.

Message from killer? Watching (victims or police or both)??
Blind. Visually impaired.

Who? Access? Ophthalmologist. Toymaker/hobbyist. Factory
worker. Taxidermist. eBay? Internet – basically anyone?

Type of glass eye/prosthetic? Human, mammal, bird,
mannequin, doll, reptile, teddy bear, fish?

Closed-circuit television cameras had been installed at the entrances to the woods a week before Adam's death. She wanted to ask Mac what had been the point of that fruitless and costly exercise, as teething problems meant they hadn't been working on Sunday. But if she spoke up, two dozen heads would twist in her direction and she wasn't ready for such scrutiny.

'Well?'

No one answered Mac. A couple of chair legs scraped across the floor as one or two officers shifted. Others gazed at their hands or pretended to take notes.

The slap of Mac's palm against the table made the room jump.

'He.' *Slap.* 'Was.' *Slap.* 'One.' *Slap.* 'Of.' *Slap.* 'Us.'

Detective Constable Bernie French's braying voice broke into the silence. Wildeve gritted her teeth again, and this time it wasn't because of the pain.

'If you don't mind me saying so, guv, I think we need to go back to the beginning and Natalie Tiernan.' His chest puffed out at having the floor. 'The Doll Maker—'

'Don't call him that.' Mac's terseness cut through French's self-importance. 'And that goes for the rest of you too.'

He didn't bother to explain why. But Wildeve knew. Mac hated these monikers. Thought it glamorized the killings and legitimized the act of murder. But that wasn't the only reason. He had told her once that it made his officers lazy and narrowed their thinking, that – subconsciously or otherwise – it pointed the investigation towards assumption rather than fact.

French snorted and looked around colleagues new and

old for support. 'I think it's rather good, actually. Bit more imaginative than the usual bullshit.'

Mac's smile was over-warm, full-blown. French clocked the DCI's expression and a self-congratulatory laugh slipped from him. But he had misread the signals.

'Here's what will be *more imaginative than the usual bullshit* if you don't shut up,' said Mac, still smiling. 'Your fucking CV. Because you'll be trying to cover up why you got sacked.' Mac leaned towards the detective constable. 'Here's a tip. When I say jump, you say, "How high – and shall I make you a brew while I'm up there?" And have some fucking respect. Adam's wife's here. Got it?'

French moistened his lips with his slug of a tongue. He stretched out his arms and locked his hands behind his head, all elbows and arrogance. He opened his mouth to argue, but Mac was staring him down, head cocked, still grinning.

French dropped his gaze. 'Got it.'

Mac raised one eyebrow. 'Got it, what?'

If looks could kill, her boss would be dead. 'Got it, *guv*.'

The rest of the briefing passed without incident, with tasks assigned, leads to investigate and interviews to conduct, but their exchange had left a nasty taste. During major investigations, it was not unusual for different teams to join forces and operate as one, but conflict was common. Different methods of working. Egos. Clashing personalities.

'Wildeve, have you got a minute?'

She put down the bin. Mac had not allocated her a specific job. She'd been taking a closer look at Victim Two – Esther Farnworth – when Adam was killed, but he'd probably written her off.

He was close enough for her to smell aniseed balls on

his breath. When he wasn't delivering briefings, he sucked them incessantly. The far wall was ablaze with orange fire, and that rise and fall of the sun, the corporate smell of the meeting room, the low buzz of an active investigation, reminded her that the world kept turning. And so did she. Thirty thousand breaths a day, one hundred thousand beats of her heart, an echo of hunger in her hollowed-out stomach. She had always marvelled at the families who kept going in the hours and days after a brutal, senseless death. But now she understood. She was here, at work. Breathing and thinking and talking. Still here. Shock, the brain's sophisticated system of protection from reality.

'We're all so sorry about Adam.'

She nodded, not trusting herself to speak.

'I hate to ask, but did he say anything to you about where he was going? Anything at all?' A gentler tone. 'Was anything going on at home that I need to know about?'

Tears filled her eyes, but they did not fall. She had replayed their last conversation countless times. 'Nothing.'

A sharp, disappointed nod. Then kindly, but direct. 'Would you – shouldn't you – why don't you take some leave?'

Wildeve pictured their home, its lonely rooms filled with memories of her husband. The pain in her head, and her heart.

'I can't,' she said.

Mac studied her. His eyes were grey and red-rimmed, and there was dried egg yolk on his tie. But appearances were deceptive. He was sharper than the blade of a carving knife.

'The Chief wants to assign you a family liaison officer.'

'No.' She was shaking her head. 'I don't want one.'

'You think you can handle this, but you're in shock,

Wildeve.' His voice was soft with sympathy. 'And the crash is going to come.'

She couldn't say it, couldn't articulate the words. Some would think her unfeeling, uncaring even, but that wasn't it at all. Not everyone would understand. She didn't expect them to. But work filled up the hollows of her heart and mind. Stopped her from imagining the horror of his last moments. A distraction from the hole blown into her life. And a way to make his killer pay. 'I'm fine.'

'Sure?'

'Yes.'

'In which case, I want you to have a poke around. See if you can unravel what Adam was up to. I know it's a lot to ask but . . .' He didn't need to finish. It made sense. She knew her husband better than anyone. 'The minute – and I mean, the *minute* – it gets too much, you tell me,' he said. 'Promise me.'

'I promise.'

'And I know you're not going to like this, but I want you to take French with you.'

Oh, Christ on a stick. The guy's a grade-A prick.

Adam's verdict was so spot-on that she almost turned around to check if he was standing behind her. French was holding court on the other side of the room, his volume control turned so high she could pick out full sentences. 'He's a dick.'

'But he's a *clever* dick,' said Mac with a grin.

A laugh slipped from Wildeve. A couple of officers looked over. She glared back, defiant. *Adam would have enjoyed the joke too.* Mac's expression grew serious again.

'Do your best, Wildeve,' he said. 'Get inside his head.

Retrace his steps. Find out what he was doing when he died.'
His voice was quiet. 'Adam was a damn hero every day in this
job. Let's make sure he dies one too.'

27

Now

Human lives are defined by secrets.

All those truths that stay hidden because we're trying to protect ourselves or others. Because we don't wish to seem stupid or vulnerable, cruel or weak. Because we're seeking answers to questions we're not yet ready to share.

Olivia Lockwood kept secrets. I know this because she told me. She'd had a lover, a younger man, and was considering leaving her husband. Garrick Lockwood kept secrets. He didn't know if he wanted to stay married to his cheating wife. Detective Inspector Adam Stanton kept secrets too. He loved you, and he had never forgotten you, but he hadn't told that police officer wife of his – he hadn't told anyone – that he was trying to find you.

In the last few months, I have learned that our secrets are never as well hidden as we think they are. A freeze-framed expression. A forgotten newspaper photograph. A bloody secret buried beneath layers and layers of paint.

When the police hunt a killer, it is always the secrets they should seek out first.

Because – and remember this, it's as important as life and death – the camera never lies.

28

26 The Avenue – 7.28 p.m.

The sky was a painting. Streaks of tangerine and gold. An underwash of rose. Yet it wasn't the colours that interested him, but the clouds.

Fletcher Parnell kept a spiral-bound notebook and fountain pen in the pocket of his jeans for occasions such as this. He'd run up the stairs as soon as he'd heard the low thrum of the plane's engine, hoping for a distrail, at the very least.

But he had not expected this.

A fallstreak hole.

He turned to a clean page in his book. Dated it. Noted its precise location. Scratched the words onto the lines.

Cavum. Layers of altocumulus. Iridescence.

He took a photograph on his phone and wished he hadn't left his camera at work. He flipped back through the pages, checking through meticulously kept records.

Fallstreak holes were rare. The last time he'd seen this natural phenomenon was nine years ago. Before all that

121

silliness. A pair of them, an imprint against the sky in the shape of lungs.

Fletcher blinked up at the sunset, mesmerized. A gap punched through cloud droplets which had frozen into ice crystals, as if the sky's mouth had opened and was trying to speak.

He laughed at himself, not usually given to flights of fancy.

Dessie would be home soon. He should make a start on dinner. She'd be tired after a day of filming, and grouchy. She despised the dismissive way that some actors treated her, viewing her as the hired help. Once, she'd deliberately over-bronzed a Hollywood name because he'd been so rude. *Never piss off the make-up artist.* She had laughed when she'd said it, but Fletcher knew she'd meant it. They'd only lived together for a few months, but he didn't like pissing her off either. Made her unpredictable. But if he cooked dinner, she'd soften, and when it came to bedtime she might not push him away.

All these thoughts were crowding his head, and he could almost smell the garlic and the tomatoes he would roast, the egginess of fresh pasta, a peppery undertone of basil leaves.

And he was turning to go, he honestly was.

But the sun fell upon the cylinder of his telescope, warming up the brass and lighting the fire within him, and the pull of the sky became too much.

As the glowing sphere descended towards the horizon, and the first, faint stars appeared, Fletcher lost himself in the wonder of the moment, the passing of day into night, the relentless cycle of time. It made him feel less than. An ant.

All around him was the sliding darkness of twilight. As

the night deepened, a tattered skein of stars was thrown across the sky. He began to catalogue the constellations, muttering the names over and over again.

But it could not drown out the knocking at the back of his head. The small, secret part that whispered to him, that offered up its seductions, nudging at him like a dog that demands to be fed.

Because if he was to aim his telescope downwards and to the left, the gentlest of adjustments, he would have a window into number twenty-five, and the family who had moved in yesterday.

Specifically, the mother and the girl.

But he mustn't.

With a jerk, he directed his finderscope skywards until his vision was filled by a darkening swathe of fabric, pricked by a thousand silver pins.

And he began to mutter again, repeating the words over and over.

But this time he was not glorifying the stars and the shapes that they made. Even their cold beauty was not enough to distract him.

If Dessie had come home at that moment, had climbed the stairs to rinse out her make-up brushes and shrug off her work clothes, if she had paused outside the door and caught the murmur of Fletcher's voice, she would have been puzzled by the incantation falling from his lips.

I mustn't. I mustn't. I mustn't.

29

25 The Avenue – 7.30 p.m.

Aster Lockwood stretched out a leg and admired its shape, the colour of her lightly toasted skin and the still-wet red nail polish.

She'd seen some boys hanging about the street earlier in the day. Too far away to work out if they were worth her time or not, but it always paid to be prepared.

Her music stopped. Fucking Wi-Fi. The crap signal was another to reason to hate this house. She'd turned up the music to drown out her pain-in-the-arse brother, but now he was crying again.

Aster swung her legs over the bed, careful not to smudge her toes, and walked into the hallway. Mum was cooking, the smell of frying onions drifting upstairs. She'd better not be doing burgers for tea. She'd refuse to eat them if she was. All that saturated fat.

She opened Evan's door without knocking, went straight for the jugular.

'Be quiet, will you? I'm trying to think.'

She braced herself for an insult in return. Evan always gave as good as he got. Her money was on 'You're too stupid to think', and she was formulating her response when her younger brother lifted his tear-stained face from his pillow.

'Sorry.'

His voice was small and tight, and the shell that Aster had constructed around herself developed a hairline crack.

She flopped down on the edge of his bed. 'What's up?'

'Mum.' His tone was sulky.

'Oh God, what's she done now?' Aster inspected her toenails, wondering if they were dry yet. She might go for a walk in a bit, on the off-chance she would bump into those boys.

'Shouted. Told me I'm selfish.'

Aster smoothed back his fringe. His face was hot and clammy and he was cuddling his old bear. He didn't seem nine, curled up on his bed, but a much younger version of himself, a throwback to a time when she'd been younger too, and interested in him. 'Sounds like Mum.'

'I wanted to ask her something, but she was too busy with her laptop and wouldn't even listen.' Evan had torn out pictures of his favourite footballers from magazines and stuck them on the wall with Blu Tack. The sight of them pulled at her in a way she didn't expect.

'Tell me if you want,' she said, surprised by an impulse to protect her brother. Evan checked to see if she was mocking him. Aster smiled to show she meant it.

From under his pillow, he pulled out the plastic rectangle he had found in the treehouse. 'Do you know what this is?'

Aster laughed. 'Bloody hell, where did you get that from? The Dark Ages?'

Evan frowned, and tried to snatch it back from his sister.

'Calm down,' she said, holding it above her head. 'Let me have a closer look.'

'Give it back.'

'Wait a sec.'

'GIVE IT BACK.' Tears welled in Evan's eyes.

'I was just looking,' she said. 'And I wasn't laughing at you, I promise.' She nudged him, trying to make him smile. 'It's a cassette, dummy.'

'What's a cassette?'

'You know, a tape. Matthew's parents have got a few. Old people used to store music on them.'

'Can I listen to it?'

'Not unless you've got a tape player.'

Evan's face fell. 'I haven't.'

Aster shrugged. 'Where'd you find it?'

'In the treehouse. Look –' Evan showed his sister the writing on the cassette label – 'what do you think it means?'

She pored over it. 'Probably someone messing around.'

'I want to listen,' he said again. 'Can you help me find a player, Aster? Please.' His fingers clutched her arm. 'Please.'

Aster took in the damp tracks running down his cheeks, the hope in his reddened eyes. He rarely asked her for anything. 'I'll do my best,' she said, already knowing it was a promise she had no idea how to keep.

Back in her bedroom, Aster gazed down on the street below. Mum had called her for dinner ages ago, but she'd pretended not to hear, and her mother hadn't bothered to fetch her.

It was darker now and the streetlamps were glowing

pink lozenges in the summer evening. She leaned out of her window, breathing in floral air underscored by the stink of muck-spreading from the fields beyond. A width of crime scene tape cordoned off the entrance to the woods, rippling in the kiss of the breeze.

In the house opposite, a shape moved behind the curtains. Aster stilled. The shape stilled too. The teenager couldn't tell how she knew this, but some instinct whispered that the shape – broad-shouldered, tall, *a man* – was studying her across the valley of the street.

A sort of trembling excitement filled her.

Aster found herself at a crossroads in her young life. She could turn her back on the shape, switch off her bedside lamp and go downstairs, apologize for ignoring her mother and seek comfort in the familiar patterns, the argument of family life.

Or she could do what she was about to do.

Aster's fingertips closed around the hem of her T-shirt and slowly, *deliberately*, she pulled it over her head, taking her own sweet time.

A buzzing filled her head, more intoxicating than the vodka Matthew had smuggled into her best friend's birthday party the weekend before Aster and her family had moved. The nerve-endings in her skin tingled, the tiny hairs on her arms raised and alert with the promise of the unknown.

The girl stood in the half-darkness, dressed only in denim shorts and a pale grey cotton bra. She flicked her gaze to the window opposite.

The shape was still watching.

Reaching behind her back, Aster felt for the hooks and unclasped them, let the flimsy slip of fabric drop to the floor.

She stretched, a purposefully languid movement, arms flung skywards, revelling in the power of being sixteen and the slow-birthing knowledge of her desirability. Of sharing her most secret self with a stranger.

The girl wrapped herself in the heat of the summer evening, enjoying the scent of her own skin, the sense of teetering on the edge of the rest of her life, filled with all the possibilities that lay before her, choices waiting to be picked like plump and shiny fruits.

The shape raised a hand.

Who knows what might have happened next? Aster had flirted with pressing herself against the cool glass of her window, of stepping out of her shorts, of walking boldly across the road and knocking on his door.

But her teenage fantasies were interrupted by a tapping on her bedroom door.

'Aster, it's Mum.' A pause. 'Can I come in?'

Aster crossed one arm across her breasts, fumbling for her T-shirt, embarrassment staining her cheeks.

'Wait a sec.'

Decent but still flustered, she opened the door and spoke to her mother through the crack.

'What is it?'

'You haven't eaten, love. Come down for a bit. There's salad.'

When it came to debating this with her mother or just having dinner, Aster considered eating the lesser of two evils.

'I'll be down in a minute.'

'Aster . . .'

'I will, OK?' She didn't mean to sound impatient but

her mother was so irritating. She waited for her to leave, desperate to see if he was still watching. As soon as she heard footsteps on their way downstairs, Aster flew back to the window.

The curtains were drawn, the shape gone. Disappointment settled on her like ash.

30

Now

The first child through the door was blonde and uncertain. She clutched her mother's hand, her body half turned, a thumb plugging her mouth.

You welcomed her with an understated wave and drew her into the shop with a lollipop from the jar. Her eyes were greedy, gorging on the new toys lining the shelves. She reached for an expensive doll with sticky fingers and I itched to slap her hand away.

Her mother gave her a gentle push and she chose a place to sit at the front of the shop, cross-legged and patient. 'This is Tallie, she's five.'

'Ten minutes.' I was still smiling then. 'We'll wait for the others to arrive.'

The bell above the door rang out. A boy a few years older was next. He was whistling when he walked in, alone and unhurried. He sat a little distance from Tallie, jiggling a string bag of marbles he had plucked from the tub by the entrance. They clanked together. The sound made my teeth hurt, like drawing nails down a chalkboard.

On the street outside, the Saturday shoppers were going about their business. I had half expected a queue, worried that the shop would be overrun and we would sell out of toys, but not this. Never this.

A breeze caught the banner – GRAND REOPENING AND PUPPET SHOW TODAY – strung across the front, and it gave an embarrassed shudder.

Another two children arrived at the same time. A girl and a boy. Then a lad on his own. He took one look inside the shop and walked out again. The trickle did not swell into a deluge.

The final two arrivals – step-brothers, by the sound of things – had a petty argument at the door and both of them left.

So that was it. Two boys and two girls. The culmination of weeks and weeks of preparation. All that expense.

The small knot of children did not know each other. Strangers flung together by fate. They sat on the floor, watching me, and my insides squirmed. Times were different then. Their parents had left them in good faith. Half an hour's guilt-free shopping time. Time for a pint, a Campari and soda.

The photographer was even more uncomfortable than I was. 'I'm sure it will pick up soon,' he said, but he wouldn't look me in the eye. He fired off a couple of shots, wrote down their names for the picture caption that would appear in next week's newspaper and left, relieved to escape the darkening atmosphere. In his hurry, he left the scrap of paper with their names by the till.

I wanted to shut up the shop and crawl away, to lick my wounds in a quiet corner.

But the show must always go on.

And out the puppets came.

31

Monday, 30 July 2018

25 The Avenue – 8.40 p.m.

The back of the house was lit up like a stage. An audience might have observed the silhouette of Garrick Lockwood as he pored over building plans on the dining-room table, a glass of wine in hand, while in the sitting room, Olivia was bent over her laptop, calculating how much she would need to earn next month.

That separation spoke volumes about their marriage.

The hulk of polished mahogany was the only furniture in the dining room, their wedding day crockery still wrapped in newspaper, chairs stacked against the wall, the cut-glass crystal tumblers she had bought him for their fifteenth anniversary buried under bubble wrap. But none of that mattered to Garrick. Once he was driving the train, there was no derailing him. He left the everyday practicalities to Olivia.

The neighbours on both sides had already lodged a list of objections, but the architect in him knew that getting them on board was the key to a happy ship. Not that Olivia

133

was ever happy. Even a beautiful home, two children and a loyal husband hadn't been enough for her.

Garrick studied his drawings. He'd done an excellent job, even if he said so himself. Shame it might turn out to be a waste of time. When they had bought this house, he'd been desperate to make a go of their marriage, and still wanted to, if he was honest, but Olivia was so distant, so painfully dissatisfied with her life, that he was considering cutting his losses.

When he had met her – in a pub in Didsbury on a summer night not much different from this one – she had been giddy on vodka and ambition. He had walked her home and they had sat on her front step, chatting for hours about the shape their lives would take.

She had captivated him with her easy laugh, her dreams about starting her own advertising agency, and with talk of the deposit she had saved for her first flat. He had revealed shyly his own plans to run an architect's practice in New York, and later, when the night sky was lightening, his hopes of becoming a father one day.

They were married two years later. She never did buy that flat or start her own business and he never went to New York. Instead, Aster came along, and then Evan, and somewhere along the way, their youthful plans were discarded for middle-aged responsibilities.

And now they found themselves here. In a marriage he wasn't sure could withstand the earthquake of her infidelity. In a house that neither of them loved and could barely afford. Aster and Evan were growing up. In another couple of years, his daughter would be gone. But what about *him*? Should he stay or go?

If he left Olivia – and who could blame him? – he would still see the children. Perhaps not as much as he was used to, but he'd make damn sure they always had a good time. No shouting or arguments. Trips to the cinema and bowling and miniature golf. Quality over quantity and all that bollocks. He'd have to sort the house out first, though. Didn't want to risk losing another truckload of money.

The doorbell rang, a discordant buzz that made him jump, but he didn't move, his hands smoothing out the tracing paper and the neat lines of his technical drawings, working out how long the building work would take and how soon they could feasibly sell.

The bell rang again. Why didn't Olivia answer it, for Christ's sake? He waited a beat, then huffed to the door.

A woman waited on the doorstep. No part of her was beautiful on its own, and she looked tired, weighted down, but there was something about the way she held herself, and the pure lines of her cheekbones and the sweep of her hair across her face.

He vaguely registered a man standing behind her, but if he'd been pushed, he could not have described him.

She did not wait for him to speak.

'Detective Sergeant Wildeve Stanton – and this is Detective Constable Bernie French.'

'Come in, come in,' he said, cringing at himself, sounding like an overenthusiastic uncle. He held open the door. 'What can I do for you?'

The police officers stepped into the hallway.

'You'll be aware there's been another murder, Mr . . . ?'

Taggart.

'Lockwood.' He'd wanted to make a joke, adopt a

faux-Scottish accent, but was worried he'd sound disrespectful. And lame. For some reason, although he didn't know her, he found he cared what she thought of him. 'Yes. We saw the police cars. We only moved in yesterday.'

'The victim was a police officer working on an ongoing case,' said DC French. DS Stanton gazed forward, back straight, mouth set in a line. 'One of your neighbours saw him yesterday morning. Did he knock on your door? Did you see him? Speak to him?'

He shook his head. 'We didn't arrive until the afternoon.'

'If you remember anything, you'll let us know?' DS Stanton pressed a card into his hand. Their fingers brushed and her skin was cool against his too-hot hand. 'You can reach me on this number if you need to.'

Before she had finished walking down the footpath, Garrick already knew that he would.

32

27 The Avenue – 8.45 p.m.

Audrina Clifton was whipping up a welcome for the new neighbours. Resting her hands on her comfortable hips, she surveyed the bags of flour and cocoa powder, the jars of sugar and candied peel, nuts and desiccated coconut. Sticky glacé cherries and plump raisins.

Her baking was legendary. She was the undisputed queen of her local Women's Institute cake-making competitions. First prize for her Dundee cake at the produce show in a nearby village for six years in a row. She had a knack for it. A gift, some said.

And success tasted sweet.

Audrina settled upon brownies. Everyone loved brownies. And she was known for them. Royal weddings and street parties. Charity bake sales. The birth of a baby. All kinds of celebrations. Although there had been too few of those lately, the murders driving their small community into their homes instead of together.

A rich, chocolatey smell rose up from the bowl.

137

Brownies had been Joby's favourite too. Her son. Even now, she thought about him every day.

Audrina sprinkled in some walnuts and opened the oven. A full-body heat drenched her. As if it wasn't hot enough already. *At least the damn mentalpause has long gone.* A smile quirked her mouth. Mavis had always called it the mentalpause. She breathed out her sorrow. She would miss her old neighbour and her unique turn of phrase.

Audrina moved her wooden spoon in a figure of eight and wondered how friendly the new arrivals would be.

Mavis and Derek Atwell had been the perfect neighbours, quiet and reserved, and they had rarely used their garden. Even in the beginning, their children had been too old to play in the treehouse and over the twenty years the family lived there, they had grown up and moved out, one by one. Mavis and Derek had always been willing to indulge in a round of canasta and a glass of sherry on a Saturday night, though. Mavis hadn't quite met her eye when she said they were moving on. To be nearer the grandchildren.

Audrina had patted her on the shoulder, despite the flare of envy. Over the years she had learned how to dampen it down, but sometimes it burned.

Cooper opened the back door. His eyes, blue and watery, snagged hers.

'Any chance of a drink? I'm as parched as this blasted grass. Damn greenhouse is so hot.'

She set down her spoon.

'Tea? Or something cool?'

His face, as familiar to her as the liver spots on the back of her hand, broke into a smile.

'Tea. And a custard cream.'

THE NEIGHBOUR

He was forking the earth by one of his bushes when she carried out the tray. She watched him through the fading light. A sprig of baby's breath poked from his pocket. He was bent over, and one of his socks had half fallen down his leg. Audrina was swallowed up by a rush of love.

He worked so damn hard. In the garden. Volunteering for charity. Neighbourhood Watch. She supposed he was consumed by the same need to forget as she was. To fill his empty spaces with dirt.

Mavis hadn't known what to say when she'd told her about Joby a week after the Atwells moved in. At seven years younger than Audrina, she had come from a family where arguments were rare, and if they did happen, they were patched up over tea or telephone calls, a race to apologize first.

'So do you have any children?' Mavis had asked, taking a sip from one of Audrina's best china cups. She had pointed to a photograph. 'Is that your son? What a good-looking boy.'

Audrina had drunk her tea too quickly and the liquid had burned on its way down. She had pressed her knuckles to the centre of her chest, trying to ease the pain of the scalding. To an observer, it looked like she was clutching her heart.

'He – we – don't see him anymore.'

It was as simple as that.

Mavis's eyes had widened and Audrina could think of only one word for her expression: aghast. All these years later, she still could not puzzle out whether Mavis had been mortified at accidentally stumbling across such a sensitive subject, or by the idea of the – she fumbled for the right word – estrangement itself.

At least she and Mavis could talk about it. Not properly, of course. Not in depth, like those young girls today, discussing their most intimate secrets over a bottle of wine. But she had shared with her old friend a little about her feelings of loss. Not the circumstances, though. That was too personal.

A bat whirled in front of her, and she envied its freedom to follow its basest desires. Evening was rubbing out the colour of the day, but the heat was unrelenting. It made her sleepy and slow. The smell of baking, warm and inviting, drifted through the open back door, competing with the arum lilies, protected by pristine white hoods.

Cooper dunked his biscuit into his tea and sucked it.

'There'll be a hosepipe ban, mark my words.'

She forced herself into alertness. 'What will you do?'

He finished his biscuit and tapped the side of his nose. 'Same as before.'

She didn't like to ask what he meant. Cooper enjoyed being mysterious, even though he was the type of man who never let his MOT lapse and expected ironed pyjamas and pants.

The doorbell rang.

She looked at Cooper and he looked back. They weren't used to visitors this late, not even when the summer evenings clung on to light for as long as possible.

'Police,' they said together.

Audrina put down her teacup and went to answer the door. Cooper disappeared into the greenhouse.

Two officers were standing on the doorstep. She hadn't seen this pair before. And she'd met a lot of them over the last few months. She gripped one of the handles of her wheelchair, and sunk into it, the strength suddenly gone from her legs.

'Terrible, isn't it?' she said. 'Another one, God rest his soul. We didn't see anything, I'm afraid. I'm so sorry we can't be more help. Would you like tea or coffee? I've made some cakes. They'll be done soon.'

She ran out of breath. She always talked too much. The police had this habit of making her feel guilty, of wanting to confess her sins. When she was growing up, officers of the law were treated with courtesy and respect. Times had changed, but that didn't mean she had to.

'Is your husband in?' said the lady officer. 'We'd like a quick word with him too, if that's possible.'

'He's in the garden,' said Audrina, lifting herself unsteadily out of the wheelchair. 'Come on through.'

Cooper was putting his tools away in the shed. Night was falling fast. Five minutes ago, she could pick out every detail of his weathered face, but now he was a smudge in the textured air.

Audrina half listened as they asked Cooper the same set of questions they always asked when a body turned up. Her husband was leaning on his fork, frowning and nodding, talking in serious tones. A jolt of pride surprised her.

In his capacity as Neighbourhood Watch coordinator, Cooper's view was frequently sought. He'd acquired a sort of god-like status after tracking down the culprit behind a recent spate of burglaries. During the window of time that spanned the afternoon school run, he'd noticed a stranger lurking on the street and carried out a citizen's arrest. Which made the police's lack of competence all the more shocking when one thought about it. Five lives taken and still no trace of the killer.

'The name Stanton does sound familiar,' he was saying. 'Dark hair, shortish?'

'Yes,' said the policewoman, a trembling excitement making her voice rise. 'That sounds like him.'

He took a pipe from his breast pocket, packed tobacco into its bowl. 'He came by early yesterday. Had a cup of tea and a slice of Audrina's famous Dundee cake.' He put the pouch away. 'He wanted to talk to everyone on the street again, to see if anyone had seen any odd behaviour near the entrance to Blatches Woods.'

'What time was this? Did he say where he was going? Who he was going to see next?' The words tumbled from her.

Cooper struck a match and lit his pipe. The smell of his smoke comforted Audrina. It spoke of a lifetime of marriage.

'About ten. He said he was on his way to talk to Trefor Lovell. Number thirty-two.'

They left Cooper puffing on his pipe and tidying his tools while Audrina escorted them back to the front door.

The policewoman studied the photographs lining the hall: Sissinghurst; Alnwick; Kew. In one of them, a man was wearing a cap and leaning against a spade. In another, a young boy was holding up a giant pumpkin. In the next picture on the wall, an older woman wore sunglasses, arms folded across her chest, sunlight catching the face of her watch. Horse brasses gleamed. A vase of flowers sat on a telephone table. The grumble of television from the living room.

'Are you any closer to finding whoever is doing this?'

The male officer shook his head and leaned towards her in a conspiratorial way. 'It's a nightmare, to be honest. It's one of the most complex and puzzling cases I've ever worked on.' He raised an eyebrow. 'Between you and me, I think our boss is a bit out of his depth.'

The woman turned around sharply, skewering her colleague with a look.

'But we *will* find him, don't you worry about that,' she said.

Standing on the doorstep, saying their goodbyes, the young lady officer – hardly older than thirty, but so tired-looking – pressed a business card into Audrina's hand.

'Please contact me if you see or remember anything at all.'

'Of course. We'll have a think.'

As soon as they had left, their voices drifting back to her in the summer night, Audrina examined the card. Her gaze was drawn not to the telephone number, but the name printed in black ink.

Detective Sergeant Wildeve Stanton.

Stanton.

Stanton.

Her back against the inside of the now-closed front door, Audrina folded neatly onto the doormat, its bristles scratching the back of her thighs where her skirt had risen up.

She hadn't heard that name for more than thirty years until yesterday.

And now twice in two days.

The sound of boyish laughter filled her ears, and she began to weep.

33

Now

The snapping teeth of the crocodile made the boy jump and he laughed until he held his stomach. The ballerina tumbled over her feet, making them gasp and point. It was exactly as I had hoped it would be, given I was not a professional puppeteer. But I had practised at home until my fingers were sore and the puppets did my bidding.

Do you remember the faces of those children? Shining lights. The shop was filled with laughter, with chatter and joy. My mood had begun to lift again. Perhaps the parents would reward our efforts by buying an expensive toy for each child when they came to collect them. Two or three of them, I thought optimistically. There were always birthday presents to lavish on other people's children. And word of mouth was a powerful engine.

But, for now, it was time for the grand finale.

Children like to be scared, don't they? I was counting on it. They enjoy the frisson, pressed up against fear, knowing that the safety net of an adult is never far away. At least, that's what I had thought. I had not been able to find what I was looking for and so I had made it by hand. Sewing and glueing. And it had seemed like such a *clever* idea.

The crow had been lying on the lawn. Perhaps a fox had claimed it, tail feathers between its incisors, claws pressing on its breast, but when I stumbled across it, the body was intact. Its head, though, had been detached, and its collar was bloodied and torn. Its beak and eyes were open. By my calculations, it would take three or four months to decompose. Enough time for my purposes.

A puppet with a bird's head and human hair stuck to its feathers and black scraps of lace fabric from an old Victorian dress I'd found amongst the costumes in Birdie's old shop.

A version of a mourning doll, my own private joke.

34

The Avenue – 9.04 p.m.

The postman unwrapped his sandwiches. Ham and mustard. He balled up the aluminium foil and flicked it into the footwell where it joined an empty lemonade can and a crisp packet. He took a bite. A poppy seed caught between his teeth and he worried it free with his tongue.

His Royal Mail van was parked at the top of The Avenue. He hadn't wanted to draw attention to himself, but tucked away near the shops gave him a decent vantage point without attracting suspicion. As soon as it got dark, he'd drive further down the road, but for now, he was content to wait.

An opera was beginning on BBC Radio 3 and he switched it off. He used to love its extravagance, the opulence of the language and vocal tone, but he couldn't bear to listen to that kind of music anymore. *Così fan tutte* had been playing when she died, and in every note, he heard the wet sound of her skin yielding to the blade. He put down his sandwich, appetite gone.

The door to number twenty-seven opened, a tunnel of

146

light on the path. Two police officers were talking to Mrs Clifton; and when she went in, they stood on the pavement, their heads bent together. He slid further into his seat.

His gaze flicked to the entrance of Blatches Woods, to the length of police tape strung between the bushes, and his heart was a hammer against his ribs.

The woman was standing there, duct tape binding her wrists and her ankles, a thin trail of blood snaking down her chin.

With her eyes, she pleaded for her life.

35

The Avenue – 9.06 p.m.

'What do you think?'

DS Wildeve Stanton was standing in the middle of the street, the night shading in around her. A few late crows flew overhead and their silhouettes were slashes in the sky.

The houses watched her. Inside those brick boxes, the unfolding of lives. Baths and televisions, music and dinner, glasses of wine and cups of tea. So ordinary. And heart-breaking.

She turned away from French, that tilt of grief again.

'It's getting late,' he said. 'We'd better come back in the morning. Can't knock on doors at this time of night.'

He was right. The older inhabitants of The Avenue might find late visitors unsettling, especially in the current climate. But she didn't want to go home.

She stared down the street towards number thirty-two, replaying Cooper Clifton's words. *'He said he was on his way to talk to Trefor Lovell.'* With his doll business and easy access to the woods, Lovell had been an early suspect, but he'd had an alibi for the second murder – an old friend had vouched for him – and they had ruled him out, taking him in for questioning and dismissing him as a harmless oddity. But she wondered how thorough her colleague's investigations had been. There had been talk of a wife, but no one had seen or spoken to her. She wracked her brains, trying to remember what information they had on file for him. Perhaps he was worth a closer look. But it would have to wait until tomorrow now.

'How long do you think Mac's going to last? I reckon he'll be out within the week.' French was jangling his keys, gleeful at the prospect.

'Don't, Bernie. He's doing the best he can.'

'Not good enough, though, is it? Sorry to bring it up and all that, but you, of all people, must be thinking if we'd caught the killer by now, Adam would still be here.'

His words slapped her. Because even though they were crass, carelessly tossed at her without compassion, there was truth in them. She *did* think it. Chest tightening, she took two or three shallow breaths and followed the progress of the birds.

'Five murders is fucking ridiculous. My mother could do a better job.'

'Well, get your mother here sharpish.' The air snapped with her anger. 'And you shouldn't slag off Mac in front of me or anyone else. It's unprofessional.' She waited for him to apologize, but he shrugged. An urge for solitude tugged at her. 'Come on, let's go home.'

Wildeve had always hated coming back to an empty house. She loved the flicker of candles against the window, lit squares of warmth inviting her in. A paper-wrapped bouquet of mismatched roses that Adam had picked up from the flower seller by the station as she was closing her stall. The smell of dinner cooking. But now there was no one to welcome her.

The pain in her head had confined itself to an occasional stretch of its claws. Sometimes an attack could last for days and days, and she would lie in bed in the mornings, still half asleep, braced for the first strike, but there was silence, and for that she was grateful.

She slid her key into the lock. French had invited her for a pint, but the idea of listening to him drone on about Mac's failings was even less appetizing than the prospect of an evening alone.

That's not to say she hadn't been briefly tempted. Time to think was the opposite of what she wanted. And she had clocked the sideways glances from some of her colleagues, could read their unspoken questions. *Why is she at work? Why isn't she crying? Do you think they were splitting up before he died? It's only been a day. She can't possibly have loved him that much.*

But she *had* loved him. All of him. The part of him that forgot her birthday, and left his trousers on the floor, and had to have the last word, just as much as the part of him that made sure she ate, and laughed at her jokes, and listened, and always, *always* smiled when he saw her.

She wasn't one for crying, that was all.

Emotion did not fill her up, it drained her until she was as empty and dry as the mud-cracked streams and gullies struggling in this unending heat.

Upstairs, she rummaged through the washing bin until

she found one of his old T-shirts. It was crumpled and sweat-stained and beautiful.

She climbed into bed on his side. His pillow smelled of the aftershave he had worn for as long as she had known him. She buried her face in it, breathing him in.

Loneliness, the heaviest weight of them all, pressed down on her. Wildeve closed her eyes, imagined herself walking through the dark universe of her grief, looking for a pinprick of light in the distance. Her body was shaking, dozens of tiny tremors that she could not control.

Five minutes passed. Ten minutes. Half an hour.

Dry-eyed, she eventually propped herself up, leaning into his pillow. A glass of stale water was on his nightstand. A photograph of their summer holiday in Sardinia. A well-thumbed thriller by his favourite writer.

He was never coming home.

Another stone settled on the pile in her stomach.

Where were you, Adam? Who did this to you? I wish you were with me now. I wish you could talk to me.

The ceiling light flickered in her bedroom and was followed by the thud of something heavy falling.

Wildeve jumped and knocked over the glass, water spilling onto the carpet. A power surge, that was all, and an attack of clumsiness. When the thrumming in her veins had calmed, she leaned over the side of the bed. The hardback had slid onto the floor, its spine cracked, its pages fanning out like the feathers of a bird. But it wasn't that which caught her attention.

Lying on the carpet was a folded sheaf of paperwork.

She gathered up the documents. Surprised, she began to read. The first was a handwritten statement about the disappearance of Bridget Sawyer, owner of a toy emporium. Dated September 1966 and covered in rows and rows of spidery writing, it was clear it had been sitting in a police file for several years. It had been photocopied three times.

There were also two photocopies of a yellowing newspaper picture caption dated nineteen years later, a row of five children clustered around a striped puppet booth in what appeared to be a reopening of the same toy shop.

She wondered how these had ended up in Adam's possession. It was a loosely guarded secret that some police officers 'lost' evidence that didn't support their theories. When they'd knocked down the old police station at Greenham Lane, twenty-seven case files had been found at the bottom of the lift shaft, the mother of all hiding places. But it looked like this case had simply been forgotten.

The light bulb flickered again, making it difficult to read. Wildeve scanned the text, and two words jumped out at her. *The Avenue.*

She stared at the writing, trying to make sense of it. Could this have been what Adam was investigating? But how were the two events linked? And what did it mean?

She looked skywards. *Is this what you're trying to tell me?*

The light flickered a final time and went out.

36

Now

The phenomenon of collective hysteria has always intrigued me.

What prompted a convent of French nuns to assume the behaviour of cats until their mewls were whipped from them by soldiers? How was it possible for eighty-five schoolgirls to faint, one after the other, like a run of dominoes?

I did not believe in the truth of it until the events in the shop on that day.

The crow puppet had not proved as successful as I'd hoped.

When it swooped down and attacked the ballerina, one or two of the children started to cry. In my haste to hide it away, to pack all the puppets back into their boxes and recapture some of the earlier joy, I didn't notice that one of the girls had become so distressed that she had left the shop floor and found her way into the old storeroom.

The door was supposed to be locked. And you were

supposed to have locked it. But it was too late to do anything about that.

Her screams fractured the peace of the shop, one after the other, layers of fear and disgust.

All of us ran towards the source of the cry. The young blonde girl. She was standing at the back of the storeroom. Thumb in her mouth. Tears streaking her face. A mangy peacock feather boa twisted around her neck.

But I wasn't looking at her.

She was standing next to a hand-carved toy chest that had been tucked away for as long as I could remember, hidden under piles of mouldering fancy dress costumes and surrounded by boxes. Those costumes were now pooled on the floor, as if she had swept them off in her fervour to reach the feather boa. The lid was an open mouth.

No.

I longed to pluck the key from a clockwork mouse and turn back the hours and minutes, to before this moment, this day.

But it was too late.

A ball of dusty candyfloss hair, the shape of a body carved from bone and wood, the remote stink of an emptied rubbish bin.

Knees pulled into its ribcage, body folded in half to fit the space. Teeth bared where the skin had retracted over nineteen years, pulling tight across the bones of the cheeks.

A leathered stick wearing a wristwatch with the sharp-edged face I knew so well.

The child took one look at my expression, unplugged her thumb and screamed again. That sharp, high sound infected the child next to her, who also began to scream. The sound passed to each child, a contagion. Within eight or nine seconds, all of them were screaming, crying, clutching at each other, pulling at their neighbour's clothes. Their screams filled all of the empty space inside the shop. Inside me. Filling my ears and my head and fuelling my anger. I wanted to shake the silence into them, to hear the snap of their necks. *Self-control.*

You did not know what to do. You ran amongst them, trying to calm them, to muffle the cries. But I knew it even then. Each intake of breath, each scream punctured another hole in the life I had built.

'It's not real.' I forced myself to laugh. 'It's another of my puppets.' I touched the grey hair to show I wasn't afraid and slammed shut the lid. 'It's just pretend, children.' I said it over and over again until the screams had subsided into gulping sobs and blotchy cheeks, and they had been ushered from the storeroom. I repeated the words until I believed them myself.

There was nothing else for it. I doled out more lollipops and invited every child to choose a toy to keep. As I handed over the beribboned bags, I bit the inside of my cheek until I tasted blood and whispered to each of them that the puppet with the grey wispy hair was cursed and would come for them and their families if they dared to breathe a word.

'Sorry,' you said, flicking anxious glances in my direction, but I was too angry to answer you.

By the time the parents arrived to collect them, the children were docile enough to go home, more than a little subdued.

I sold one paltry toy that day.

37

27 The Avenue – 12.01 a.m.

A boy's laugh was playing on repeat.

Audrina sat up in bed, placed her hands over her ears and began to sing loudly to herself.

'*Who would true valour see, let him come hither; one here will constant be, come wind, come weather . . .*'

She stopped singing. The laughter was gone. The lamp in her bedroom was throwing down shadows, but the echo of his childish joy filled her heart. *Oh, Joby.* The arrival of the boy next door had unsettled her, that was all. Filled her head with memories best forgotten.

She switched off the light and lay in darkness. A rhythmic buzzing filled her up, like the march of a hundred-strong army of tin soldiers.

She curled herself into a ball and drew the pillow over her face. But when Cooper joined her half an hour later, she was still awake. He drew her shaking body to him, and it calmed her.

THE NEIGHBOUR

The night rolled into early morning, passing into yesterday.

But her sleep was restless, the voices of the past crowding her dreams. Joby. Mavis. The dead who haunted the woods across the street.

When she awoke, sweat gathered in the small of her back, nightie stuck to her skin, the room was in darkness save for a patch of moonlight, the air so warm it seemed to breathe.

Too overheated to do more than lie still, Audrina listened for the voices, but they had quietened for now, disappearing through the cracks in the walls.

The clock on her bedside table ticked away the minutes. *2.57 a.m. 2.58 a.m. 2.59 a.m.* She stared at the hands as they continued their inexorable progress, unable to relax, to even shift herself into a more comfortable position. She was wide awake, her body tensed and waiting, biting the skin around her nails. She listened for a while longer, trying to catch the sound of the en suite toilet flushing, but there was no doubt about it. The room was too quiet, the absence of his heavy breathing louder than he was.

Audrina lay motionless under the rose-patterned bedspread, and she knew what all this silence meant: Cooper's side of the bed was empty and she didn't know where he had gone.

38

25 The Avenue – 3.01 a.m.

On the other side of the wall, Olivia Lockwood was also awake.

Garrick's snoring had dragged her from sleep and now it was eluding her. She was worrying about money and whether the children would settle into their new schools and if this house was a millstone they would regret for the rest of their lives. She blinked into the darkness, fully alert now. A distraction was needed. She felt on her bedside table for her Kindle, but found only tissues and a packet of throat lozenges. And then she remembered: the journey from Cheshire. She had left it in the car.

And, Lord, the heat. The energy-sucking heat. Even though she was only wearing a T-shirt, she wanted to tear off her skin. The back of her neck, where skin met hair, was damp. The sheets were damp. A motorbike revved its engine somewhere in the distance. This place was not home. It was strange, full of unfriendly noises. She licked her dry lips. Imagined a tall glass of juice. Her mouth watered. She slipped on her dressing gown, decorated with the urgent red of poppies and their deep black eyes, grabbed her mobile and walked softly across the bedroom.

It was thirty-one hours since he had texted her. In that time, she had checked her mobile fifteen, twenty times for every hour that passed, but there had been no more messages.

She should delete his number. Block him. She had promised Garrick it was over. It *was* over.

Except she missed him. And she wanted him to miss her too. To fight for her. Which was pretty shitty when one thought about it.

The kitchen floor was cool underfoot, the grapefruit juice tart and cold. The hit of sugar did not encourage her back to bed.

Instead, she refilled her glass, rummaged in the drawer for the car keys and quietly opened the back door, heading for the patio outside. She sat on the edge of a wooden chair, her phone on her lap. Play it cool. Let *him* contact her.

The dazzling white of a security light flooded next door's garden. She looked up sharply, a wash of anxiety dampening her top lip. Fox. Or badger. The estate agent had mentioned this area was a haven for wildlife, and there were occasional sightings of muntjac deer. A moth bumped repeatedly against the ancient outdoor light above her head. So much wasted energy. Her fingers played across the cool metal casing of her phone.

Don't do it.

Her thumb brushed the screen, bringing it to life. She knew he'd be awake or dozing. He was a night owl like she was.

Next door, a noise shattered the silence, the sound of a terracotta plant pot being knocked over and breaking. Olivia jumped, her heart knocking in her chest. She held herself still, listening to the sounds of the night, for the footsteps of an intruder. She rose from her seat, prepared to investigate.

A dark shape crossed the garden and she inhaled sharply, then laughed at herself. The badger was making its presence known.

She collapsed back into the chair, sipped her juice and typed a single word.

Hey.

Within a minute, he had replied.

Hey. How's it going?

OK, I guess.

Only OK?

She drew in a breath, held it. What could she say? A tiny message icon appeared on her screen, sparking another powerful adrenaline rush.

Liv, I thought we weren't going to do this. But for what it's worth, I miss you.

A surge of elation. And then another message from him.

I'm down south for work. Do you want to meet?

Ten words that might just change her future. Did she *want* to meet him? She was hooked on the excitement of illicit texting, she was honest enough with herself to admit that. But they had drawn a line under their affair, knowing how much it had hurt others. If she were to meet him, it would mean that her family's move – which had come at great financial and psychological cost to all of them – would have been for nothing.

She gazed across her new garden and then up to the

window above, where Evan was sleeping. He was still so young. Aster would be all right, she was tough as nails. But her son was much more sensitive. Another five years, that was all. Then she would be free.

Her phone was almost out of battery, but the charger was upstairs and she wasn't ready to go up yet. In a couple of minutes, when she had replied to him, she would wander down the driveway to retrieve her Kindle from the car. Then she would return to the garden and sit a while longer until her eyes grew heavy enough for sleep.

A fierce expression crossed her face. She tapped out her reply. Deleted it. Tapped another.

Can't. I'm sorry.

It was the last message she ever sent him.

39

26 The Avenue – 3.12 a.m.

A mass of noctilucents.

Fletcher Parnell pressed his face against the window and breathed out his admiration, misting the glass. Imagine if he had missed out on this.

He often had trouble sleeping. Sign of a guilty conscience, his mother used to joke. Back when she was alive. Back when everything was different. But not tonight. Tonight he was awake because it was the start of one of his favourite events in the celestial calendar: the Perseid meteor shower.

A streak of silver lit the darkness. It burst through the skyscape, the briefest waterfall of light. Reminding him that he was a dot on the earth, that the world would still turn when he was dead and buried.

Fletcher recorded his observations in his notepad, taking his time, trying to rein in the gallop of his heart, but it was no use. He could sense the flutter of rising panic. During the day, he could button it up and hold it in. But in the small hours, when the world softened and held its breath, their faces taunted him.

He lifted his telescope and stared up at the sky.

The wisps of beauty anchored him. Layers of bright hope in the darkness, the highest clouds in the earth's atmosphere. When he was logging his findings, he went to great pains to use the correct scientific terminology. He liked things done properly. But he made an exception for this particular type of cloud phenomena because he loved it so much.

Night shining clouds.

His gaze stretched to the street. It was quiet and dark, save for the ugly glow of the streetlamps. So intrusive. He hated the way they polluted his nightscape, had even considered throwing a rock and smashing the bulb. He'd have done it too, if he wasn't so worried about drawing attention to himself.

He scanned the hulking shapes of the cars on their driveways. The indistinct masses of bushes and trees. The sheer ordinariness of the street. But a light burned inside him. Waiting, that's what it felt like. For something to happen.

He turned his attention back to the telescope. The stars were clear and watchful. They did not judge. They did not point and laugh and accuse. They just *were*.

Time flowed into itself when he was studying the sky in all her glory, great chunks of it passed without his knowledge. That often happened to him. Sometimes, he would come to, and find that he couldn't remember what he'd been doing. It was a worry.

The hoot of an owl distracted him, dragged his gaze

from the sky to the street. A movement caught his attention. He leaned forward, trying to get a better look.

Blood thundered in his veins.

The new woman from across the road was standing on her driveway by her car.

His brow furrowed. It was late, gone 3 a.m. He peered through his telescope. She was wearing a long T-shirt and a silky dressing gown with poppies on it that had fallen open at the front. One of its pockets was hanging low, as if it held something heavy. He focused his telescope. Small and rectangular, most likely a mobile phone. In her right hand, she carried a set of car keys. It looked like she was crying. He dithered for a split second, uncertain what to do.

He mustn't.

The woman was opening the passenger door and he watched her bend over and reach for something, her legs long and tanned. She straightened up, holding a Kindle. He heard the thud of the door closing and watched her turn her back to him. As she walked towards the side gate that led to her back garden, the belt of her dressing gown snagged on a bush and his eyes followed the vivid slash of red. All at once, he longed to feel the silk against his skin.

He mustn't.

But a compulsion as powerful as the gravity that weighted his feet to the ground yanked at him, hard and unforgiving.

And Fletcher Parnell moved silently down the stairs and made the second biggest mistake of his life.

40

18 The Avenue – 3.15 a.m.

Trefor Lovell was awake too.

He was in his workshop, sorting through a box containing dozens of sets of glass eyes, seeking out a particular colour.

When he couldn't find what he was looking for, a sense of nausea settled on him.

He swore, rose from his chair and headed to the back of the Doll & Fancy Dress Emporium. He ran through his checklist again. A galvanized tin bath, a small bladed knife and six tins of red paint. Powdered chemicals. Sodium chlorate and sulphur. For his latest project. The internet was truly an Aladdin's cave of treasures. A crude handmade shotgun leaned against the wall of the shop.

It was going to be spectacular.

His knees were aching but the pull of the kettle was stronger. Hot chocolate made with water. Never mind the weather. Warm drinks cooled him down.

The dolls' heads lined up across the shelves of his

workroom watched him move about the place. He mock bowed to them as he waited for the kettle to boil.

Pitiful. That's how he would describe today's efforts, too distracted by those feral children to focus on what he was supposed to be doing, which was completing the orders he needed to ship.

Thanks to them, he'd been working most of the night.

He picked up the telephone, dialled the number he knew by heart, but no one answered. That unsettled him.

He spread out several sheets of that evening's newspaper across his bench, the headlines full of the latest murder. The glass eyes. The unsullied body. The flawless painted face.

Trefor dipped the tip of his brush into the water to clean it, and the colour swirled like blood. But it was too late. He couldn't concentrate now.

Leaving the lights on, he slipped out into the heat of the night.

41

25 The Avenue – 3.17 a.m.

Olivia was walking through the side gate that led from the front driveway back into her garden when she heard a low cough and caught the scent of tobacco smoke.

She froze, keys dangling from the end of her finger, Kindle in hand. She turned around to look behind her but the street appeared empty. A convoy of ants crawled across the back of her neck. She pulled the gate closed, but the latch was stiff and didn't catch properly.

Olivia wandered over to the patio table and put down her things. She drained the rest of the grapefruit juice, but did not sit, her eyes scanning the night garden. The tiny hairs on her arms stood upright, despite the heat. Something felt *off*.

She wandered further down the lawn until she was about halfway between the house and the fence at the bottom of her garden. The fence had its own gate into the copse beyond their boundary, with public access from an entrance

167

on the north-west side. It was one of the things that had attracted them to 25 The Avenue, but now it felt like a threat.

She stood still and listened.

There was a light wind, a drift of breeze that exhaled softly through the trees. But she could hear twigs breaking, the crackle of dry leaves underfoot. Something – or someone – was in the undergrowth.

She walked nervously towards the gate. The sounds were coming from beyond it. It was probably the badger again, but then she remembered the cough. Olivia hesitated, tempted to run back to the house and wake Garrick. But if she was going to leave him, she would need to learn to be strong on her own terms.

Entering the copse was like plunging into darkness. No glow from the patio, just a sliver of hope from the moon. The noises were louder here, and coming from somewhere to her right. The breeze was picking up and it nudged the gate shut behind her. Through the lines of trees, she saw a pinprick of light that bounced wildly. A torch.

She fumbled in her dressing-gown pocket for her phone, ignoring the low battery warning and intending to switch on its flashlight. But it was too dark and she couldn't see properly, and as Olivia stumbled forwards, thorns catching against her dressing gown and scratching her bare legs, her head exploded in pain, and her world tipped and turned off.

42

The Avenue – 4.01 a.m.

The postman walked down The Avenue and back to his van, his flashlight safely in his pocket. The houses were cloaked in silence. He breathed in the warm air. He felt at home in the night.

There was no one about, which was a very good sign. He shouldn't be here, but he couldn't keep away. He mustn't stay much longer, though. What if somebody saw him? And if he didn't leave now, if he didn't try to grab an hour's sleep, at least, he'd never get up in the morning, which would bring disaster of a different kind down on his head.

He unlocked the driver's door and climbed in.

She was sitting in the passenger seat, brown hair spilling down her back. Her skin was grey, her lips colourless. The duct tape was gone, but there was a hunting knife sticking out of her chest, pinning her in place. Her head turned towards him and she mouthed these words. *You promised.*

The postman reached for the knife, his fingers closing

169

around its handle, but before he could pull it free it dissolved into dust, and the passenger seat was empty again.

He was still crying as he started the engine and drove home, the dawn marking the beginning of another lonely day.

43

Now

For months, the police have been visiting every house in The Avenue, each fresh killing sparking a flurry of activity.

Did you see anyone suspicious at the mouth of Blatches Woods? An unusual car in the street? A stranger? Please, try to think. Are you sure?

I have grown accustomed to it. A formality. I say the right things. I do not lie. I have learned that most officers cannot recognize the truth even when one draws back the curtain and offers them a glimpse. That the threads of a police investigation are far more tangled and messier than they would have us believe.

But when Detective Inspector Adam Stanton came calling, I knew that steps would need to be taken before matters went too far.

He was friendly, at first. Interested and chatty. He talked about the weather and his job. Pretended to drink his tea. Asked to look around the house. The garden.

And then he brought up the shop. Enquired about Birdie. About you.

The roof of my mouth feels dry. A breeze is nudging the leaves. I hear the chimes of the ice-cream van, and beneath that, the sirens. The police are at the bottom of Rushmore Lane now. Two minutes, I'd guess. Perhaps more. I wonder if Olivia Lockwood hears them too.

Detective Inspector Adam Stanton was shaking his head. 'It doesn't make sense,' he said. 'Help me to understand.'

He showed me an article from our local weekly newspaper dated Thursday, 25 July 1985, five days after the Grand Reopening. He pointed to each of the faces of the children in the photograph: two boys and two girls. And a fifth child.

He looked me in the eye and asked me a question that no one had ever asked me before. I told him the truth.

And then I killed him.

44

18 The Avenue – 9.21 a.m.

DC French was hungover.

His breath smelled of stale alcohol, he was wearing the same clothes as yesterday and he hadn't shaved. He grunted a greeting. 'Stayed at a friend's.' But there was no hint of embarrassment, no sense of apology. 'Missed the alarm.'

'Clearly,' said Wildeve, who had been waiting for twenty minutes in a heat so intense she'd developed circles of sweat beneath her arms.

She, on the other hand, had been up since dawn. She had finally fallen asleep on the pile of documents she had found amongst Adam's things at around 2 a.m. When she had turned over, they had rustled and woken her up. The sun had been shining and the pain in her head had eased. For two and a half seconds it was a promising start to the day.

And then.

Adam is gone.

She had drawn her knees into herself and listened to the

173

birds outside her window. No tears. But a space as desolate as a desert plain.

Five minutes. Ten. An hour. And then she had crawled out of bed, put on her clothes and forced herself to drive to work.

Five decades after the police statements about Bridget Sawyer's disappearance had been taken, the Doll & Fancy Dress Emporium was still standing on the corner of The Avenue. Built at the start of the post-war economic boom, its signage was now faded, the paint flaking and cracked.

Wildeve didn't trust French with Adam's secrets, but she owed him some explanation, and offered the scantest of details about the shop owner who had gone missing fifty-two years earlier.

'Bridget Sawyer. Known as Birdie. Forty-six. One day she was there, eating breakfast, drinking coffee, the next she had vanished into thin air. Her purse and keys were gone. She left behind a teenager, a home, a business.'

He raised his eyebrows. 'Clutching at straws, though, isn't it?' But he hadn't challenged her.

It was gone nine, but there was no sign of life and the shop was shut up. She pushed gently against the door but it was locked, so she knocked on the glass.

French watched her, swigging from a bottle of Lucozade. 'Not in,' he said.

'Wow, thanks. I'd never have guessed.'

She surveyed the street. The early-morning commuters had long gone, and it was quiet, families enjoying a lie-in during the summer holidays or away on their annual break.

All except the postman, who was walking up the road towards them.

'Doesn't open until twelve, sometimes later,' he said. He smiled at her, but it lacked commitment. She looked away, wrong-footed although she couldn't explain why.

'Funny sort of a business,' said French. 'Missing half the day's trade.'

The postman shifted the bag to his other shoulder. 'Most of his business is online, I gather,' he said. 'Shop's just a base for him, I reckon. He's an old guy. Has the occasional customer, but not so you'd notice.'

'It's Trefor Lovell's place, right?' said Wildeve.

The postman waved a couple of letters at her. 'One and the same.' He leaned forward and posted them through the shop's letterbox, then raised a hand in farewell. 'Good luck.'

Wildeve and French exchanged a glance.

'It's a bit of coincidence, don't you think?' said Wildeve. 'That a woman who owned this shop went missing, and now one of our early suspects runs his doll-making business from the same shop. The same man that Adam told Cooper Clifton he intended to go and see next.'

French shrugged. 'Life is full of coincidences. It doesn't have to mean something. Sometimes it just is. And he has an alibi, remember.'

'Alibis don't always stand up to scrutiny. You know that as well as I do. I think it's time for us to pay Trefor Lovell another visit, don't you?'

DC French held up his hand to stop her. He sagged against a garden wall, empty Lucozade bottle in his hand, face the colour of curdled cream.

'I feel sick,' he said.

Wildeve stared down at this crumpled excuse of a human being. An intense longing for Adam claimed her. 'For pity's sake, Bernie, pull yourself together.' She marched off down the street and didn't look back.

Trefor Lovell's house was at the end of The Avenue, as tired-looking as the old man himself. The roof had a couple of tiles missing and the gaps were like broken teeth.

The grass was brown and thirsty. High up, beneath the top left window, was an oversized plastic butterfly fixed to the wall. Its yellow and blue markings were not quite garish enough to offset the ugliness of the house's pebble-dashed exterior.

The building wore an air of sadness, and reminded Wildeve of a place that she and Adam had once viewed, belonging to an elderly widower moving into residential care. Not quite clean, vaguely unkempt. The old man had shuffled about in too-loose trousers, sorrow scratched into the lines of his face, the absence of his wife more powerful than her presence had ever been.

Wildeve swallowed down the lump of grief in her throat and pressed the doorbell.

No answer. She pressed again. Nothing. French bent down and lifted up the letterbox.

'Jesus Christ,' he said, staggering upwards, his hand over his mouth.

'What is it?' she said. 'Hangover taken a turn for the worse?'

French retched, and the rough sound of it made Wildeve gag too. He jerked his head from side to side, a violent gesture.

She remembered the postman's words. *He's an old guy.*

This heat was punishing. Autolysis, the first stage of decomposition when enzymes consume the body's cells from the inside out, wouldn't take long.

'Oh, fuck,' she said. 'You don't think he's dead?'

'Who's dead?' said a thin voice behind them. 'And who are you?'

Both police officers turned around.

An older man blocked the path. He was average height, hair the colour of dirty grouting. Despite the weather he was wearing a coat, over a pair of faded shorts. Even from a couple of feet away, Wildeve could smell his unwashed clothing. He was holding a carrier bag with vertical blue and white stripes. Through the stretched plastic, she could see a loaf of bread and a tin of soup.

'Mr Lovell?'

'Aye,' he said. Not Scottish, but there was a memory of an accent in there somewhere.

'I'm DS Stanton, this is DC French, we're—'

'Here about that copper's body. Aye, I know.' He let his eyes leave her and settle on French. 'Rough night, was it, pal?'

French's eyes narrowed. 'No, sir. I stumbled across a rather nasty smell.'

Lovell gave him a level stare. 'Did you now?'

'Aren't you going to invite us in?' said French.

'Reckon not,' said Lovell. 'No law against that, is there?'

'No, of course not,' said Wildeve. Mr Lovell smiled at her with such tenderness that the grief she had swallowed down threatened to engulf her again. She cleared her throat, buying time to compose herself. Kindness, it always undid her.

'You'll want to know if I spoke to him,' he said, still looking at her. 'Word's already flown around the street.'

'Did you?' said Wildeve, urgency sharpening her tone.

''Fraid not,' said Lovell. But he couldn't quite meet her gaze.

'Yeah, right, course you bloody didn't,' muttered French. Wildeve glared at him, skewering his sarcasm with a stab of her eyes.

'Look,' she said. 'If there's something you'd like to share with us, Mr Lovell, we can be very discreet.'

He studied her, considering his next move. He opened his mouth to say something, but French made an elaborate gesture of looking at his watch and Lovell's face closed up. 'I was working when they found him,' he said. 'But I'd like to catch the bastard, before another one turns up.' His voice hardened. 'Can't let them get away with it.'

'We don't intend to,' said French. 'No way.' He pasted on his most synthetic smile. 'Actually, I feel a sudden urge to use the conveniences. Not going to refuse an officer of the law the chance to exercise a basic human right, are you?'

'Toilet's broken,' said Lovell, his gaze pinning French in place. 'It's full of shit.' The police officer blushed but he didn't reply. The two men stared at each other for a too-long moment until French looked away.

Lovell coughed and loose phlegm rattled in his throat. 'Now, if you don't mind, I've been working for most of the night and I'm going to make myself some breakfast.'

'Mr Lovell . . . ?' Wildeve could feel his attention slipping and she made a grab for it.

'Aye?'

'How long have you had that shop?'

'More years than you've been alive, miss.'

'Does the name Bridget Sawyer mean anything to you?'

'Never heard of her.' But his eyes flickered.

'Are you sure?'

'Listen, I've been awake for a very long time and I'm tired and I'm hungry, but if you come back later, we can talk then.' He brushed past them, heading towards his front door.

'What about your wife – Annie, isn't it?' said Wildeve. 'Can we talk to her instead?'

Lovell became very still. He turned to face them, his movements unhurried and his gaze steady, but Wildeve noticed the hand holding his door key was trembling.

'I said later.'

'When?'

He spoke carefully, as if choosing the words most likely to make them leave. 'This afternoon? Three o'clock?'

'We'll be there,' said Wildeve. 'In the meantime, if you remember anything, however small, do let us know.'

Lovell touched her arm with a rare sort of gentleness, as if he somehow suspected the horrors she had seen during the last twenty-four hours. 'I promise,' he said, and she believed him.

The police officers watched Trefor Lovell go into his house. As soon as the door shut behind him, French turned on Wildeve.

'We need a warrant. Call Mac. Tell him what's going on.'

She couldn't help but laugh. 'On what grounds? A terrible smell?' She began walking briskly up the street towards her car. French had to half jog to keep up with her.

'Oh, come on. He's dodgy as fuck. Anyone can see that.'

'I think he knows more than he's letting on, yes, but we'll get that out of him this afternoon.'

'After we've given him a few hours to move the body.'

'He said his toilet is broken.'

French grabbed her arm, forcing her to stop. 'He's lying.'

Her temper was rising with the heat. She didn't appreciate being interrupted or manhandled. 'Maybe. And maybe he's telling the truth.' But French had a point. What if there was something sinister inside Lovell's house? A part of her wondered whether her reluctance to take French seriously was less about distrusting his instincts and more about her dislike of him. She hesitated, unsure about what to do next.

French noticed her indecision. 'He's been out all night, he admitted that himself. So what was he up to? Why wasn't he at home in bed?'

'He was working, Bernie.' Her car was a few metres ahead and she upped her pace, needing time to think.

'Doing what? It's too much of a coincidence. That, and the stink. How would you feel if he's got some poor fucker holed up in his house, all ready to dump in the woods tonight, and we did nothing? Because that's career-ending, and I'm not ready to throw in the towel yet.'

She forced herself to breathe deeply, and dug in her pocket for her keys.

'I thought you didn't believe in coincidences.' She turned to face him. 'Look, I hear what you're saying but we have no reason to suspect him of that. You can't just go around accusing people of murder. We'll take a closer look at his alibi and we'll go back at three, and talk to him then. And hopefully, his wife. If we're still uneasy, we'll raise the issue of a warrant with Mac. Happy?'

'And give him a chance to hide the evidence? Are you fucking mad?' French slammed his hand on her car roof. The violent sound surprised them both. 'I knew you shouldn't be at work. It's too soon. It's skewing your judgement.'

A white heat consumed Wildeve. 'Don't you dare.' The low throb of her anger was palpable, and it grew more intense. All-powerful. Her shout splintered the quiet of the street. 'Don't you fucking dare.'

'Why not? It's fucking true, isn't it? Everyone thinks so.' He was shouting too, spittle flying from the corners of his mouth. 'This is not fucking playtime. This is life and death. You should be at home, before you condemn some other fucker to an early grave.'

His words were like punches. Hard. Fast. Brutal.

She was vaguely aware of a woman walking past, craning her neck to watch them. A desire – hot and immediate – to claw at the skin of his face took hold. She wanted to hurt him. To make him feel pain.

And then DC French's mobile began to ring.

He stalked away from her, but she could still hear him, loud and overbearing, brusque, full of his own self-importance.

'What is it, mate? I'm up to my eyes.'

He was in profile, and she studied the outline of his strong-featured face, his aquiline nose. He could have been a good-looking man, but arrogance made him ugly.

He's a prick, Wild. We both know it.

The warmth of Adam's voice nearly destroyed her. He'd have listened carefully to her point of view, not shouted at her like French had. Her fury wilted. Sadness, keen and quick, took its place.

French was pacing the pavement, but he stilled and the anger building in his eyes and in the lines around his thin lips began to slide, a landslip of emotion. The corners of his mouth twitched upwards.

'You've got to be joking.'

He threw his head back and laughed, an extravagant sound from deep in his stomach.

'I knew it. I fucking *knew* it.'

A pause. And then he threw her a sly look. 'Oh, yes,' he said. 'It will give me the greatest of pleasure.'

When he had cut the call, he swaggered back to Wildeve. She knew from the confident strut of his body that this was bad news for her.

'Go on, then,' she said.

'The Assistant Chief Constable's finally grown a pair,' said French. 'We've got to go back in. Mac's been kicked off the case.'

45

Now

Birdie's remains ended up in the reservoir and I shut the shop for a month. The low humidity and lack of air in the wooden chest had contributed to her mummification. If any of the children had confided in their parents, I hoped enough time had passed for their outrage to weaken. To dismiss it as childish imaginings, and move on.

But that was not the only reason.

I had someone else's blood on my hands.

Your blood.

And I needed time to process what I had done.

46

Tuesday, 31 July 2018

25 The Avenue – 9.37 a.m.

The smoke alarm would not stop beeping.

'Mum!' The kitchen smelled of burnt toast and a coil of smoke rose up from the grill pan. Evan doused a tea towel in water and threw it over his blackened breakfast, like the fire safety officer had shown his class when he'd visited last term. He flapped his arms and shouted for his mother again. 'I've had a bit of an accident.'

He waited a few moments, but his mother didn't appear. The smoke alarm continued to blare, the sound drilling its way into his head. The kitchen was full of smoke. He was in big trouble. But he'd only made his own breakfast because he was still feeling sulky with his mother. Wearing his goalie gloves and an anxious expression, he ran down the hallway and called to her through the study door.

'My toast is on fire.' Strictly speaking, that wasn't *exactly* true, but he thought the dramatic sound of it would rouse her from her work.

Silence.

184

He hesitated, and went in. His mother's computer was on the desk and the bag she used for work was slung in the corner. Her glasses case was by the keyboard, a thin cardigan draped across the chair's arm. A notebook with *Olivia Lockwood* embossed on its front sat next to a silver pen and a coffee mug.

It looked like she had only popped out for a minute.

He called again, irritated and hungry. '*Mum.*'

Evan checked the downstairs toilet, the dining room and the garden. An empty glass sat on the patio table, a wasp crawling across the residue of stickiness at its bottom. The patio light was still on and her Kindle was on the table next to her car keys, as if she had just put them down.

There was no sign of his mother.

Through the open window, Evan could still hear the smoke alarm. He went back inside and stood, uncertain, in the hallway. He switched tack. 'Dad?' A pause to see if his call would be answered. 'Where are you?' And then he remembered. His father had an all-day job interview in London and had left before Evan woke up.

The boy went back into the kitchen. The smoke alarm had stopped now, but the silence rang. He put the toast on a plate and covered it with a thick layer of chocolate spread. But it didn't satisfy his hunger, it made him feel sick.

He cast around for a note but the worktops and table were empty.

His mother would never have gone out without telling him.

She would be back in a minute.

47

26 The Avenue – 9.41 a.m.

Fletcher Parnell wasn't just playing with fire, he was sticking his hand into the flames.

He adjusted the finderscope until he was zoomed in on the female police officer. She was shouting at the man with her, and her face was all twisted up. The anger pulsed off her in waves like an *asperitas* formation. The air shimmered with heat.

They were walking up the road, in the direction of his house. For a moment, she looked straight up at the window and he panicked, swinging his telescope wildly until it pointed the opposite way. He crouched down beneath the sill, his back to the cold radiator, heart in his mouth.

'What are you doing?' Dessie was standing in the spare-room doorway, wearing her running gear and a perplexed expression.

He laughed, patted his palms across the carpet. 'Dropped my cufflink.'

She peered closely at him. 'You look tired.' Glanced at her watch. 'Shouldn't you be at work?'

'Shouldn't *you*?'

'Job's been cancelled, smartarse.'

He laughed and made another performance of looking for his cufflink before standing up and pulling her into a hug.

Her body stiffened, but then relaxed. 'Seen any good clouds?' she murmured, biting the lobe of his ear.

'Clear skies today.' He nudged her away. 'I better get going,' he said.

She followed him downstairs, chatting as he tied up the laces of his brogues. The sun poured through the front door's stained glass, reds and blues and greens pooling on the hallway floorboards. A sweat was rising on his forehead. Another scorcher.

'Did you think any more about our holiday?'

Shit.

'I fancy America. Or Canada. What about Niagara Falls?' She reeled off several other places she would like to visit.

'I'm not sure if I'll be able to get away. Work's crazy at the moment.'

It was her turn to laugh. 'Everyone deserves a break, Fletch, even if it's just for a week.'

'I don't know where my passport is. I've got a horrible feeling it's expired.'

'Well, get a new one,' she said, impatience creeping in. A sudden thought. 'It's not money, is it? I mean, it's not as if you pay me much rent, is it?'

'It's not the money.'

'So you'll book the time off?'

'We'll see, OK?'

Dessie pouted. 'Sounds like you don't want to go on holiday with me.'

He pocketed his keys and reached for her hand. 'I do, it's just difficult with work at the moment. But I'll do my best.'

'Promise?'

'Promise.'

Fletcher had a high, tight pain in his chest as he left the house and headed towards the train station. The police officers were climbing into separate cars and he looked away, keen not to make eye contact. If he'd been honest from the beginning, he wouldn't be in this situation.

He wouldn't be living a lie. He wouldn't be full of regrets. He wouldn't be worrying about paperwork and visa applications, pretending to be someone he wasn't.

But there was no way he could come clean now.

He flicked his gaze towards number twenty-five. The windows were open and he could hear the urgent call of a smoke alarm. He started towards the house, but as he reached the gate leading up their path, he faltered and turned away.

No, stupid to get involved.

This was his new beginning. He mustn't fuck it up.

48

Major Incident Room, Rayleigh Police Station – 10.56 a.m.

The whole investigating team had been recalled to the incident room for the 11 a.m. briefing.

A metallic taste filled Wildeve's mouth. Her anger had gone. Now she was wrung out and empty. Her legs felt weak and she gripped the back of a chair to anchor herself.

Voices rose in the airless space. A babble of gossip and rumour. She tried not to look at the bank of photographs on the wall, but she was drawn to Adam.

His pale face. Bloodied eye sockets and their glass imposters.

A tunnel opened up in front of her. A black void. She blinked several times and felt an arm steady her; realized, too late, she had been swaying. She flashed a grateful smile at the female sergeant. Her tongue was thick and dry in her mouth.

French was beside himself, jigging his foot, arms flying about as he talked to Detective Chief Inspector Roger Sampson. Not only had French's nemesis Clive Mackie been

189

pulled from the case, the replacement was his own chief inspector, drafted across from the Brentwood murder squad.

Parking had been a nightmare and it seemed French had arrived back before her, dripping poison in Sampson's ear.

Because of the media outcry and the scale of the inquiry, the investigating team had been drawn from four different homicide teams, pooling expertise and manpower, but the divisions between them were clear to see. French had commandeered a chair near the front, leaning back to chat to colleagues behind him. DC Jim Sheridan was sitting on the other side of the room next to Adam's best friend, PC Simon Quick. They had saved her a seat and she slipped in beside them.

DCI Sampson turned to address the assembled officers. He didn't beat about the bush. The rigours of the case had been too much for Mac and he was retiring with immediate effect.

A collective gasp spread out across the room. Wildeve and Sheridan exchanged a glance. Sampson had made it sound as if their boss had made the decision himself but everyone in the room knew Mac's demotion had left him no choice but to leave.

Then it was down to business.

Sampson was meticulous and organized. He allocated every officer a job and a ticket. He wrote each ticket number in his book so he remembered who was supposed to be doing what. He barked orders. He demanded that his best officers go over each of the murders again, starting with Natalie Tiernan, the first victim. He was tough and thorough and switched-on.

The team began to drift away. All except Wildeve, who was still awaiting instruction.

'What do you need me to do, guv?'

'Wildeve Stanton, isn't it?' said Sampson.

She was aware of French lingering near the door and turned away from him. 'Yes, guv.'

'I'm so sorry for your loss. We all are. I didn't know your husband, but I understand he was an excellent officer.'

'Thank you.'

'Clearly, this is an extremely distressing time for you. Why don't you take a few weeks off? You need a chance to process what's happened. Come back when you're ready.'

'That's kind of you. I appreciate it. But I'd rather be at work.'

DCI Sampson blew out a long, slow breath. 'Look, I'm not quite sure how to put this and it's understandable, of course, but there have been some concerns about your ability to focus fully on the job.'

Her stomach plunged. Adam whispered in her ear. *Keep your cool.* 'They're unfounded, guv. I'm entirely focused. I don't want to be at home. I know you need officers on the ground and I want to help find Adam's killer.'

'It's not a question of choice.'

His words took a moment to sink in before the penny dropped. He was ordering her to go home. A heat suffused her face and she glanced at French, who smirked before slipping through the door.

'It was Bernie French, wasn't it? Who raised these "concerns". With all due respect, he's lying, guv. We had a difference of opinion, that's all. Did he tell you he turned up for work late this morning? That he was driving, still hungover, reeking of alcohol? No, I bet he didn't.' The words tumbled from her, the injustice oiling her tongue and her temper. 'He's lazy, sir. And indiscreet. He jumps to conclusions. Doesn't pull his weight.'

DCI Sampson patted her arm.

'This is exactly what I'm talking about. You're overwrought and emotional. Unsurprisingly so. I need clear thinkers on my investigation. I don't care for petty politics between my officers. I want results.' His voice softened but there was steel in it. 'Do yourself a favour, Wildeve, and get yourself home.'

She slammed the door behind her on the way out.

49

25 The Avenue – 11.29 a.m.

Evan was sitting on the treehouse roof.

He liked it up there. Hidden away from his sister and the rest of the world, his face obscured by branches and leaves, the sun on his skin.

He was bored. B-o-r-e-d.

His mother was *somewhere*, but he didn't know where.

His father was still in London, but had promised to get home as soon as he could.

His dumb idiot of a sister was supposed to be looking after him, but she was pretending to walk up to the shop to buy a magazine so she could hang about and meet boys.

He flicked a nervous glance at the house. The smoke had finally dispersed after Aster, dragged from bed by the noise, had panicked and called their father mid-interview. He'd told her to turn off the grill and open all the windows and doors. He'd also shouted the F-word down the phone, Aster said. Now he was getting the train home early from his Very Important Interview. Evan had a bad feeling about this.

His stomach rumbled. He pulled a plum from the tree, but as he lifted it to his mouth, a wasp crawled from a hole in its flesh and Evan dropped it. The sound of it hitting the grass was thick and wet.

In a flash of inspiration, he remembered a half-eaten packet of Jammie Dodgers in the treehouse. As he prepared to climb down, a movement from next door caught his eye.

An old lady was hurrying down the garden.

'Cooper,' she called. '*Cooper.*'

An old man appeared in the greenhouse door, secateurs in one hand, plant cuttings in another.

'What is it, my love?'

'I've been checking over those drawings again.' Her voice was loud. Animated. 'Not only are those people next door planning to dig up the foundations for a basement kitchen, they want to build a two-storey extension and a garden room—'

'Hush, *hush*, my love.'

'Oh, don't worry about that,' she said. 'He's gone out. I saw the taxi this morning.'

'Well, now,' he said mildly, scratching his head and pulling out his pipe. 'There's not much we can do about it.'

Evan inched forward, half on the metal roof and half on the branch of the tree, trying to catch her reply, but it was muffled and indistinct.

'Don't upset yourself, my love.' That was the old man. 'These things take time.'

Her voice rose again. 'He's an out-of-work architect. He has time.'

The old man chuckled. 'Why don't we go and discuss it

with them? Talk it over. They're new. They won't want to make trouble.'

The old lady was pacing up and down the garden. 'Imagine the noise and disruption. Loud radios. Diggers.' She plucked a dead leaf from the laurel bush and let her complaint hang in the air.

At any other time, when the sun was so bright it was difficult to see and the birds were full of song, Evan's eavesdropping might have passed unnoticed.

But at half past eleven on that late July morning, after days and days of unremitting heat, the branch of the tree the boy was leaning on snapped and tumbled to the grass, taking Evan with it.

He let out a yell before hitting the ground, landing on his arm.

He began to cry.

The old man from next door called over the fence.

'Young man, are you hurt?'

Evan cried louder.

'Is your mother there?'

'No.' The boy breathed out his reply in the gaps between sobs. 'She's out.'

The fence panel that separated their gardens began to lift upwards, and before Evan realized what was happening, the old man was kneeling beside him, examining his wrist.

'Looks swollen. Why don't you come and sit with us until your mother gets back? Or at least let me put some ice on it.'

Evan did not want to go with the old man, whose face reminded him of a well-worn football. Not when he had never met him before. But he'd only be a minute, and his arm was hurting, and his natural instinct was to let an adult take charge.

He stepped awkwardly across the gardens, leaning on the concrete fence post with his good arm. Their garden was much neater than the Lockwoods'. An ornamental pond with its own fountain commanded the centre of the lawn. Several tall plants with blousy purple hoods stood by a wall. Inside the greenhouse, Evan saw plump tomatoes, ripe strawberries and a giant marrow. A row of seedlings in pots. He followed the man through the back door.

Their kitchen smelled like his granny's house, of air freshener and leftover roast beef.

The old lady ran him a glass of water. She was wearing an apron. There were lines on her face, like cracks in old soap. Her hair was permed, but the curls were loose waves. Her face was set into neutral.

As she put the glass on the table, it made a hard, heavy sound and Evan guessed that she was still annoyed with his parents.

But then she smiled at him and her face broke open, a shaft of sunlight through the clouds, and her eyes softened.

'I'm Audrina,' she said. 'And this is Cooper. What's your name?'

'Evan.'

'Welcome to the neighbourhood,' she said.

'Right, Evan,' said Cooper. 'Let's have a closer look. Love, I think we need some ice.'

Evan winced as his elderly neighbour manipulated his wrist, but the pain had begun to wear off. The old lady appeared with a bag of frozen fish fillets which she wrapped in a tea towel.

'I don't think it's broken,' said Cooper.

They sat for a while, the rough fabric pressed against

Evan's wrist, dampening in the heat. The boy couldn't think of anything to say and, after a while, began to fidget.

'I better go home now,' he said.

Cooper adjusted the ice pack, pressed his palms on his knees and leaned forward. A bluebottle buzzed lazily around the kitchen. 'How old are you, Evan?'

'Nine.'

'And do you often stay at home on your own?'

'Um, sometimes.'

'Shall I tell you something?' It was the kind of question that did not allow for an answer. 'I've been many things in my life. Mostly a gardener on those big country estates you might have visited with your mum and dad, but, in my younger days, I used to be a school governor. And I think nine's a bit young to be left on your own.'

'My sister's looking after me today.'

'Is she now? Doesn't seem to be doing a very good job of it, if you ask me.' He laughed. 'You fell out of a tree.'

'She'll be back in a minute.'

'Well, I'd feel happier if we can keep an eye on you until she gets back. Did you bump your head?'

'No.'

'Looky here,' said the old man. 'I appreciate this isn't the way you wanted to spend your morning. Come on upstairs. There's a few things up there that might interest you.'

The door creaked as it opened. Evan's eyes widened. A single bed neatly made with a blue and white patchwork quilt was tucked in the corner of the room, a well-worn teddy leaning against the pillow.

Mr Men books filled shelves that ran the length of the

room. Evan recognized *The Complete Tales of Beatrix Potter* nestled beside Enid Blyton's *The Castle of Adventure* and half a dozen *Shoot* football annuals.

An AT-AT walker – he recognized it from the *Star Wars* films his father made him watch – stood proudly on the windowsill next to boxed figures of Luke Skywalker and Jabba the Hutt. A flat, red computer with a handle and a yellow and blue keyboard caught his eye on the bedside table. Speak & Spell. He could see action figures and boxes of Lego and a whole selection of Matchbox cars.

'Go in,' said Cooper. The old lady was pegging out the washing and for that Evan was grateful. He couldn't put it into words, but the room seemed faded, like an old photograph brought to life.

'This was my son Joby's room.' Cooper's smile was sad. He made a sweeping gesture. 'Please, have a look around. But be careful. His things are very precious to us.'

Evan moved hesitantly into the room. He felt uncomfortable, like he shouldn't be there. It was stuffy and sort of unhappy. Cooper opened a window and waved to his wife. He was wearing a pullover, despite the heat, and reminded Evan of his own grandpa.

Evan picked up the AT-AT walker and put it down again. Pressed a finger against a cyclist on a stainless steel bicycle sculpture. It began to move rhythmically, insistently, the rider swinging back and forth.

'Perpetual motion,' murmured Cooper. 'A little bit like life, eh?'

Evan had no idea what he meant so he opened the bedside drawer to find pens, pencils and a Tupperware box full of rubbers. Evan opened the tub and a faint fruity smell filled the room.

A Rubik's Cube. A small maze filled with liquid mercury. An ancient box of candy cigarettes.

And a set of headphones plugged into a yellow box emblazoned with seven letters. WALKMAN.

'What's this?' He held it up for Cooper to see.

'It's a cassette player. Plays music and stories. You know, tapes.' He pointed to the drawer under the bed. 'There's a heap of them in there.'

The doorbell rang.

'Back in a tick,' said Cooper and hurried from the room.

Evan turned over the Walkman in his hand. He should put it back. It didn't belong to him. But he didn't move. Instead he chewed on his thumbnail. Borrowing wasn't stealing, was it? Before he could change his mind, he undid the hoodie that was tied around his waist and wrapped it around the Walkman.

A voice he recognized drifted upwards. Evan heard his name being mentioned.

'I'm Aster from next door. We've just moved in. I don't suppose you've seen my younger brother. I saw the fence had been—'

He tucked his prize into the crook of one arm and barrelled down the stairs. 'I'm here,' he said. 'I'm here.'

He wasn't often pleased to see his sister but the sight of her warmed him. Evan didn't wait for Cooper to speak, but grabbed hold of his sister's hand and tugged her down the path, calling out a goodbye.

* * *

Even the soft tread of Audrina's footsteps on the carpet was not enough to drag Cooper's gaze from the window and he felt rather than saw his wife's presence.

The old couple stood side by side at the window, not touching, looking down on the garden next door, watching the boy who vibrated with life and youth and reminded them of the son they had lost.

All those memories, all those choices, buried deep in the earth of their lives. Both of them carrying the scars, not on their skins but beneath the neighbourly smiles and the warmth of their welcome, Audrina and Cooper from number twenty-seven.

Audrina dragged a finger along the sill, searching for non-existent dust.

'I better get back to the greenhouse,' Cooper said, dabbing at his watery eyes with a tissue.

She didn't try to stop him.

But as soon as she heard the back door click, Audrina lay down on her son's bed and closed her eyes. If she listened carefully, she could hear the low thrum of the Matchbox car engines, the march of a thousand tin soldiers, the clink of marbles on the drain covers.

The shouts of her son and his best friend playing in her garden all those years ago.

50

The Avenue – 12.11 p.m.

'You look like you could do with a drink.'

Nine words that would change both their lives. He had passed a weary hand across his eyes and rested his elbows on the bar. The woman with the long dark hair had poured him a whisky and when he'd downed it, she'd poured him another. The music was loud. The club throbbed with it.

He had held out his hand, ready to shake. 'I'm—'

'I know exactly who you are.'

Chilled by her reply, he had thrown a glance over his shoulder, half expecting to find his exit blocked by security. But it turned out she hadn't known who he was. Not then. That came much later and it cost them everything.

A car door slammed, and the postman was back in The Avenue, sun on his neck, still on his delivery round. He mustn't allow himself to be distracted. He walked up and down the driveways and garden paths, letters gathered in his hand like gifts.

Even now, fourteen months after that night in the club,

the postman could pinpoint the moment a line had been crossed. As they had dangled their legs over the seawall near Southend, a few weeks after they had met, she had lifted her lit cigarette to his lips, and he had taken a drag. Their eyes had held each other's through the smoke, and they had both known. But she wasn't his to love.

And trusting him had killed her.

51

Hanningfield Reservoir – 1.12 p.m.

The sound of beating wings startled Wildeve and she watched the flock of geese land with grace on the sparkling skin of the water.

From her perch on the decking of the cafeteria, she could see knots of families, spreading out rugs and unpacking their picnics and cricket sets, the drift of merry voices through the air.

Adam had wanted to be a father, had often talked about surrounding himself with a brood of children – a legacy of a childhood without siblings to share the well-meaning but suffocating attentions of his parents. His friends had filled the gap of brothers and sisters but had fallen away as he'd grown older. When they had first moved back to the Essex town where Adam had spent his childhood, he'd wanted to find them again but had never seemed to have the time. A few months ago, he'd been invited to a school reunion. He'd spent a couple of evenings on social media, tracking down his former classmates. *I'd like to connect with old friends,*

Wild. Recently, he had spoken of one in particular he was still trying to locate, muttering about credit checks and electoral roll searches that had drawn a blank. But life and work had got in the way and he hadn't mentioned it again.

Wildeve had been less certain about children, concerned about how weighty she might find the burden of responsibility. At thirty-six, she had experienced no maternal pangs, no longing for motherhood. Now she might never know.

She wrote a single word on a piece of paper: *Funeral.*

A man with silver at his temples and pouchy eyes approached her table. She stood and reached out a hand to greet him, but he pulled her into a rough hug. He smelled of aniseed balls.

'What a bloody mess.'

'I can't believe this, guv,' she said, mouth pressed against his polo shirt. She let him go. He was wearing knee-length shorts and deck shoes. She tried not to stare, more used to his smart trousers and ironed shirts.

He ran a hand through his hair. 'What can I do? I messed up.'

'You didn't,' she said hotly.

'Didn't catch him though, did I?' He smiled at the waitress and she came over to their table. Wildeve tried not to mind that she had been trying to catch the young woman's eye for ten minutes. Mac seemed to have that effect on both sexes. Objectively, he was a good-looking man, but she loved him because in the four years she had known him, he had never flirted or been overfamiliar, talking proudly of his wife and boys.

'I can't believe Roger Sampson has been put on the case,' he said. 'Or that he sent you home.'

She fiddled with a sachet of brown sugar, absently tearing the paper. Tiny grains scattered across the table. 'He's come in with all guns blazing,' she said. 'They're going back to square one, to Natalie Tiernan.'

Mac sighed. 'That's a mistake. They don't have the resources. And we've already spent more on that strand of the investigation than the rest of the victims put together.'

It was an unfortunate perk of being the first to die.

The waitress brought over their drinks, smiling at Mac. The ice cubes in their glasses of lemonade clinked as they both took a sip. A frivolous sound, unsuited to a grieving widow and a career copper put out to pasture.

'So what are you going to do?'

He put down his glass. 'Get under Peggy's feet. Help Harry get ready for university.' His laugh was hollow. 'What about you?'

'I can't sit around at home. I just can't.' That hot pricking behind her eyes again. She took another sip of her drink because it was a way to stop herself falling into the dark spaces.

'I know, lass,' he said, all his decades down south not quite drowning out the music of the Tyne. 'I know.'

They sat in silence for a few minutes, watching a small boat meander home to the jetty. A jabber of swallows or swifts, she could never remember the difference, swooped and spiralled above the water, an aerial ballet.

'I don't know what more I could have done,' he said, and Wildeve had to lean forward to catch the shape of his words. 'But we've missed something important.'

'No persons of interest?' She knew the team would have

checked out anyone with convictions for violence or sexual assault, but she wanted Mac to confirm it.

'Nothing, or at least, nothing relevant.' He sighed again. 'There's nothing we can do about it now, though. We're out of the game.'

Wildeve pushed the police statements and a photocopy of the faded newspaper clipping that she had found at home across the table.

Mac stared at them. 'What's this?'

'I found them in Adam's things.'

Mac scanned the paperwork while she talked, determined to convince him. 'We need to speak to a man called Trefor Lovell. He's expecting me this afternoon. He owns the shop now. I think he knows more than he's letting on.'

He looked up. 'You know we can't do that. We're off the job.' He gave another laugh, laced with bitterness. 'And, in my case, out of the police.'

'Why can't we?'

'It wouldn't be right.'

'Guv, they've treated you like shit. And you've left Essex Police now, remember?'

'I know that.' His delivery was considered, as if weighing up the consequences of what she was suggesting.

'We won't tread on anyone's toes. We'd just be . . .'

'Interfering with an investigation?'

'Of course not. We'll be discreet. We won't get in anyone's way. We're only going to ask a few questions, that's all.' She spoke quietly. 'I need to do this. For Adam.'

Mac stared out across the reservoir, a muscle in his cheek twitching. He drained his drink, pushed back his chair and stood up. Pulling out his wallet, he placed a ten-pound note on the table.

Wildeve's stomach plunged. He was a proud man, a respected police officer with a varied and decorated career, and she had offended him.

'Where are you going?' she said, a dark hole about to swallow her up.

'Can't conduct interviews in this T-shirt,' said Mac, holding out his hand to her and pulling her up from her seat.

They walked back to the car park together. 'A couple of ground rules, Wildeve. No treading on anyone's toes. No breaking the law. No obstructing justice. We operate under the radar and we give anything we get to the team. Got it?'

'Yes, guv.'

'And one other thing.'

'Yes, guv?'

'Call me Mac.'

52

Now

What is the opposite of a crime of passion? A crime of apathy? Indifference? Of calm?

My belief is that death should never be inflicted from inside the blinding mists of fury or because of a lack of control. It is much more deserving than that. Planning and preparation are required. As little mess as possible. A method that is meticulous both in execution and aftermath.

The research was less difficult than I had anticipated.

Three of them still lived in this town. They were easy to find, even though two of them had married. Internet searches. Public social media accounts. A list of friends and followers – husbands, brothers, sisters, mothers – helped me to identify them. It never ceases to surprise me how much of their lives people choose to give away. Photographs of their houses or new cars, children in school uniforms, detailed plans for the evening, a window into their lives for a motivated stranger.

One lived in London but made regular visits home.

THE NEIGHBOUR

It was easy.

If I was forced to make a guess, I would say the sirens will be passing Mayflower Road in approximately one minute. My suitcase is packed, the keys are in my pocket. I could run. I could go now and they would not find me.

Stop and smell the roses.

A favourite phrase of Birdie's. I have tried to live by that adage, to fill my home and my heart with the scent of flowers. To sweeten the bitterness of what I have lost.

It is fitting that Natalie Tiernan was the first. First through the shop door. First to find Birdie. First to die.

Little Tallie. Except she was not so little anymore. Thirty-eight years old, a mother and a wife.

As I brushed her hair in the shadow of the trees, the cursing of the birds filling the silence, I smiled at the sight of the silken strands, as golden as her five-year-old self.

53

18 The Avenue – 1.15 p.m.

Four porcelain dolls were hanging upside down by their pretty ankles from a light fitting inside Trefor Lovell's workroom at the back of the shop.

He liked to test his craftsmanship in this way, to make sure the hair he had glued to their heads was unlikely to detach. They watched him, long strands waterfalling beneath them. Lovell did not use synthetic hair. Mohair was expensive, and his second choice. Human hair, his favourite.

Lovell spread out a square of plastic sheeting across the concrete floor and placed an old tin bath on top of it. Next, he carried through several cans of paint, a sheathed blade inside his boot.

He fiddled with a piece of wire, and laid out several batteries on his worktop. The chemicals he had bought from the internet had done their job, and the pellets had dried nicely. The shotgun was waiting, propped against the wall.

From the street outside he heard the lift of teenage voices, and the sound of his own name.

THE NEIGHBOUR

Lovell drew the knife from his boot and drove its tip beneath the lid of the first can to loosen it. Paint sprayed across his shirt like warm blood.

Then he picked up the gun and went outside.

54

Tuesday, 31 July 2018

25 The Avenue – 1.17 p.m.

As soon as Aster heard the voices under her window, she slicked on some lip gloss and flew down the stairs.

'Back in ten minutes,' she called out to Evan, who was sitting on his bedroom floor with the tape and Walkman.

'But you've only just got back,' he protested. 'You promised you'd help me with this.'

She tuned out his whine and ignored a stab of guilt. 'I will,' she said. 'As soon as I get home.'

'What about Dad?' he said as the front door slammed. 'And lunch.'

The sun was so bright it turned everything into a washed-out white and she blinked as she stepped outside, struggling to adjust to the switch from the gloom to this unforgiving glare.

Three boys around her age were standing near a house at the bottom of The Avenue. They all had bikes with them, and one was holding a carrier bag. She'd seen them outside the newsagent's earlier. One had nodded to her, said, 'All right?' She had smiled brightly. 'Great, thanks.' She had spent the walk home groaning inwardly at how gawky she had sounded.

She hovered on her front step, not quite brazen enough to walk over to the boys. But the one from earlier – tall and blond – beckoned to her and she flushed, managing to refrain from pointing at herself in a cartoonish *Who, me?* fashion.

'You new, then?'

'Yes, we moved in a couple of days ago.' She didn't know where to put her hands so she ran one through her hair.

'Sweet.' He dragged out his vowels. 'What's your name?'

'Aster.'

'Has-ter-be what?' said another of the boys and they all laughed.

She rolled her eyes and pretended to inspect her nails, even though her heart was pounding, embarrassment burning through her veins. 'Like I haven't heard that before.'

The blond boy looked sheepish. 'Just messin'. I'm Bailey, this is Charlie and Marco.'

'Hi.' Aster's greeting was cool. 'So, what you doing?'

The trio exchanged looks and Bailey shrugged, appeared to think for a moment and then nodded to his friends.

'See that house over there,' said the boy called Marco, pointing to a run-down property with a butterfly pinned to the brick. 'The guy that lives there murdered his wife.'

Aster's eyes widened. 'No way.'

Charlie grinned. 'He's a fucking weirdo. Always staring out the window and working on his creepy dolls, the goddamned freak. He doesn't bother to wash or anything. His shoes have got holes in them.' He laughed as if this was the funniest thing he had ever heard.

'We think he's behind all these killings,' said Bailey. 'And he deserves to be punished for his crimes.'

'But surely the police . . .' Aster didn't want to say it aloud, to undo the fragile peace, but the boys frightened her with their cavalier attitude to justice.

'. . . are doing fuck all.' Bailey grinned around the group. 'So we're going to do it for them.'

'What are you going to do?' She flicked a wary look at her own front door. She didn't want Evan to be privy to this.

'You'll have to wait and see,' grinned Bailey and they laughed again, but there was a cruel edge to it. 'Come on.'

The boys began to wheel their bikes up the path of the house. Aster hovered uncertainly behind them. Charlie unhooked the carrier bag from his handlebars. A fly buzzed around the opening and the boy swatted it away.

Aster felt sick. She sensed something bad was coming, but she lacked the strength to walk away.

'There,' said Bailey and pointed to a trailing rose growing around a wooden stake in the old man's front garden. He loped onto the lawn, grabbed the stem of the plant and yanked it free. 'Shit,' he said, sucking the bloom of blood from the bulb of his thumb. 'It's stuck.'

'Let me see,' said Aster. Her fingers closed around Bailey's warm palm. A thorn was embedded in his skin. She pulled at it gently and it came free, leaving a streak of blood on its barb.

'Thanks,' said Bailey, and winked at her. Aster's insides liquefied.

'Hurry up,' said Marco, throwing a glance up the street, 'before someone comes.'

Bailey flung the ruined rose onto the grass. 'Come on, Charlie. You're up.'

Charlie swaggered onto the lawn and stuck two fingers up at the window. The carrier bag was swinging from his other arm and Aster caught a stink of iron earth and death.

She put her hand over her mouth.

None of them noticed the old man standing at the top of The Avenue, too intent on watching Charlie, a butcher's son, plunge his hand into the bag and pull out a pig's head.

Aster took one look at the snout, the closed eyes, the rough tufts of hair and gagged. Charlie waggled it at them, and Bailey and Marco nudged and pushed each other towards it, swearing and laughing, full of boyish bravado, but desperate not to touch its leathered skin.

Charlie glanced at Lovell's front door and, with as much strength as he could muster, drove the pig's head into the top of the stake.

The butcher's carcass swung lopsidedly, as if the pig was still alive, dancing at its own funeral.

Several things happened at once.

Aster screamed.

Charlie wiped his fingers frantically against his shorts.

And the old man appeared on the pavement behind the teenagers and pointed a shotgun at Aster's head.

55

Now

What is it about the inanimate that frightens us so much? Is it fear that the shuttered face of a doll might open up as we turn away, that skin-crawl sensation of being watched? Do we suspect their eyes will blink, heads twist, a grin twitching into life, laughing at our trust?

Or is it that these dolls, and the puppets we use our hands to move, to bring to life, represent our most primal hopes of raising the dead?

I do not have the answers to these questions. I try not to think on them too long. I have no desire to bring anyone back. Except you.

Some days, though, when I am going about the business of living, I am reminded that most of us discard the identities we once inhabited.

The cruelty of the children we were. The shy lover we pretended to be. The manic depressive who was once the class clown.

THE NEIGHBOUR

Perhaps this is why the inanimate frighten us so. Because the faces we turn to the world are ever-changing while they are condemned to never grow old.

56

26 The Avenue – 1.21 p.m.

When Dessie Benedict had completed a three-mile run, finished cleaning the house she had owned for eleven years, hung out two loads of laundry and eaten lunch, she stretched out on the sun lounger in her back garden.

This glorious weather was all well and good, but it wasn't the same as being on holiday. Her make-up artist friend Alexis had just got back from a month-long road trip in the southern US – Nashville, Memphis, New Orleans. Dessie longed for an adventure of her own, but Fletcher seemed reluctant.

Maybe he was going off her. They hadn't been living together for *that* long – only a few months – but sometimes he seemed distant. A secret part of her couldn't help thinking he had landed on his feet with the peppercorn rent he paid her. He'd be a fool to leave.

Dessie closed her eyes, enjoying the warmth on her skin. Perhaps it *was* about the money and he was too embarrassed to tell her. Pharmacy dispensers didn't earn much.

She sat up, sunglasses sliding down her nose. That *had* to be it. His budget wouldn't stretch to the kind of holidays she could afford with her extensive list of well-connected and lucrative clients.

A seed of an idea began to flower.

She would surprise him with a holiday. Book it. Pay for it. Surely he couldn't refuse such a generous gift.

Excited by her plan, Dessie ran through a list of possible destinations and dates. The Amalfi coast in late September. Or autumnal New England with its spectacular display of colour. Perhaps, if she could bear to hold on a few months, they could take a springtime trip to Japan, and see the float and drift of its cherry blossom. She'd always wanted to do that.

During awards season, her career as a make-up artist had seen her flown into some of the world's most exclusive hotels. She didn't stay there, of course, but the 'talent' did. Still, she might be able to hunt down a deal. She'd need to book flights too, and for that, she'd need their passports.

Passports.

A bud of doubt.

If Fletcher's had expired, she assumed he'd had one once, though she couldn't remember seeing it. They'd been away for weekends together, but never abroad.

She slipped on her flip-flops and went inside. When he'd moved in, she'd noticed he kept his important documents in a large box file. Perhaps it was in there and she could secretly renew it for him.

An hour later, Dessie was still looking. She'd checked the spare room, the space above the wardrobes, under the bed and in the attic. The only place she hadn't tried was the garage.

She unlocked the side door and walked into a mouthful of cobwebs.

He better bloody appreciate this effort.

She peered around, her eyes adjusting to the gloom. The skeleton of her old bike. A Black + Decker Workmate. Some half-used tins of paint and crusted brushes.

And there it was, sitting on a shelf.

With a sense of triumph, she edged her way through the assorted detritus of her life and lifted down the box.

A stash of A4 plastic folders was crammed into the space. Each was neatly labelled. *Bank Statements. NHS Card. National Insurance. Certificate of Immunizations. Birth Certificate. Passport.*

A grin split her face. She flicked through the passport's pages and there he was, sober-faced, but still handsome. A quick check of the expiry date confirmed he'd renewed it last year, a couple of months before they'd met. *Excellent. This was going to be fun.* She slipped it into the pocket of her shorts.

But as she tried to lift the box back onto the shelf, her ankle bone grazed the pedal of her bike. The flash of pain tipped her off balance and the box slid from her hands, spilling the slippery plastic folders across the garage floor.

'Shit,' she said. 'That hurt.'

And then laughed because she was talking to herself.

Dessie crouched down to gather them up. One or two of the folders had lost their contents and she picked up the papers, trying to match them to their rightful homes.

Most of them she recognized, but one official-looking

document was unfamiliar to her, typed, signed and witnessed, a large red stamp on the bottom corner. She wasn't one to pry, but curiosity won its battle over decency and she began to read.

CHANGE OF NAME DEED

I, the undersigned Benjamin Turner of 14 Deepdale Road, Lincs, now lately called Fletcher Parnell a Citizen of the United Kingdom by birth do hereby . . .

Dessie reread the words until the letters jumped about in front of her eyes. She was trying to find her way through the language, to untangle the truth of what she was reading. Her eyes strayed to the date at the bottom of the signature. Last spring. Three months before they met, four weeks before the date on his passport renewal.

Her hands were shaking so much that she dropped the piece of paper and it fluttered to the floor, taking her hopes for the future with it.

She drew in a breath – *Calm down, Dessie* – and forced herself to think it through.

At once, the rational part of her began to justify her discovery, to consider all the possible reasons why her live-in boyfriend – the man she loved – might have such a document in his possession. Fletch was a good man. He treated her with kindness and compassion. He wasn't a liar. She would ask him and he would explain. Simple. But the ringing of the death knell drowned out every one of the excuses she made for him. Cut through the legalese and what was left? His name was not Fletcher Parnell. Or rather, it *was*, but only because he had officially changed it by deed poll.

The blood thundered through her veins as she tried to organize how she felt about this and what it meant.

Technically, he had told her the truth. In the eyes of the law, his name was Fletcher Parnell. So why did it feel like a lie? Surely, there had to be a reasonable explanation.

Dessie crouched down to retrieve the piece of paper that had blown a hole into her ordered existence. All her life, fate had smiled on her. Exam results, job interviews, relationships, even the process of buying this house – success had been an easy road, smoothed by invested parents and the gift of emotional and financial support.

But this was the equivalent of a tyre blow-out on the motorway, spinning her off in a terrifying and wholly unexpected direction.

On autopilot, she eased the document back into its plastic wallet, sealed the box and placed it back where she had found it.

As she stepped out of the shadows of the garage and into the blinding light of a summer afternoon, only two questions were on her mind.

Why had Fletcher – she could not think of him in any other way – gone to the trouble of changing his name?

And who the hell was Benjamin Turner?

57

32 The Avenue – 1.24 p.m.

If she lifted her head, Aster would be looking down the twin barrels of a shotgun. As it was, she stared at the cracked soil of his undernourished garden and prayed that whatever he was planning would be over soon.

Mummy.

A longing so intense filled her up. She hadn't called Olivia that for years and years. But all the anger, all the hurt was stripped away in a moment, and she wanted the warmth of her mother's arms, her calm, reassuring voice.

The boys – although a shotgun pointing at them on that empty summer's day did more to turn them into men than years of furtive cider-drinking and stolen cigarettes – were mostly silent.

Charlie – at least, she assumed it was him – muttered something like, 'You'll pay for this, you prick,' but he was shushed by Bailey, and the four of them stood next to each other, suspects in a police line-up.

Old Man Lovell shoved the muzzle into Charlie's chest.

223

The front of the boy's pale green shorts darkened. Aster felt laughter stir inside her like an air bubble, but it wasn't down to Charlie's lack of control, but at the sheer awfulness of the predicament they were in.

'If you *ever* come onto my property again, you will regret it.' He pushed the muzzle deeper into Charlie's chest, making him stumble backwards. *He'll have a bruise there tomorrow.* Again, a bubble of laughter threatened to burst from her and she clamped shut her lips.

'Get rid of it.' He jerked the gun towards the pig's head.

The boys exchanged glances and Bailey stepped forward. He tugged at one of the ears, but Charlie had impaled it with such force that it would not budge. He shot a panicked look at his friends.

Marco moved hesitantly towards it, grabbed the other pig's ear and yanked. The combined strength of both boys freed it from the stake and they staggered backwards. Flecks of raw meat and pale, bloated fat flew through the air and landed on Aster's bare arm.

She screamed.

Lovell turned his attention to her.

'You're one of the new family.' It was a statement, not a question. He already knew.

She nodded, not trusting her voice to remain steady, her eyes drawn to the stiffening splashes of red on the front of his shirt.

'A word of *neighbourly* advice.' The corners of his mouth were white with spittle. 'Stay away from this bunch of no-hopers. They're not worth it.'

Bailey kept his gaze on the ground, but Aster saw Charlie roll his eyes behind the old man's back.

'Now fuck off.'

He did not need to tell them twice. The boys grabbed their bikes – Bailey still holding the pig's head – and were off, cycling up the street at speed, leaving Aster alone in a stranger's garden.

'See?' said Lovell, shaking his head. 'Told you they're not worth it.' He went inside and shut the door.

Abandoned in the flat, hard sun. True, she barely knew them, but they had left her behind. No one had done that before. Tears of self-pity filled her eyes. She missed Matthew and her friends from home. This was not home. It would never be home.

And then, at the top of street, a bike came into view.

Bailey pedalled furiously down the street towards her.

'Get on,' he said.

She stared at him for a moment, confused by what he meant. But then he eased himself forward until he was standing upright over the crossbar, feet on the ground.

'The seat,' he said, flashing an anxious look at the house. 'Hurry up.'

A thrill of excitement rushed through her. She climbed awkwardly onto the seat, resting her feet on the rear wheel axles, but there was nothing to hold on to except Bailey's waist.

She slid her arms around him. His stomach was flat and hard, and she could feel the heat of him, even through his T-shirt. She blushed, self-conscious, worrying about whether she was too heavy and would slow him down, but enjoying his proximity too.

And then Bailey pressed his weight against the pedals, and she laughed and so did he, and they were cycling up the road, away from Old Man Lovell, away from her house and her little brother, and into the bright, shining lights of a new friendship.

Charlie and Marco were waiting for them on a patch of grass by the newsagent's, their bikes tilted loosely beneath them. They were talking furiously. Aster switched her gaze from one boy to another. It was like watching a table tennis match.

'He's a twisted fuck.'

'*Duh.*'

'So let's do something about it.'

Marco nudged the toe of his trainer against his pedal, making it spin. 'You're joking, right? He told us to keep away.' He glanced at Bailey and Aster. 'I get the impression he means it.'

Charlie flattened his lips. 'Uh-uh, my friend. We're going to pay that old bastard back for what he did to us.' He gave a thin smile. 'Total. Humiliation.'

'Come on, Charlie.' Marco's tone had become pleading. 'He's got a gun, for fuck's sake. Let it go.'

Charlie narrowed his eyes. He was a tall, heavyset boy. Glasses. A sweep of acne across his forehead. 'Bailey?'

Aster got the impression that although Charlie was the muscle of the gang, Bailey was its leader. He steadied the bike, and held her hand as she dismounted inelegantly. Aster was glad she was wearing denim shorts and not a skirt.

Bailey gave a half-shrug. 'Could be fun.' He was still holding Aster's hand. His thumb brushed hers. *Don't let go.*

'What do you think, Aster?' He had an amused expression

on his face. The other two boys looked at her, Charlie with a hard, appraising stare, Marco with a kind of hopeful relief.

Aster's insides squirmed. Her conscience warned her away from Lovell, from this whole sordid situation. But Bailey's fingers were threaded through hers, and she was lonely and weak.

'I'm *always* up for some fun.' She cringed inwardly, but the reaction from the boys was instantaneous.

Charlie's face broke open in surprise and he saluted her, a new respect in his eyes. Bailey squeezed her hand, hot breath in her ear, 'I knew you were one of us.'

Only Marco shook his head slowly, naked disappointment on his face.

'Tonight,' said Charlie. 'Here. Two a.m. And cover your faces.'

58

The copse – 1.54 p.m.

All around her the birds were singing.

Olivia Lockwood ran her tongue across her cracked lips. She could taste blood and mud, and she felt like her legs were on fire. From a faraway place, she could hear the low growl of machinery. She groped for the word, but could not find it, although she knew it had something to do with cutting grass and the garden and a fresh, sweet smell.

Her eyes would not open, and when she tried to move, to relieve her body from the discomfort of the twigs and stones digging into her back, pain was everywhere, setting off flashes of light. From somewhere inside came the knowledge that she should not be here and that something terrible had happened, but she could not untangle these thoughts or smooth them into sense, and instead, with barely a sigh, she tumbled back into the black hole of unconsciousness.

59

32 The Avenue – 1.55 p.m.

DC Bernie French sniffed his armpits. Fresh as a fucking daisy. He had a spring in his step as he walked down The Avenue, the bounce of a man who had got his own way.

He checked his watch. He wasn't a stickler for punctuality, but he was excited and had arrived early for his role as ringmaster in this particular circus.

Mr I'm-too-tired-to-talk Lovell was about to get the shock of his life.

The sun made his shirt stick to his back, and the baton he'd slipped into his pocket was digging into his thigh, but even those inconveniences were not enough to put French off his stride. Today had been a good day – and it wasn't over yet. Clive Mackie off the case, that emotionally derelict copper back in her box, and DCI Sampson – and now the on-call magistrate – approving his request for a search warrant. *This is a major manhunt, your honour. The public is terrified. It is imperative we leave no stone unturned. Imagine the outcry if we overlooked an obvious suspect.* Never mind that

229

he'd over-egged the pudding. He grinned. Minor details. Lovell was as off as three-day-old fish.

He checked his phone. Less than an hour until he was supposed to hook up with some detective constable he barely knew. He'd texted him to say he was following up a lead in Leigh-on-Sea and would probably be late. Sometimes, a man needed to be alone.

Translation: he wanted to have a little fun before the others got here.

A seagull wheeled overhead, blowing in from the coast. French looked up at the sky. It was flat and blue with cigar-shaped clouds. The perfect day to fuck up someone's life.

The curtains were drawn at 32 The Avenue, but DC French considered that to be an advantage. It meant that Lovell couldn't see him coming.

Strictly speaking, he should wait until the rest of the team had arrived. He'd even dithered about delaying until tomorrow. His favourite kind of raids were the 5 a.m.-ers, when suspects were pulled from their beds without warning, vulnerable with sleep, pale-faced and exposed. He got a kick out of rummaging through their dirty washing baskets, seeking out worn clothing and potential DNA. Relished the penny-drop moment when the gawping idiot he was investigating realized he'd left it too late to destroy the evidence. Revelled in the power of having one over on another human being.

And Sampson would frown on this. No question about it. But while French wasn't one to play by the rules, he had no intention of getting found out. This is what happened when you pissed off a police officer. And Lovell had pissed him off.

Plus, he wanted to catch him in the act.

But if he had planned to wrong-foot Lovell, it was Lovell who wrong-footed him. As if the old man had been waiting for French to return, the door opened before he could knock.

'You're early.'

'I have a warrant to search these premises. If you'd like to step aside, please.' Admittedly, that last sentence was a bit unnecessary.

'Can I see it?' Lovell's tone was mild. His hair was wet and he smelled of soap, as if he'd stepped out of the shower.

French hesitated. He didn't actually have the court order on him. The DC from Rayleigh was supposed to bring it with him. And most suspects didn't ask. They were usually too shocked to remember their rights.

But then Lovell surprised him.

'Come in, I suppose.' He stood back to let French enter. 'Remind me, what do you think I've done?'

French coughed. The house reeked of lavender, its floral scent catching at the back of his throat. And an undertone of something thicker, uglier. The residue of the rotting-meat smell that had prompted him to apply for a warrant, but it was faded, like an old memory.

French ignored him. 'Can I have a look around?' he said, although it was a perfunctory question. He was already opening doors and cupboards.

Lovell's house was neglected and unloved. Motes of dancing dust were illuminated by the sun. The dirty shadows of boot prints were visible across the hall rug, as if no one ever bothered to sweep up. Piles of cat hair and dried mud lifted gently as the air moved with unexpected activity. A patch of something unidentifiable marked the carpet on the stairs.

'Ever heard of cleaning, mate?'

'My wife used to do it.'

French muttered under his breath. 'Why doesn't that surprise me?'

Lovell's eyes narrowed as French stared him down. The old man was wearing a clean white shirt and a jacket, with a gold pin that was vaguely familiar on his lapel.

In the kitchen, the back door was open. A pallet truck stood on the patio, a sheet of MDF positioned across its forks and attached with a length of rope. A blanket rested on the ground. French could see a garage, and through its open door, a large chest freezer. His fingers tapped against his leg, nervous energy thrumming through his veins.

He would take a closer look outside when he had finished in the house.

The rotting-meat smell was stronger upstairs, but it had not reached the gagging stage yet. A tiny part of him – the part that occasionally doubted himself – wondered if he should have waited for the others, but he silenced it. This was his lead. His discovery. Lovell had been discounted early on, yes, but in the heat of a rapidly moving investigation mistakes were often made. Evidence was overlooked. Corners cut. If Lovell was the Doll Maker – *Fuck you, Mac* – then French would claim this victory all on his own.

Promotion. Pay rise. Pussy.

French opened the spare-room door, and stumbled backwards, hand over his mouth. The air was thick with heat and the sweet, sickening smell of decomposition. His memory threw him back to Christmas Eve a decade ago.

He'd been called to an elderly woman's flat by her alcoholic son. No response for a few days. His colleague had stayed with the man while French had broken a kitchen window. At first, he'd assumed her blinds were black, pulled tight against the cold glare of daylight, but the glass had been darkened by flies. They'd crawled over his arm as he'd shattered the pane.

As soon as the air from inside the flat had reached him, he'd known that she was dead. The weather was stone-crackingly cold, but the windows had been shut, the gas fire blazing. She had died sitting in front of it.

He had flicked her a brief glance, disturbed by the ghost of Christmas Yet-to-Come. Her nose was not where it ought to be, and it had taken him a minute to register that her face had slipped off in the fierce heat, and it was not her nose, but her tongue.

She'd been wearing a nightgown with pockets, filled with cash she had squirrelled away to give to her grandchildren as Christmas presents. The notes had stuck together with the fluids that had leaked from her decomposing body. French had collected them in an evidence bag and stashed them in his locker. The stink had permeated the station and put him off his fish and chips.

That night, the son had turned up at the station, half pissed, demanding his mother's money.

'I can't give it him,' muttered French to the desk sergeant. 'It's a public health hazard.'

The sergeant had shrugged. 'Nothing we can do about. Legally, it belongs to him now.'

French still felt queasy when he remembered the stench that had risen from the damp notes as he had peeled them apart to count, and the idea of them being passed back and forth to customers in the pub.

But that was a long time ago. And this was now.

Because ten years later, lying on the bed, was another woman in her nightgown, and she was staring at him, eyes wide and fixed. Her arms were straight and stiff, hanging over the side of the coverlet, and her skin was blanched like a piece of freezer-burnt meat.

Her face was painted, her cheeks stained pink, lips a deeper red. A few drops of water were visible on the carpet.

And she was unquestionably dead.

60

Now

I tried so hard and for so long.

I learned to garden. I planted and tended and watched life grow. I made things. I observed other people. I cooked and read and listened to the radio. Got on with the business of life.

And I tried to rub out the scars that both of my mothers – and you – had left upon my soul.

I folded up my past until it became a forgotten slip of paper, buried at the bottom of a drawer. Formed friendships. Tried to behave in the ways that others did. I watched and learned and copied.

I was a decent person. Paid my taxes. Put litter in the bin. Helped old folk to cross the street and contributed to society.

But as the seasons moved on, I did not.

I found it hard to see clearly, to shine as brightly as I might. I was obscuring a part of myself, like a smear on glass.

Because through the years of living my life, the old-jumper-ordinariness of it all, death whispered to me. It still does. Lures me. Teases me with its *what ifs?* I tried to ignore it. And I managed to do so for such a long time. I fought to nail it down. And I would have succeeded. But the interference of others denied me a future.

They held a special service for Natalie Tiernan. With counsellors on hand. The school she taught at established the Natalie Tiernan Prize for Academic Excellence in her memory.

First through the shop door. First to find Birdie. First to die.

Her murder was as perfectly executed as clockwork. She had no reason to suspect. Invited me in with a smile on her lips. It didn't take long for her to stop smiling.

I developed a taste for it once I had started. And I claimed them, one by one.

Oh, the newspaper stories. Reams and reams of them. Enough to paper a house. All asking the same questions. Why paint the faces of the dead? Gouge out the eyes? Why hide the bodies in the woods?

And the naming. Always the naming. Drum roll, please. Step forward, *The Doll Maker*.

There's a pleasing symmetry, don't you agree? The Doll Maker and the man who makes dolls. Clever of them. The press, I mean. But not quite clever enough.

I have read all the stories, I have watched the television specials, and their theories are wrong.

There is no mystery behind the paint. A final gift to bestow upon the lost, to rescue them from the ravages of decomposition, to ensure they face the darkness as the best versions of themselves. An apology too, I suppose. A way of making amends for the act of murder, of repaying what I have stolen by using their skin as my canvas, breathing youthfulness back into them. And, most importantly, a sleight of hand, a misdirection.

The eyes are different.

I took those because of what they had seen.

61

Tuesday, 31 July 2018

25 The Avenue – 2.06 p.m.

The first thing Garrick Lockwood noticed was the silence.

'Liv.' His voice rang out in the stillness. Again, with urgency: 'Liv, I'm home.'

Nothing.

He rested his portfolio against the wall, his chances of a job at the cutting-edge firm of architects blown by his early departure. The only sound was the shifting of gears as his taxi drove off and the thrum of next door's lawnmower.

He stood at the bottom of the stairs and called again. '*Liv.*' A pause. 'Hello? Anyone home?' But the house had the feel of emptied pockets about it.

The edge of panic that had haunted his journey home – on the Tube, the broken-down c2c train that had sat on the track for what felt like hours and the car ride from the station – tipped into a creeping kind of worry.

Where was Olivia?

He popped his head around the study door and saw her handbag hanging on the chair. She had not mentioned what she was doing today. He searched his memory, sifting out clues. Last night, she'd said something about a briefing from a client, but he'd tuned out after that.

Her mobile phone was still off. After Aster's panicked call, he'd rung his wife every ten minutes, with no success. But the car was on the drive so she couldn't have gone far.

For the first time, he appreciated the enormity of moving to a place without friends or family. He'd had no one to call on and ask them to check on the children.

Aster was old enough to look after Evan, but the incident with the grill had made him doubt the wisdom of leaving them alone. He wasn't convinced his daughter could be trusted.

Back in Cheshire, a few weeks before they had moved, he and Liv had spent the evening at a gallery opening. Aster was supposed to be babysitting. Instead she had met friends at a roller-skating rink and left her sleeping brother on his own. Her irresponsible behaviour had only been discovered because he and Olivia had argued and come home early.

And his daughter had a teenager's flair for exaggeration. He'd fully expected to find his wife at home, full of apologies. But there was no sign of her. Concern stroked its fingers across his neck.

Evan burst in, face pink, hair damp. He was wearing his goalie gloves. 'Hi, Dad. I was in the garden. Heard you shouting. I'm hungry. Where's Mum?'

'I don't know, son.' Garrick glanced at his watch. 'Where's Aster?'

Evan flushed. 'I don't know.'

His father narrowed his eyes. 'Has she gone out too?'

Evan scratched his head. 'I'm hungry, Dad. Can I have something to eat?'

'For Christ's sake, I can't believe she left you by yourself again.' He sounded angrier than he meant to and knew he was projecting it onto the wrong target. He forced himself to calm down and assess the facts.

He hadn't seen Olivia since they had both gone to bed at a quarter to twelve the previous night. Her mobile phone was switched off, her handbag discarded. She had not left a note for the children or told anyone she was going out.

Put like that, it didn't look good.

'Come on,' he said to Evan. 'I'll make us both a sandwich and we'll decide what to do.'

'I'll be there in a sec, Dad. Just want to get something from my room.'

Evan sat down on the edge of his bed and tipped up his Magic 8 Ball.

'Is Mum safe?' he whispered, a twist of worry in his stomach.

The words took a couple of seconds to appear. *Reply hazy, try again.*

At the same time, his father's voice drifted up the stairs.

'Is that Detective Sergeant Stanton? I'm so sorry to trouble you, but I don't know who else to call. My name is Garrick Lockwood and I think my wife is missing.'

62

32 The Avenue – 2.17 p.m.

A flare of adrenaline lit French from inside. Instinct switched itself on. He must read Lovell his rights, handcuff him, call for immediate back-up.

Don't touch anything. Stop Lovell from leaving. Oh, fuck. Fuck it. I've done it. I've caught the fucking Doll Maker.

Like electrical sparks, his thoughts jumped and arced, and he turned to Lovell, baton raised, ready to arrest him.

Lovell took a step towards him and French brought his baton down on the old man's arm with a smacking sound.

'Hands on your head. Stay where you are.'

A livid red mark was rising on the skin above Lovell's wrist bone. 'Now why did you have to do that?' he said, rubbing it. He took another step towards French.

'Stay back,' said the police officer, his voice cracking on the last letter. French hit him again.

But although Lovell was older, he was rangier and stronger, and now he was up close, French could read the writing on the pin – *Per Mare, Per Terram.* He had half a

241

second to register *Royal Marines* before Old Man Lovell squeezed his fingers against French's throat, putting pressure on his vagus nerve.

His vision blurred, and a strange popping sensation in his ears deadened the sound of the birds and the drone of a passing car on the street outside. He could smell Lovell's breath – sour coffee and plaque – and noticed the old man had blackheads on his nose, and that his mouth was shaping a single word.

Sorry.

In less than eight seconds, French was unconscious.

63

25 The Avenue — 2.22 p.m.

DS Wildeve Stanton was the first to arrive.

She parked by the Lockwood family home and considered her position. Technically, she was on leave. She should pass the details of Mr Lockwood's call to the investigating team and stay out of it.

But empathy was opening her car door and pushing her up the path. A woman had disappeared. A wife and a mother. Wildeve knew what it was to lose someone.

To lose everyone.

In the garden next door, a bank of stargazer lilies was in flower. Their scent was dense and cloying, and it transported Wildeve back to her teenage self. To the feel of the wooden bench beneath her knees. The heavy crematorium curtain. To the sound of crying and the weight of anxious glances and her folded hands, pink with cold.

So excited, she'd been. Alone overnight for the first time. Her parents were visiting family in Glossop, taking her younger sister with them. They'd tried to persuade her to

243

come, but she'd begged off, citing revision. No need to mention her friend Lily's party.

Fifteen years old. Loosening the strings. Flirting with adulthood. Studying for exams, acquiring a taste for white lies and alcopops. Discovering herself.

When she'd returned home at half past eight that Sunday morning – her mother had arranged to ring the landline at nine – a police car was waiting outside.

She had pulled her coat tighter, last night's mascara smudged beneath her eyes, hair mussed up from sleeping on the floor, and reached for her door key. A cursory glance, that's all she had given them. Her mind had been full of the way that Martin Stokes had kept staring at her and their brief kiss in the downstairs toilet, and how he had promised to phone her from the call box on the corner of his street that evening. In that self-absorbed way of teenagers, she had not – for even a beat in time – considered they were there for her.

The WPC – they were called that back then – had droopy eyes and smelled of coal tar soap. She had made Wildeve a glass of lemon squash. Even now, she couldn't bear the taste of it.

She had been brief and matter-of-fact.

A head-on collision with a lorry crossing Snake Pass.

All three of them killed at the scene.

Instantaneous.

The police officer had tried to comfort her, had offered to make calls on Wildeve's behalf. Had fussed about who was going to take care of her and where she would live.

'I'm sixteen tomorrow,' Wildeve had said, head bowed,

staring at her Doc Marten boots. Dull-voiced. In shock. 'I'll stay here. I'll be fine.'

Fine.

And she had been. Not immediately. The loss of her family had almost broken her. She had cried for months for the future no longer promised to her. No mother, warm and sensible, to offer advice on relationships. No proud father at her graduation. No sister to share secrets and clothes with. The loss of unconditional love. But she had survived. Friends and family had rallied round. Shopped. Cooked. Washed her bedding and driven her to school. But the kindnesses had gradually faded, as most kindnesses do. And she had been left on her own. Not yet seventeen and already self-sufficient.

She might have veered off the rails, but her desire to join the police had fuelled her study. She had filled her family's absence with schoolwork, and she had excelled. As soon as she was old enough, she had applied to join the Force.

But she had never sought promotion at work, had actively shied away from it. Not because she was daunted by the responsibility of becoming an inspector, but because she remembered being that teenager, the *fear* of it all, and wanted to stay at the coalface of policing.

And she *was* fine. But the abrupt ending of her childhood had left its scars. Youngsters who experience tragedy in their formative years often struggle to cry later in life, even in the eye of fresh trauma, Wildeve had learned during her police training. And so it was for her. Sometimes she wondered if she had cried so much as a teenager there was nothing left but dust and ashes. In the dark hours of the night after Adam's death, she had longed for release, the *relief* of tears, but it was denied her. Every now and then, the dam broke, but it was only a temporary respite. It might be years before it happened again. And it didn't mean she didn't care. Never that. Adam had shown her that she still had the capacity to love.

But she knew she would survive. She had done it before.

Garrick Lockwood opened the door, the beginnings of a five o'clock shadow on his chin.

'I hope I'm not wasting your time,' he said.

Her second visit in less than twenty-four hours. If she hadn't been on her way to see Lovell, she might have called it in to another officer. But it suited her. She could keep an eye out for French while she was here, and make sure their paths didn't cross. She followed Mr Lockwood into the kitchen. He was washing a plate and his hair was sticking up, as if he'd been clutching at it.

She had decided on a compromise. Not a lie, exactly. But not the whole truth.

'I'm not sure I'm the best person to be talking to,' she said. 'I can pass on your details to the team, if you'd like.'

He had his back to her, fiddling one-handed with the sponge. 'I'd rather speak to you. You've met her.'

Let it go, Wild. If you think it's got legs, you can pass it on yourself.

Adam was right. For now, she would listen.

Garrick talked her through his wife's disappearing act. The empty glass on the patio. The lack of a note. His assumption that she had been asleep in the spare room with the door shut when he'd left for his interview at the crack of dawn.

'Phone?' said Wildeve.

'It's off. I can't find it.'

'You've tried friends and family?'

'Yes, no sign of her.'

'Purse, house keys?'

'In her handbag.'

Wildeve inspected her bitten nails before looking up at him. For an adult without ongoing mental health issues, in the absence of a suicide note, without any other indicators of harm, Olivia Lockwood fell under the umbrella of low-risk. She'd only been gone a few hours. Not long enough to panic. But what elevated this case was the nine-year-old boy. Few women willingly walked out on their responsibilities without some kind of explanation. But their father seemed invested, so it wasn't a social services job. Not yet.

'Mr Lockwood?' She met his gaze. His reaction was important. So many husbands were behind the disappearances of their wives. This wasn't a formal interview. No caution given. No record taken. Technically, she wasn't on duty. But it would help her decide what to do next.

'I know this is a difficult question, but do you have any reason to suspect she might be with someone she doesn't want you to know about?'

A light went off in his eyes. He was drying the plate with a tea towel and kept rubbing the same spot.

'Mr Lockwood?'

He turned to her and she saw his despair. 'It's possible.'

'Tell me everything,' she said.

His name was Orson Heller. He was four years younger than Olivia, and they'd worked at the same advertising agency in Manchester.

Late nights working on pitches with tight deadlines had turned into drinks had turned into a sixteen-month affair.

'How did you find out?' Wildeve felt the pull of pity.

'Same old story.' He placed two mugs of coffee on the table and sat down opposite her. 'She'd left her phone on the armrest when she went to answer the front door. I picked it up to check the time because I was supposed to be collecting Evan from football.' He sighed. 'A message popped up. It was clear they'd fu—' His son clattered into the kitchen, helped himself to a biscuit, and left again. 'Slept together.'

'Is it over?'

'So she says.'

'When did it end?'

'About six months ago.'

To Wildeve, a complex equation of emotion was written across his face. Concern, warmth, a sense of holding oneself at arm's length.

'But you're still together?'

His laugh bulged with bitterness. Then, as a concession to Wildeve's question, 'We're doing our best. That's one of the reasons we moved here.'

'And is it working?'

He shrugged, as if he didn't care. 'Who knows? But if we're to make a new start, I – it's – this state of limbo is damaging to us all.' His voice cracked. 'I don't think she loves me anymore.'

He started to cry and her own eyes pricked. In his loneliness, she saw the reflection of her own. Wildeve got up from the table, stood behind his chair and touched his shoulder to comfort him. He looked up at her and she looked back, and then, from nowhere, the moment stretched into something else, and he was half out of his seat, moving towards her, his hand drifting up her back, and she didn't move. Didn't know what to think or what to feel except that she didn't want to pull away because the touch of someone, anyone, was better than nothing at all.

The front door slammed. Both Wildeve and Garrick jumped. He dropped his hand and started out of the chair.

A mumbled apology. And then, 'Liv?' The hope in his voice was convincing.

The kitchen door flew open.

But it wasn't Olivia Lockwood. Instead it was her daughter, tallow-faced and trembling.

'Aster?' He was sharp with disappointment, and shame at his own behaviour. 'Where have you been?'

'Is Mum back yet?'

'No, love.'

Aster burst into tears. 'There's a man on the street who's killed his wife and he's got a gun and he was shouting and what if he's got Mum?'

The detective moved so quickly she knocked into a chair and it scraped across the kitchen floor.

'Who is he?' she said. Again, more urgently. '*Who is he?*'

Aster could hardly speak because she was crying so much. 'I think his name is Trefor Lovell.'

Wildeve's stomach plunged, and she was running down the hall, and all the while these words beat a drum in her brain: *French was right, French was right, French was right.*

64

32 The Avenue – 2.23 p.m.

Trefor Lovell was screwed.

He knew it, and when the police officer lying on his bedroom carpet woke up, he would know it too.

Trefor crouched next to the man and eased a pillow under his head. Tilted his chin in case he was sick. Five minutes or so. If he hadn't come round by then, he'd call the ambulance himself.

'I'm sorry,' he said again. Muttered an expletive and placed his fingers on the pulse point at the base of the detective's throat, to make sure he was still breathing. He was. Trefor thanked the heavens for small mercies.

The afternoon sun spilled into the bedroom. Even in the last couple of hours, the heat had intensified the smell. The bunches of lavender he'd hung from the curtain pole and the lamp shade and door handle had helped to mask it, but it hadn't been enough to smother it completely.

For the last few months he'd been dreading the fall of the guillotine, but now it had happened, he felt strangely calm, as if he had been poised for it all along, neck exposed on the block.

He looked at his wife and he thought he might cry.

He had kept her safe for eight months. Placing her in the chest freezer in the garage a couple of days after she died, almost breaking his arm as he slipped on the icy path. Bringing her back into their home on the nights his grief threatened to swallow him, a black mouth of sorrow and despair. Laying her on the bed, still wearing her favourite nightdress.

Light as a feather, she'd been when she died. A sparrow. That first time, he'd carried her body by himself. But the freezer had weighted her down. Now he couldn't manage on his own. He had to use a pallet truck to lift the rigid shape of her, and tie a sheet around her waist to drag her upstairs.

They'd accused him of killing her, those dirty-mouthed kids. The police would think the same. But it wasn't like that. He could never have hurt Annie. But the disease had eaten her from the inside without either of them knowing.

First symptoms in November. Diagnosed in December. Dead by January.

Her hands had been like paper at the end, dry as dust. She had placed one on his cheek.

'Let me go,' she had said.

His sorrow had spilled over, tears streaking the hollows of his face. He had turned away from the bed so she wouldn't see.

'I'm sorry,' he had said, wiping his eyes with the sleeve of his jumper.

'Don't be sorry.' Her voice was soft. 'Your tears show me that you still feel something for this old, useless body of mine.' She'd tried to laugh, but it had turned into a cough and she'd squeezed his hand. He'd stroked the back of hers with his thumb. The hand he had held for fifty-nine years, that had guided and steadied him, that had shown him love in a thousand tiny ways.

He'd stayed with her for hours, listening to the rattle in her throat, the rapid breaths and then the long pauses between breathing, reluctant to leave, even to use the bathroom or fetch himself a drink.

He was still holding her hand when her grip slackened and the room flatlined into silence.

It wasn't planned. Not at first. He'd had every intention of calling the doctor, of registering her death and organizing her funeral. But he was lost in the woods, couldn't find his way out.

They'd never been ones for central heating. And those bitter January snows had helped preserve her body for the first couple of days. He'd found himself talking to her of his loneliness and grief, confiding his feelings as he'd always done.

They'd had few friends and fewer relatives. They'd always been the type of couple who had done everything together. And he was a shy man, reclusive. It was easy to withdraw into himself, to bat away concerned enquiries with a shake of his head. *Annie's too weak for visitors.*

And then, when the neighbours became too interested, *She's gone to stay with her goddaughter.*

As the weeks had passed, as the state of her body had continued to deteriorate, he'd used his skill with the paintbrush to preserve her face, to keep her looking as Annie-like as possible.

But he'd known it couldn't continue. That he was on borrowed time and the clock was ticking. That he would be discovered. That the continued cycle of freezing and thawing was accelerating the destruction of the tissues of her already-decomposing body.

But when the police came they would never believe him. He'd looked it up. They'd charge him, he was sure. Concealing a body. Preventing a burial.

The detective on the floor moved his head, groaned.

Trefor Lovell checked his watch. It was almost half past two. The officer was coming to. No need for an ambulance.

If he was going to run, he would have to do it now.

His wife's eyes were closed, her lips the same deep pink as they'd been when he'd met her. If he shut his own eyes, he could hear the sounds of the dance halls, the fizz of the trombone, the swish of Annie's skirt.

'I love you,' whispered Trefor, and blew her a kiss. He patted his pockets, making sure he had his wallet, the keys to his car.

As he left the room, he turned to look at his wife for a final time. For a moment, he stayed perfectly still and then, with a flicker of incredulity, he started back towards her, running those few steps across the room because Annie's face seemed to be moving. He let out a bark of despair.

The maggots had found her.

65

Now

Smoke. Mirrors. Secrets. Lies.

We believe what we want to, don't we? Our version of the truth. But there are many layers, many truths.

We sift and curate and cherry-pick the parts that best suit the face we present to the world. Nobody is a true version of themselves. Everyone pretends.

Take the telephone calls.

I knew that Mr Lovell was making them. But I did not let him know. I did not let anyone know. I allowed him to make them. I allowed him to telephone the house and whisper his threats because I knew he had a secret too.

And his truth became a telescope turned back onto him.

I knew what he was doing when the sun went down and why he was visiting the garage and where Mrs Lovell had gone. I *saw* him. And I knew what he had discovered about me.

It was a risk, of course. To let it lie.

But I knew that Mr Lovell – a painter of dolls clinging to

the body of his dead wife – would become a prime suspect for the murders bringing this town to its knees.

And he was.

My plan worked perfectly. Until Olivia Lockwood ruined everything.

66

The Avenue – 2.32 p.m.

Wildeve ran into the street at exactly the same moment a police car sped down The Avenue and braked sharply outside Trefor Lovell's address.

She started towards the house, but two officers she didn't recognize jumped out and sprinted up the path, and an ambulance, sirens blaring, pulled in behind them.

Guilt needled her, pricking at her conscience. French's instincts had been spot-on and she had ignored them. A knot of self-doubt wound itself more tightly. She shouldn't be here.

An unmarked car roared past her and down the street, blue lights flashing, and she turned away, spotting DCI Roger Sampson in the passenger seat. Officers of such senior rank rarely turned up on the doorstep, so she guessed it must be serious.

Shit.

She lingered by the Lockwood house, uncertain what to do next. It was clear that things had moved on since that morning. French had been right. Leaving Lovell until this afternoon had been a serious error of judgement.

Trust your instincts, Wild.

Adam's voice, so familiar and gentle. But this time, it did not have its usual calming effect. Instead, she longed to scream out her frustration at the sky, to demand of him answers to the questions that were haunting her.

Cooper Clifton had said that Adam was going to visit Lovell. Was it possible that he was the last person to see her husband alive? She *had* to speak to him. But it looked like her colleagues would be arresting him, and then it would be too late.

The afternoon air shimmered with heat. A skin-sticking sort of a day. Another car drove slowly down the road and pulled in next to her. Mac. His T-shirt and shorts had been replaced with his customary uniform of a shirt and trousers, and he was sucking an aniseed ball. It comforted her. In a world where everything else had gone wrong, this was the correct order of things.

'Sorry, I got stuck in hellish traffic. What have I missed?'

But Wildeve did not answer his question because an elderly man had just emerged from the bushes at the entrance of Blatches Woods. He threw a glance down the street and walked briskly towards the parade of shops on the corner of The Avenue before climbing into a battered blue Ford Fiesta parked outside the Doll & Fancy Dress Emporium.

Wildeve pulled open the door and slid in next to Mac.

'That man,' she said, pointing to the car. 'Follow him – and whatever you do, don't lose him.'

67

26 The Avenue – 2.33 p.m.

Dessie settled herself at the kitchen table, the neat rectangle of her laptop in front of her.

She stared at it, knowing that by opening its lid and switching it on, she might be risking everything she held dear.

Since Fletcher – *Benjamin*, a tiny voice whispered – had come into her life, she'd found a new sense of belonging. She'd dated men – and a couple of women – and enjoyed a handful of long-term relationships, but none had made her feel as Fletcher did, both safe and seduced, that rarest of feats.

From the first time they'd got talking at the station and both missed their trains, he'd struck her as a decent guy, ordinary, straightforward. He'd lived an itinerant lifestyle, swapping jobs, moving from one town to the next because he 'liked meeting new people and experiencing new things'. But they had connected and the weeks stretched into months, and before long, she had invited him to move in with her. With a well-paid job of her own, she didn't want him to impress her with Michelin-starred restaurants or expensive weekends in luxury hotels. She could pay for those herself. What she enjoyed most were the simple things. He called when he said he would and showed up to dates on time. When she was cold, he took off his coat and placed it around her shoulders without being asked. He didn't indulge in mind games or petty jealousies, and had never given her cause to doubt him. Until now.

'What's going on, Fletch?' She muttered the words into the stillness of the kitchen, as if the universe might answer her and she wouldn't have to wade through the murky waters of secrets and lies. But she lacked the temerity or strength, she couldn't decide which, to turn a blind eye.

She switched on her computer, drew in a breath and typed in *Benjamin Turner*.

68

London Road – 2.41 p.m.

The traffic on the London Road was lighter than usual, the holiday season in full swing. Wildeve's gaze was fixed on the blue Ford Fiesta three cars ahead.

'I think we should call this in,' said Mac.

'No.' She sounded sharper than she meant to. 'I need to speak to him first. We'll take him in ourselves.'

A cloud passed over Mac's face. 'We're inviting in a world of pain if we do that.'

How could she make him understand that this was a compulsion for her? That the desire to untangle the truth about Adam was the only reason she was able to keep going. That she was certain Lovell had some answers.

'I'll keep you out of this, Mac.' Softly. 'I promise.'

He drummed his fingers on the wheel. His face was baggy with concern. 'Look, there's something you should—'

'Wait.' She held her hand up, interrupting him. 'I think

260

he's turning left.' She waited a beat. 'OK, he's parking by the church. Let's keep our distance. We don't want to spook him.'

The choir was practising in St Margaret's Church and their voices rose in joyful song as Wildeve and Mac pushed against the church doors.

Lovell was sitting four pews from the front, his head bowed. The scent of incense weighted down the air, underscored by the heaviness of lilies in several vases and wood polish, freshly applied. The pompous drama of the organ was fitting.

Wildeve walked down the central aisle and slid in on one side of Trefor Lovell. Mac took the other side, blocking his exit. For a brief moment, it looked as if the man they had come to question was going to climb over the back of the pew and make a bid for freedom. But when he saw them, he collapsed onto his knees, the floor cushion beneath him.

As one, the choir filled the spaces inside the church with their song, and Lovell clasped his hands together in prayer.

Time seemed to slow down and still. Wildeve was aware of the singing, the sun seeping through the stained-glass windows, the presence of Lovell, and the rising smell of his sweat. She was not religious. But there was something about being inside a church that moved her. Sometimes, it would have been much easier, a comfort during her darkest days, to believe in a higher power, a force for good, the reassurance of Heaven.

But her mother had always insisted that if one believes in God, one must believe in a counterpart, the Devil.

Wildeve had seen enough of the destruction that

261

humankind inflicted on one another to know there was evil in the world. That while most people were decent and kind, others were possessed by a malignancy, a cruelty. Despite the heat of the day, the coolness of the church made her shiver.

Several minutes later, when the choir had finished its rehearsal and were calling out their farewells, Wildeve touched Lovell on the shoulder.

He lifted his head and she was surprised to see he was crying.

'Mr Lovell—'

'I didn't do anything,' he said, wiping his sleeve roughly against his face. 'I didn't mean to—'

'Did you see Adam Stanton on Sunday?' Mac was unflinching, the authority in his voice unmistakeable.

'Yes.'

'And what did you talk about?'

Lovell wiped his eyes again. 'I can't remember. Lots of things. My doll business. The bodies in the woods.'

'Did you kill him?' There was an unrelenting hardness to Mac's voice, and Wildeve flashed him a surprised look.

Lovell's eyes widened. 'Of course I didn't bloody kill him. He was as right as rain when he left my house.'

Wildeve cut in. 'So why are there police surrounding your property at this very moment?'

His face collapsed. 'That man. French. He was hitting me with a baton. I . . .'

'You did what, Mr Lovell?'

'I hurt him.' He whispered. 'I didn't have much choice.'

'Did you hurt your wife too?'

'No, I would never hurt Annie.' He lifted his head and

slammed a hand against the polished wood. The pew vibrated with his anger. 'I can't believe you would ask me that question.'

'Is your wife alive, Mr Lovell?' She did not know if this man was telling the truth. Originally, she had believed him, but it was clear he had a temper.

Lovell buried his face in his hands, but not before he shook his head.

'And those bodies in the woods? Did you kill them?'

Lovell lifted his face to hers, and she glimpsed a flicker of something in his eyes, although she wasn't sure what it meant.

'No,' he said, a quiet defiance infusing his words. 'I did not kill anyone.'

Mac and Wildeve exchanged a glance. Although she was officially off duty, DS Wildeve Stanton still had a responsibility to uphold the law. For Mac, it was different. He was officially retired. He owed nothing. But she had always believed in the importance of doing the right thing.

'Trefor Lovell, I am arresting you on suspicion of assaulting a police officer.'

'I didn't kill my wife,' he said again. 'And those murders, you're looking in the wrong place.'

69

25 The Avenue – 4.23 p.m.

Evan Lockwood was sitting on his bedroom floor surrounded by sweet wrappers and a thin, brown ribbon of unspooled tape.

His sister stuck her head around his door. Despite her summer tan, she looked heavy-eyed and pale.

'Can I come in?' she said, leaning against the door frame. She didn't give him a chance to reply. 'Look, don't tell Dad I left you on your own. He doesn't need to know.'

'He knows already.'

'Shit.'

'That's a swear, Aster.'

'Sorry, buddy. You're right. Naughty Aster.' She mock slapped her hand and sat cross-legged next to him. 'I know things are a bit weird at the moment, what with Mum and everything. Are you all right?'

'No. I. Am. Not. All. Right. The tape's broken because you weren't here to help me.' Tears swam in his eyes like silvery fish.

THE NEIGHBOUR

'I told you to wait for me,' said Aster, trying to button down her impatience.

'You were gone for ages.' A whiny, stubborn tone crept in. 'It's not my fault.'

Aster bit her lip. It wasn't her fault either, but nine-year-old boys could be irrational, and he was worried about their mother, and she didn't want Evan telling their father any more than he already had.

'Let me see if I can help,' she said, offering an olive branch. Evan accepted it with a tremulous smile.

The tape was strewn across the place like a streamer. Aster wasn't sure it could be rescued. She pulled out her phone, searching out solutions on the internet.

'Have you got a pencil?' she said.

Evan jumped up and scrabbled around in his drawer for his favourite, with its *My Neighbor Totoro* topper. He thrust it at Aster. 'Here.'

She slid the pencil into one of the holes in the middle of the cassette, and slowly began to wind, sucking up the tape like a strand of spaghetti.

'Is it working?' asked Evan, peering over her shoulder, his bony knees pressing into her back.

'Not sure yet.' She glanced at him and the doubt spreading across his face. She softened. 'Patience.'

Evan flicked through his pile of football trading cards. Leafed through the pages of a *Knock-Knock* joke book. Whispered questions to his Magic 8 Ball. The sun dappling the walls of his room was deepening into a molten bronze, throwing down shadows. The day was thinking about ending, and Aster still hadn't decided if she was going to meet the boys. She didn't want to. That old man scared her. But she hated the idea of them dismissing her as a coward.

'Where did you go, Aster? Earlier, I mean. It doesn't take that long to go to the shops.'

'I got distracted.'

'Were you talking to those boys?'

Aster did not lift her eyes from the cassette, but pink roses bloomed on her cheeks. 'What boys?'

'The ones on their bikes. I saw them out of your window. You were with them, remember?'

She wanted to shake him for going into her bedroom, but instead said, 'Oh, *those* boys. I said hi, that's all.'

Her answer seemed to satisfy Evan, who turned his attention back to her slow-turning pencil.

'Have you done it yet?' He leaned against her, knocking her slightly off balance. He was skinny and warm, and smelled faintly of orange Fruit Pastilles.

She inhaled, and imagined she was breathing in calmness and tolerance and all those qualities that a good big sister should possess.

'Almost. But I'm not sure it's going to work. See, the tape looks a little twisted.' Her fingers worked to smooth it out, but she couldn't make all the kinks disappear.

Evan rolled back and forth on his heels. Then he jigged his leg and stuck his finger into his nose. Eventually, he sat next to her on the carpet and watched her nimble fingers do their work.

Time rolled on. Evan's stomach rumbled. Aster's phone pinged with notifications. And finally, with a triumphant flourish, she held up the tape. 'Finished.' She smiled at him. 'Come on, then. Let's see if it works.'

THE NEIGHBOUR

Evan bounced on the balls of his feet, grinning at his sister. 'Thank you,' he said, throwing his arms around her. Aster blushed and hugged him back. It felt good to do something nice for her brother for a change. He handed her the borrowed Walkman and she slid in the cassette. They huddled together, each claiming an earphone. Aster winked at Evan and pressed play.

A high-pitched voice was singing about eagles flying higher and higher and something called St Elmo's fire. The voice then adopted the over-the-top drawl of a radio DJ, introducing the next song. Both children started to laugh. The voice was an excellent mimic.

And then it stopped.

If someone had filmed that very moment – in the half-light of a summer holiday teatime in an ordinary bedroom on a not-so-ordinary street, two heads bent together – they would have witnessed the anticipation on both young faces dim into darkness.

At first, the hum and crackle of recorded silence, a sense of waiting for something important to happen, of drawing in their breath and holding it.

And then a voice, whispering, urgent, the words tumbling out so quickly it was almost impossible to pick out the distinctions between letters, the vowels and consonants running together to form a plea, yearning down the tunnel of the years.

helpmehelpmehelpmehelpmehelpmehelpme

Sister and brother looked at each other, half laughing, waiting for the voice to say it was all a joke. But then a clatter and scrape, like a cassette recorder being hastily dropped and pushed out of sight. The sound of somebody new

267

climbing a ladder. And then the voice was crying, and apologizing over and over again.

A muffled thump, as if something heavy – a body, thought Aster – was hitting the floor, a shift in volume, the voice pressing closer to them, begging for whoever it was to stop, locked inside their heads, and the sound of fear saturating everything, past and present.

Evan clung to his sister, his eyes screwed shut, his fingers trembling like dead leaves in the breath of the wind.

Aster tugged at the earphones, but the wires were tangled, wrapped around each other, and she was not quick enough to save her brother from the climax of the recording, played out by a macabre conductor of death, saving the greatest symphony until the last.

A scream, long and loose. Swollen with the kind of horrors that no one should witness. Another thump. A series of breaths, fast and ragged. A wet sound like meat on a chopping board.

And then nothing, except the sound of footsteps walking away and the hiss of the still-rolling tape.

Aster and Evan locked eyes, falling into the well of each other's shock, frozen and unable to move. A few seconds later, just as it occurred to them to switch off the tape, they caught a sound, like a sack of potatoes dragging itself across the floor.

Evan squeezed his sister's hand.

And then the voice was up close again, a thickened, halting mumble, telling them that it was bleeding and it hurt so much and it was scared of dying but it might be better than living. That it was going to turn off the tape, and take it out of the Walkman and hide it inside a cushion. That it hoped someone would find it. That the person who had done this was—

The Lockwood siblings leaned forward, desperate to help this stranger, this voice from the past, but the Walkman stopped playing, the abrupt pop and click of its buttons making them jump.

The tape had run out.

70

26 The Avenue – 4.38 p.m.

Five seconds, sometimes less.

That's all it takes to turn a life inside out. A moment of inattention changing lanes on the motorway. A shortcut down an alleyway on a rain-dirty night. The discovery of illicit texts. A luxury hotel on an itemized credit card bill.

A newspaper story.

Dessie stared at the computer screen without blinking until her eyes swam and she had to rub at them with her knuckles to clear her vision.

Finally.

Now breathe.

A part of her wished that she had never begun this journey down the rabbit hole, filing her discovery under Forget as Quickly as Possible and burying her head in the sand.

But that had never been Dessie's way. She did not shy away from uncomfortable truths. That was why, two hours after opening her laptop, she had found what she was looking for.

After multiple references to multiple Benjamin Turners, she had narrowed her search to include Lincolnshire. The newspaper story was dated six years previously and she had known it was him because the photograph, although the size of a thumbnail, was clear as the estuary skies.

A pharmacist caught spying on women with a telescope has escaped jail.

Benjamin Turner, from Lincoln, spent hours at a time watching his victims in their own homes without their knowledge or consent.

Turner set up a telescope in the spare bedroom of his parents' home to observe women as they undressed.

Prosecutors told Lincoln Crown Court he had 'waged a sustained campaign on the vulnerable women in his street, including a young mother and a pensioner.'

Turner insisted that he had 'made a mistake' and had originally intended to use his telescope for documenting cloud formations and stargazing.

Turner pleaded guilty to two counts of voyeurism between 2011 and 2012 and was sentenced to a three-year community order. He was ordered to sign the Sex Offenders register for five years.

He was sacked from his job in March.

Dessie was finding it difficult to breathe, the truth as cold and stinging as winter rain.

Five dead bodies had been found in the woods a stone's throw from her house. No suspects. No arrests. Nothing. And here she was, living with a stranger who had lied about his past.

A lump of iron settled in her chest.

Fletcher Parnell had changed his name to escape his criminal record. He had preyed on vulnerable women. He had kept a terrible secret from her.

The question was, what else was he capable of?

71

25 The Avenue – 7.31 p.m.

Their father was on the telephone to their mother's sister. Aster emptied half a saucepan's worth of baked beans onto her brother's toast and sat down opposite him. Both children picked up their knives and forks. Put them down again.

'I can't stop hearing it.' Evan seemed shrunken, a shadow of himself. Aster's mouth was still dry from fear. She nodded, surprised by a wave of tearfulness.

Her brother pushed his plate away. Dark patches beneath his eyes. A scar on his cheek from a toy car she had thrown at him when he was a toddler and had scribbled on her drawing of a cat.

He looked across the table at her, seeking reassurance and guidance. His expression said *what shall we do?* But she didn't know.

'Who do you think it was?' He poked at a bean with his finger.

'I haven't got a clue.'

'Do you think it was a child or a grown-up?'

'Evan—'

'Do you think we should tell Dad?'

'I think Dad's got enough on his mind at the moment.'

'Do you think we should tell *someone*?'

Aster picked up her plate and scraped its contents into the bin. Ran warm water into the pan. From her vantage point at the sink, she could see a police car parked on the street outside. Perhaps Evan was right. They could tell the police. Or Bailey and the other boys. But the idea of talking about the contents of the tape made her squirm with embarrassment and fear. It had upset her more than she was letting on.

Evan dug up a forkful of beans. Took a sip of his milk. Aster smiled to herself. It looked like her brother's appetite had returned. Some things never changed.

'I've got an idea.' His mouth was full of beans and toast.

'Go on.'

'I found the tape in the treehouse, right? Why don't we see what else we can find? Maybe there are other clues in there.'

'I don't know, Evan. It might be best to let sleeping dogs lie.'

'What does that mean?'

'It means not poking about in stuff that isn't our business.'

His mouth set in a line, but he didn't argue.

The floorboards above their heads creaked. Their father was pacing about, still talking to their Auntie Carol. The house felt empty without their mother. She was the one who cooked dinner, and made them read and shower and tidy their rooms. The steady hand on the tiller. Aster missed her.

'Do you think Mum's OK?' Evan's voice was small, as if he needed to ask the question, but didn't want her to hear.

'She's just gone out for a bit.' Aster picked up his empty plate. 'She'll be home soon.' She didn't believe that, but she didn't want to frighten him.

Dusk slid into darkness. Their father sat in the armchair, nursing a bottle of beer, the shadows deepening around him. He didn't say much. Earlier that afternoon, he had knocked on every house in the street but no one had seen her. Both children cleaned their teeth and changed into their nightclothes without being asked.

An air of expectancy hovered around the house like an unwelcome guest. All of them were waiting for something to happen, for Olivia to call, for the sound of her key in the lock or a knock on the door from DS Stanton. *Anything.*

But time pressed on without empathy or compassion, as time always does. The clock in the hallway marked out the minutes, two children went to bed that night without a kiss from their mother and Olivia Lockwood still did not come home.

72

4 Hillside Crescent – 9.11 p.m.

'Thank you, Wildeve. We'll take it from here.' A pause. 'Let's hope you haven't screwed things up for the rest of us.'

Those had been DCI Roger Sampson's precise words when she had delivered Trefor Lovell to the officers still gathered outside his house that afternoon. Mac had stayed in the car, and she had escorted the old man across the road, knowing he wouldn't try to run, all fight sucked from him.

She wasn't certain what Sampson was driving at. Although off duty, she had only behaved as any other half-decent cop would have done. But that wasn't the issue. Instead, she suspected he was alluding to the fact she should have been at home on compassionate leave. Any solicitor worth their salt would use it as a stick to beat her with, calling into question her judgement and challenging her ability to stick to the rules, seeking out that kink in the tracks that would derail any potential case.

She cast her mind back, trying to reassure herself that

276

she had followed procedure to the letter. She knew she had done the right thing.

His words still stung, though.

She had hoped that Sampson would urge her back into service, that her arrest of Lovell would make him realize she was an essential cog in the machinery of the investigating team, but his clipped tone had told her everything she needed to know. *Run along now, there's a love.* He had even threatened her with a disciplinary if it turned out that she had messed up Lovell's arrest, the collapse of a future trial. Naive, that's what she'd been.

The news had broken within a couple of hours. She'd heard it on the radio, driving home. '*Police investigating the Doll Maker murders have a suspect in custody. The body of a woman has been recovered from a property in The Avenue near Rayleigh, Essex.*'

Put like that, it didn't look good for Lovell. Naturally, the press office hadn't confirmed his arrest for murder, because it wasn't true. Yet. But they hadn't denied it either, simply stating that a seventy-seven-year-old man had been arrested on suspicion of assault. It would quieten the detractors for a while, at least. Give the team some time to search Lovell's house and gather evidence. Breathing space.

The incident room would be buzzing with this injection of adrenaline. She could almost taste the stale water and feel the glare of the strip lighting on her skin. If she closed her eyes, she could hear Adam's voice, calling across the room to another officer, the rumble of discussion and debate and the best way to proceed. The gritty tiredness behind her eyes. They would be taking Lovell's house apart, looking for clues, examining what they had discovered and what they already knew. She should be there.

Adam.

Come back to me.

Grief, with its teeth, its hungry mouth, swallowed her. An hour, that's all it would take to rub out the pain. A handful of pills. The bite of a kitchen knife against her wrists. A step off a bridge and the cold, hard welcome of the concrete below. What did she have to live for? A job where she didn't matter. No family left. All gone. Everything.

She sat in the darkness of their home. If Adam was here, he would be preparing a late supper, opening the wine, cutting up cheese, listening to her day, sharing his. Music. Slow dancing. The press of his mouth against hers.

And now all she had left was the bumping up against his absence, the understanding that all the routines of their lives together – *her life* – would have to be remade.

For so long, she had been alone. Functioning. Capable. An island. But Adam had thrown her a rope, and she had held on, tentatively at first. Allowed herself to scale it, little by little. Put her trust in the strength of this stranger who she had come to love with a force she'd forgotten she had.

They had made her greedy, those glimpses of a life long forgotten, filled with the glitter of compassion and warmth and equality. A sense of coming home. She had grabbed for it, clung on to that rope with everything she possessed. But somewhere along the way she had taken it for granted. The rope had slackened. And here she was again, drifting on her own.

In the medicine cabinet in the bathroom upstairs were several boxes of painkillers.

Fifteen steps or so. And she could turn herself off.

The doorbell rang.

It was so late. She ignored it.

Her mobile phone beeped.

It's me. Open the door.

Mac.

She thought about ignoring him, but he pressed down on the bell again, and she knew he wouldn't go away. Mac wasn't a quitter.

He grinned at her and held up two white plastic bags, filled with food. In the kitchen, he unloaded containers of fragrant curries, pilau rice, tarka dhal, thick naan studded with coconut and raisins. Tall bottles of beer. Her mouth watered at the smell of spices and comfort.

'I knew you wouldn't bother to eat,' he said. 'And you don't have to, but in case you're hungry . . .'

She didn't say much, but touched his arm to show her thanks.

'You get the plates,' he said, 'and I'll find a bottle opener.'

Her mouth was full of cardboard, but she managed a couple of spoonfuls of curry, some rice. Mac took a swig of beer. 'Lovell's hiding something.'

She shook her head. 'No way. Sampson's warned me off. I need this job, Mac.'

Mac tore off some naan, swiped it in his leftover sauce. 'Look, I wouldn't sanction breaking the rules, but there's more at stake here than you realize. I – it's not my place, but you have to trust me on this.'

'What are you talking about?'

'I haven't been entirely honest.'

She looked at him, surprised, but he met her gaze.

Defiant, almost. Authoritative. As if he still occupied the role of her superior.

'I can't tell you why,' he said. 'It will compromise the investigation. But I will in due course, I promise.' He wiped his mouth with a napkin. 'Sampson's blinkered, he's gone off half-cocked after Lovell, probably because he was stupid enough to attack French, but my instinct tells me that although he's holding something back, he's not responsible for the murders.'

'Oh, come on. He lives in The Avenue. His wife is dead. He makes those creepy little dolls, for Christ's sake. One of the Scenes of Crime guys said she even had the same weird painted face.'

'Think, Wildeve. You're not the only one who spoke to the SOCO guys. She's been dead a long time. That's not how this killer operates. And yes, Lovell has got opportunity, there is some circumstantial evidence, but it's not enough, is it? What about motive?'

He was right, of course. Wildeve's head whirled, filling with questions. Was it possible her own instincts hadn't been off-kilter after all?

'But you said Lovell was hiding something. How do you know that?'

Mac pushed a hand through his hair. 'I should have told you this yesterday. Adam was on to something. A few hours before his body was found, he left a voicemail explaining that he needed to speak to me. He was in The Avenue, he said. He sounded excited, that he had a theory and he'd explain when he saw me.'

He fumbled for his mobile. 'Adam didn't show up when he said he would, but he did send this text.' He passed it to

Wildeve. LOVELL KNOWS. Mac shook his head. 'I don't know what he meant by that, Wildeve, and my hands are tied. I'm just a retired copper and Sampson won't listen to me. But if you could somehow speak to Lovell again, and persuade him to tell us what he told Adam, we'll have the key to unlocking this case.'

73

25 The Avenue – 2.06 a.m.

At first, she thought it was rain, throwing itself in angry handfuls at her window.

She rubbed her eyes, swimming up through sleep. But there was no trickling sound of water from her open casement window, no drumming on the roof. The glowing numbers of her alarm clock informed her it was six minutes past two. She switched on her light and saw two or three pebbles lying under her sill.

She padded over to the window and looked out on the street below.

A mass of blond hair, a face grinning up at her. Bailey. And a couple of shadows behind him. Charlie and Marco, she guessed. They were all dressed in black.

'Come on, sleepyhead,' he called softly through the darkness. 'Time to go.'

She folded her arms across her chest, her vest top making her feel exposed. She wanted to refuse, to fetch her

282

father and make them go away, but it was harder to speak up for herself now they were here.

'My dad will kill me.' The murmur of her voice sounded too loud in the stillness of the street.

'So don't get caught,' said Bailey. He smiled at her and her stomach turned inside out. 'Get dressed. We'll wait for you.'

Despite the late hour, the air was swollen, like overripe fruit. When she walked up to them, Bailey slung an arm around her shoulder, claiming ownership. The weight of it was uncomfortable, but she didn't want to shrug him off, seduced by the fickle allure of belonging.

She flicked a glance back at her house. Evan had cried out as she'd crept down the stairs, and she had paused, half hoping her father would wake up and put a stop to this nonsense. But her brother had settled back into sleep, and Aster blew out a breath, not in relief, but reluctance. Still, she had pressed on and now it was too late. She'd aligned herself with them.

'So, what's the plan?'

The others had barely acknowledged her, and she was hit by an overwhelming sensation that she had been wrong, that she didn't belong here at all, but was simply a stranger who had no other purpose than to serve as a distraction. Or worse still, a patsy.

'Well,' Bailey offered her another lazy grin, 'my mother always encouraged me to think big.'

She grinned back at him, but nerves boiled inside her.

'How do we know we can trust her?' That was Charlie.

She glimpsed his face, the black camouflage markings raked across his cheeks, his nose.

'You can trust me,' she said. It was true. She'd never been one to betray a confidence, but they weren't to know that.

'She's here, isn't she?' said Bailey. 'She's part of it now.' He opened the inside of his jacket. Aster glimpsed a bottle of white spirit, an old rag and a box of matches.

A sharp intake of breath before she had time to think about stopping herself. 'You can't do that. You might kill him.'

Charlie shrugged. 'Serves him right.'

Aster wanted to turn and run, to burrow down into the safety of her bed and forget that this night was happening. This was not what she had expected. Yes, in some distant part of herself, she had suspected they might try and spook him, but never this. This was on a different level.

'It's going to be magnificent.' Charlie's eyes gleamed in the dark. 'Teach that old bastard a lesson.'

Marco threw them a sharp look. 'Shut up. If someone sees us, we're all going to be in the shit.'

The boys hid their bikes at the entrance of the woods. The police tape was still there, but the officer had gone. They nudged each other, ducking and feinting with their fists, fired up with the thrill of making trouble. Of crossing a line.

Aster trailed behind them. Bailey was whispering something to Charlie. Marco slowed down until he fell into step with her.

'I don't think this is a very good idea,' he said, low enough for the others not to hear.

'Then why are you here?' Aster wasn't being sarcastic. She wanted to know.

Marco laughed but it lacked humour. 'Same reason as you. It's impossible to refuse Bailey when he wants something.' A sideways glance. 'In his world, you're either with him or against him.'

She swallowed, trying to clear her throat, which was closing up with anxiety. A breeze was picking up. She could smell the sea. The sickly sweetness of a plant she didn't recognize. Most of the houses were in darkness, one or two had security lights that spotlit the four of them as they passed by on the pavement. It made Aster think of those old films her father enjoyed, of criminals snared in helicopter search lights.

'Let's walk in the middle of the road,' said Bailey.

Trefor Lovell's house was at the end of The Avenue and surrounded by police tape. A patrol car was parked by the kerb, but of the two officers inside, one had his eyes closed and the other was glued to the screen of his phone.

This was not what Bailey had been expecting.

'Back up,' he hissed to the others, and they pressed themselves into the high hedge of the house next door.

Marco and Aster started to walk back up the road. 'Hey, where do you think you're going?' Bailey's voice jerked them back, like fish on a hook. They clustered together, hidden from the police car by a bend in the road.

'Let's cut and run,' said Marco, not quite meeting Bailey's eye. 'It's way too risky.'

'What's wrong with a little risk?' said Bailey with a grin.

'You can't be serious,' said Marco, meeting his gaze head-on this time. 'The police are sitting right there.'

'So what?' said Charlie, standing next to Bailey, choosing his side. 'Makes it more interesting.'

'No,' said Marco. 'No fucking way.'

'Don't be a pussy,' said Bailey. He pointed to Aster. 'You're more of a pussy than she is, and she's a girl.' He held out his hand, beckoned with his fingers. 'Come on, Aster.'

Aster wanted to ignore him. To tell him he had no right to order her around. To turn her back on him and walk away. Marco was right. It was time to go home. But her instincts warned her that Bailey could get ugly. And she didn't know how far he would go.

'Why don't we come back tomorrow night?' she said, buying time with a compromise, already plotting her excuses.

'Let's just get on with it,' said Charlie. 'All of us agreed to this. Let's not pussy out now.'

He shoved Marco back towards the house, and the boy, who was slighter and a couple of inches smaller, lost his balance and stumbled. Aster waited for him to push back, to insist on leaving, but his head was bowed and he didn't speak.

Panic began to tap its finger on her shoulder. She trawled the silt of her memory, seeking inspiration. Desperate. Determined.

'Let's head round the back and climb over the fence,' said Bailey, already heading for the garden.

'Wait.' Aster blurted out the words. 'I've got a *genius* idea.'

The display window of Lovell's shop was a tangle of faded fancy dress costumes and toys that had seen better days. The four teenagers stood in a semi-circle on the dead grass that hemmed the pavement, the moon fat-faced and silver. Bailey and Charlie were whispering and laughing. Aster and Marco could not look at each other. Both were ashamed of their weakness.

Across the shop's door was a link chain secured with a padlock. Dirt smeared the glass. A length of blue and white tape – POLICE LINE DO NOT CROSS – moved in the breeze.

'Do you reckon Lovell keeps his gun in here?' Bailey's breath was warm in her ear, his lips grazing her skin. But it didn't excite her. It made her feel sick.

She faked a smile. 'Maybe.'

'Right.' Bailey rubbed his hands together. 'Let's do this.'

Aster had half expected to see a police cordon around the shop, but even then, she did not appreciate its seriousness. She did not understand that Lovell was still in custody, that they were trespassing, and that officers were due to return at first light with an extension to the search warrant that had been executed on his house and garden a few hours earlier. That they were contaminating a potential crime scene. Breaking the law. But she knew on the most basic level that what they were doing was wrong.

Charlie unzipped his rucksack, slipped on some gloves and produced a pair of bolt cutters. As he did so, Aster glimpsed the teeth of a hacksaw and a coil of rope. He saw her looking. 'In case we need to tie the bastard up.'

Aster felt something inside her break.

Bailey was soaking a rag with white spirit. The fumes hit the back of her throat and made her cough. He rattled the match box at her. 'Want to do it?'

Aster shook her head. She might be easily led but she

wasn't stupid. 'I think that privilege belongs to you,' she said.

Bailey grinned, wolf's teeth in the dark.

Marco had moved to the corner of The Avenue and was keeping lookout. 'Hurry up,' he said. 'Before someone comes.'

'Hold the torch.' Charlie handed it to her, heavier than she expected. She shone it on the door as he snapped through the padlock and pulled it apart from the hasp.

'Showtime,' he said.

Bailey stood in front of the door, Charlie at his heels. He hadn't outlined his plan, but Aster suspected he was going to toss the rag into the shop and follow it with a lit match. A warning to Lovell of what they were capable of. Of what was to come.

But Bailey's plan was about to backfire in the most spectacular of ways. Because Lovell had anticipated an attack on his property of exactly this kind and he was ready for them. As the teenager pushed open the shop door, a loud crack went off.

'What the fuck?' said Charlie.

Bailey let out a yell and stumbled forward, clutching his arm. He tripped over the lip of an ancient tin bath placed just inside the door of the shop and fell in, headfirst.

The others heard splashing, and then a strangled cry, followed by sobbing, ugly and raw. 'Fuck. Fuck. Fuck.' Bailey was muttering that word over and over again and each time it was striated with fear and disgust.

He tipped out of the shop door backwards and swung around to face the three teenagers, pawing at his eyes. He spat on the grass, two or three times. Aster's torch was strobing wildly as she ran forward to help him, but the light touched his face and she balked, backing away from him.

'Help me,' he said.

Bailey's clothes were clinging to him and his tears were carving tracks down his face.

His skin was no longer pale. Rusty patches were daubed across his cheeks and forehead, in the fine hairs of his eyebrows and the folds of his ears. His haystack of hair was much darker and so wet that droplets rolled down his neck and hit the grass in a steady rhythm, like the beat of a heart.

A baptism not of water or fire, but of blood.

They all stared at him, frozen by the sight of the boy in his ruined clothes, clots sticking to his skin.

'Oh my God.' Marco breathed out all their fears.

Bailey was still holding his arm, still crying. 'It hurts.'

'Let me see,' said Aster, waking up. She could not bear to touch him, struggled to be close to him, but her compassion would not let her ignore him. And when she stepped nearer, she realized that instead of the animal stink of copper and spoiled meat, there was a familiar, synthetic odour.

Not blood, but red paint.

She touched his arm lightly, just below the sleeve of his T-shirt. And there it was. A hole in the skin, a puncture wound.

'I think you've been shot,' she said. 'You need to go to hospital.'

Charlie was there in an instant. 'Don't be fucking stupid. *Yeah, sorry, we were setting fire to a shop and our friend got shot.* We'll go back to yours. You're the nearest. We can clean him up there.'

Aster imagined Bailey trailing paint on the pale floorboards of their new house, Charlie opening cupboards in the kitchen, looking for food, loud and aggressive, Marco, sweet but ineffectual.

'Not all of you,' she said. 'Just Bailey.' She turned to him. 'Can you walk?'

'Yeah.' But when she looked in his eyes, she read pain in them.

Charlie was shoving the bolt cutters back into his rucksack, muttering to himself. Marco was speaking to Bailey, low and comforting. She swung the torch around the entrance of the shop, searching for the bottle of white spirit, the incriminating rag. With the toe of her trainer, she kicked them towards Charlie and he picked them up. She wasn't going to get blamed for this.

Her torch swept across the surface of the tin bath, still rippling, deep and wine-dark. She picked out splashes on the tiled floor, spattered walls. A bloody-looking footprint. She must remember to wipe her own feet on the grass outside.

She backed away, her torch swinging in wider circles, making sure she had missed nothing. Eyes watched her. Porcelain dolls sat in rows, an army of the lifeless who might blink and twist their heads at any moment. Boxes of marbles. A handful of old batteries. A rusted jack-in-the-box. Against one wall of the shop was a long, narrow table. The light landed on a box of dominoes. An old wig. A can of WD-40.

A black wallet.

Aster paused and swung back the torch, seeking it out. There it was again. A piece of leather decorated with an insignia that she couldn't read but looked like a coat of arms. The light wavered as she took a step closer, reached for it and flipped it open, loose threads at one end.

A name and a face.

Her eyes darted across the identification.

Detective Inspector Adam Stanton. The dead police officer.

74

Now

I have been observing the lives around me fall apart. I do not wish to gloat, I despise self-aggrandizement, but there is a pleasure in watching others falter, don't you think?

If one is honest, most of us take joy in the stumbling footsteps of our enemies and, occasionally, our friends. Especially those who glitter with confidence, strutting through life. As for rudeness, I cannot abide it, or the arrogance of those who talk over me or look through me. I will them to trip and fall. I want them to skin their knees and bloody their noses.

The shop was closed for a month and it never recovered. Neither did I. Because the past has a way of catching us up. Of eating us from the inside.

I had to bury the secret in the dirt with their bodies.

Like we buried you.

75

26 The Avenue – 2.07 a.m.

Dessie was in bed, but she was not asleep. She switched on her lamp at the rattle of Fletcher's key in the front door.

She waited.

First, the sound of the handle being worked up and down, then the thump of his shoulder against the door, trying to force it. She wondered how long it would take him to realize that she had left her own key in the lock, deliberately shutting him out.

She had never imagined herself to be one of those women who throw their lover's clothes out of the window, screaming and making a scene. Sewing shellfish into the hems of his trousers or cutting up suits. She still wasn't that woman. But she had packed most of his belongings into a case and it was waiting in the hallway. He could collect it in the morning.

A hammering on the door.

She rolled onto her side, pillow over her head. The

hammering stopped. Her phone vibrated with a message. She turned it off. The hammering began again.

Dessie pulled on her dressing gown and went downstairs. As soon as she switched on the hall light, the noise ceased.

'Sorry to wake you,' he said through the letterbox. She had no idea where he had been. He had not mentioned he was going out after work, and certainly not so late. 'I think you've locked me out.'

'Yes,' she said. '*Benjamin.*'

She had half expected him to deny it, but his silence told her everything. Eventually, he spoke, but there was no fire in his voice, just defeat. 'How did you find out?'

That admission of guilt was all it took to douse the outrage that had driven her since her discovery. She slid down the wall by the door, too tired to fight.

'The garage. I was going to book us a surprise holiday.' Her voice cracked on *surprise.*

'Let me in, sweetheart,' he said. 'I can explain everything.'

'Like why you were spying on unsuspecting women?'

'It was a horrible mix-up, Dessie. An awful fucking time. I was cataloguing clouds, but they thought I was a pervert. I had to plead guilty, or they'd have sent me to prison.'

'So why didn't you tell me?'

'You wouldn't have given me the time of day,' he said. 'You wouldn't have given me so much as a second look.' He started to cry. 'Would you? *Would you?*'

Dessie could never bear the sound of someone crying. And she had always tried so hard not to make judgements about people.

'I might have done.'

THE NEIGHBOUR

'No, you wouldn't. Nobody would. No smoke without fire, isn't that what they say?'

He was right. She would have run a mile if she'd known about his conviction. But he might not be lying about his motivations. She'd heard the same from one of her sister's friends, whose brother *had* gone to prison. He'd refused to admit his guilt and, in her summing up, the judge had remarked on his lack of remorse and sentenced him to seven years.

She loved Fletcher. But she didn't know if she believed him.

All afternoon she had trawled their relationship, picking it over, holding up a magnifying glass to its imperfections. She'd remembered a night, a few months back, when she'd come in from drinks with friends, her mouth tasting of garlicky olives and red wine. She'd thrown off her jeans and silk shirt, collapsed into bed without brushing her teeth and fallen into a deep sleep.

A couple of hours later, her eyes had opened. She wasn't sure what had disturbed her, but there was a man standing over the bed. She'd screamed before she'd realized it was Fletcher, and he'd soothed her, his hand on her arm.

'It's only me. Go back to sleep.'

He'd lain down next to her, on his stomach, stroking her hair, and in that vague, half-asleep way of the middle of the night, she'd registered a slight thud, the sound of something heavy being placed on the carpet before she'd drifted off again.

It was only when she awoke in the morning that she'd noticed Fletcher's camera on the floor. Her underwear had also been removed, but she had no memory of taking it off.

At the time, she'd dismissed it to the black hole of drunkenness, had barely given it a second thought. Now she wasn't so sure.

She had trusted him. She had invited him into her home and her life, allowing herself to be seduced by the man she thought he was. A part of her could not understand how she might have got it so wrong. How was it that she had not sensed this darkness in him, that her judgement had been so skewed? Was it because he was telling her the truth?

The letterbox lifted again. 'I do understand how you feel, you know.' And then he was standing up, preparing to leave. She could see the shape of him behind the stained glass. 'I'll go far away from here and you'll never have to see me again, I promise.' His voice sounded muffled against the door and then she picked up the sound of footsteps, of him walking away.

She crawled over to the letterbox, lifted it. 'Fletch, wait.' The footsteps stopped. 'Why did you change your name?'

He crouched down and she saw his mouth, the stubble on his chin, through the open flap.

'I wanted a clean page, a new beginning. Everyone deserves a second chance.' A hopeful lift to his voice. 'If you let me in, we can talk about it properly.'

Dessie remembered their holiday plans, their first Christmas together, the way he made her laugh.

She unlocked the door.

76

4 Hillside Crescent – 2.08 a.m.

DS Wildeve Stanton was many things, but she wasn't a fantasist.

By her reckoning, Trefor Lovell had been in custody for eleven hours. The police had another thirteen hours to charge him or let him go. But if they'd found enough evidence to hold him for murder, it could be another three days before he was released. Or remanded in custody. Without bail. Which was no good to her. She needed to talk to him now.

But it was gone two, and killer or not, he had a legal right to sleep, and she was banned from the investigation anyway. It was game over.

Or was it? She just had to find a way in.

Wildeve sat on the edge of her bed, revived by Mac's offering of food and the warmth of his company, her mind too noisy for sleep.

Adam.

She needed to see him.

His old photograph album was in the drawer under his side of the bed, and she pulled it out, careless and frantic, tossing bits of paper and receipts and his leather belt aside, desperate to see him, consumed by the fear that one day she might forget the shape of the mole by his ear or the arch of his eyebrow.

She had a pain in her temple, running down the side of her face and along her jawline. She flipped the pages. There he was. Laughing with his mates at a beer festival; a young man, in his police uniform, upright and proud; on a ferry to Ireland with his parents, gap-toothed, freckles spreading across his nose; a picture of him on his first day at primary school.

She stared at the pictures of her husband, drinking each one in, until the first bird of the day began to sing. A blackbird, perhaps. Or a wren. Her eyes – sore and gritty – told her it was time to sleep.

She was about to put the album away when she noticed a cardboard photo frame slipped into the back. Embossed on the bottom in gold lettering were the words *Croft Lane County Primary School, Class of 1985*, but the photograph was missing.

Adam's primary school.

Something shifted in her brain. Where was the photograph? Had he taken it to the school reunion? No, he'd gone to the pub empty-handed. She remembered because she had given him a lift. And yet it couldn't have slipped from the frame by itself. Someone – Adam – had removed it. But why?

Round and round. All the dead ends and loose ends. None of it made any sense. And yet, some instinct told her she was within touching distance. The corners of her puzzle were in place. Now she needed to find the rest of the pieces. She lay on her bed, the minutes ticking on.

And then her phone began to ring.

77

26 The Avenue – 3.37 a.m.

He was asleep.

Fletcher had talked and cried until there was nothing left. 'I was as much a victim as those women were,' he'd said, his face breaking open as he'd relived his ordeal. 'It was horrific.'

He was frank and honest, told her everything. 'We can start again, Dessie,' he'd said, and touched her hand, offered up a hopeful smile. She had smiled back and nodded, let him think that she'd believed him.

His breathing was slow and steady, the rhythm of untroubled sleep. Who was the vulnerable one now? She gazed at the cupid's bow of his lip, the stubble shadowing his chin and felt – nothing. When he began to snore, she slipped from their bedroom.

His work bag was in the hallway. She'd never had a reason to go through it before, would never have intruded on his privacy in that way, but this was a necessary evil.

She unzipped it.

A weakness in her legs.

Boxes and bottles. Dozens of them. *Phenobarbital. Diazepam. Zolpidem.* She'd had enough celebrity clients to recognize sedatives when she saw them. Fletcher must have stolen them from work. A thought – traitorous but resonant – popped into her head. The bodies in the woods. *No visible signs of injury.*

Her mouth was dust.

She kneeled down, rummaging through the medication and tossing it aside, desperate now to find what she was looking for.

And there it was. At the bottom of his bag. The rectangle of his digital camera. In her hands, it flickered into life.

She scrolled through the pictures, dozens of images of cloud formations, each of them filled with a kind of mystery. A halo around the eye of the sun. The bruising of a storm. A belt of trees silhouetted against a mackerel sky. For one, glorious moment, relief sluiced through her. She had been mistaken.

And then the landscape changed.

Sky became skin. The branches became arms and legs. Hundreds and hundreds of pictures. Of her, asleep or lying in the bath. Of women she did not recognize and who did not know they were being photographed. Some blurry, some in sharp, precise focus. All unguarded. The intimacy floored her.

They were time-stamped. Three months ago. Last week. On Sunday.

Several photographs of the neighbours who had just moved in across the road. The teenage daughter. The woman who was now missing.

A drum began to beat in her head. *Where had he been all evening?*

Dessie put her thumb to her mouth, tore at the nail until it was ragged and sore. She huddled against the wall and tucked her knees up under her chin. She was trembling, despite the suffocating heat.

She scrolled through the pictures again and the fire that had been smouldering in her belly since she'd discovered the lies about his past blazed into life, the flames leaping high. Her anger was the petrol, fuelling it.

On the telephone table was the card of the female officer who had knocked on the door yesterday. Dessie registered it was late, but she did not much care about the time. All she knew was that she needed to contact the police.

As she reached for the handset, a noise made her lift her head.

Fletcher was coming down the stairs.

In his hand, he was carrying the silken noose of a dressing gown, its poppies like splashes of blood.

78

25 The Avenue — 2.22 a.m.

Evan missed his mother.

Yes, she shouted at him, but her cuddles were the best. When Lucas Naylor had directed all the boys to gather around, pinching and punching him as he'd walked through the school gates on the first day of June, she had taken one look at his face at pick-up time and headed straight for the ice-cream van.

She hadn't probed, not at first, but later, arm around him on the sofa, she'd extracted the full story. She hadn't taken her eyes off the film they were watching, but she'd pulled him to her and said, 'Those who feel small inside might feel a little bigger by knocking down others, but it never lasts. We should feel sorry for them.'

He hadn't understood what she had meant. But later, when he'd had a chance to think about it, he wondered if she was saying that Lucas acted the way he did because he felt bad about something else.

A few days later, Lucas had stolen Evan's lunchbox and

eaten his sandwiches. Evan's mother had made her son some toast when he'd got home. 'Lucas doesn't have a mum,' she'd told him. 'And his dad isn't well.' Evan knew then that he'd been right. For all her impatience, his mother hid a kindness beneath her quick temper.

A thought occurred to him, and despite the warmth, he shivered, sitting up in bed in his thin pyjama top.

What if she had left because he was rude and naughty? Was it his fault? But then he remembered the way she laughed when he tickled her feet, and the expression on her face when Aster was singing, and he didn't think she would *choose* to leave her family.

And that made his stomach turn over, like falling off a wall.

He kicked off his covers. The house was quiet. Evan shut his eyes and tried to reclaim sleep. He tossed about, trying to get comfortable, but his room was airless, the heat a heavy blanket across his chest. He gave up and climbed out of bed, drawn to the window.

High and bright, the moon was lighting up the garden with silver and shadow. The treehouse was a dark secret at the end of the lawn.

Staring at it for too long made his eyes play tricks on him. His tired brain saw smudges peeping though its windows and shapes in the darkness. He rubbed at his eyes, but he could not stop thinking about the tape.

He never, ever wanted to listen to it again, and had hidden it in one of the unpacked boxes of toys so he didn't have to see it. But the sound of that cry was imprinted in his mind. His heart hurt. It made him afraid. He knew why.

The handwriting, almost the same as his own.

THE NEIGHBOUR

A cry – high and familiar.

A child, like him.

He wondered who it was. And where that child was now.

The branches of the trees were lifted skywards in worship. His vision blurred and they seemed to beckon to him, urging him outside.

The curious part of his nature – the part that pored over maps of the world and took apart his wind-up alarm clock to discover how it worked – burned to find out more.

But the young boy in him – nervous of the dark, who put his hands over his ears when the house shifted and creaked – was resistant to wandering into the garden alone with the night so black and watchful.

He stood at the window for a while, watching the treehouse. A breeze breathed through the leaves and they waved at him like tiny hands. The plums were glossy, their skins dark and lush amongst the branches.

What secrets were hidden amongst the wooden slats of the treehouse? What had happened there?

He reached for his Magic 8 Ball and whispered his question: *Should I go back to the treehouse?*

Screwing up his eyes, he tipped the ball over and waited for its answer to appear. After a minute, he could wait no longer.

It is certain.

Evan put on his slippers and headed into the night.

79

Southside Hospital, Essex – 2.24 a.m.

The mortuary was in darkness, save for a lamp in the exam-ination room at the front of the building. A blonde head was bent over a stack of post-mortem reports. She lifted her glasses and rubbed her eyes.

Mathilda Hudson did not have to be there. She could have packed the paperwork into her briefcase and taken it home to read on the sofa, legs tucked under her, an icy gin and tonic on the table. She could be in bed. But instead she had set up a makeshift desk in this sterile stainless-steel room. It was her penance.

She was having trouble sleeping, anyway.

Yesterday, a broadsheet newspaper had printed a detailed analysis of the murders. A pathologist who knew nothing of the case had criticized her lack of progress. A public skew-ering. It wouldn't have hurt so much if it hadn't been true. It was her job to find out what had killed them. But she still didn't know. Guilt impaled her. And professional shame.

The reports were full of medical technicalities that would

have baffled the families of the victims, but they were poetry to the pathologist, full of meaning and depth. Held between those pages was the key to the Doll Maker murders, but Hudson hadn't unlocked the puzzle yet.

What had caused all five of these victims to display signs of cardiogenic shock and respiratory distress? The answer to this question was at the heart of the police investigation. It was her responsibility to find that answer. And she took her professional duties extremely seriously.

But she was missing something vital.

She had examined and photographed every inch of their bodies, every bruise and laceration, every graze and imperfection. She had clipped hair and nails and sent the samples for testing. She had made a careful note of body temperature as soon as the cadavers had come into her care, to narrow down the time of death. She had detailed the effects of *rigor mortis*, she had studied and documented the pathology of their organs, she had taken bloods and ordered extensive toxicology reports.

But they were still keeping their secrets from her.

Mathilda was an experienced pathologist and she understood that death was not always clear-cut. That the weather, the age, the weight of a victim could skew the results, even if they had all been killed in the same way. Her job was to seek out the common link, to interpret the architecture of the deceased's body and construct her case.

But she had run out of building blocks.

The bodies had not yet been released to their families. They were being kept in the freezer to preserve evidence, and in case the defence team in any future murder trial exercised the accused's right to an independent postmortem.

Adam Stanton was still in this mortuary, waiting to be transferred.

Mathilda had worked in this place for more years than most, and she was used to keeping company with the dead. Some of her colleagues found it too unsettling to stay there alone, the metal trays of refrigerated bodies enough to spook even the most rational of minds.

But she had always found a comfort in their presence. In all the time that she had been a pathologist, no corpse had ever got up and talked to her. In some ways, she wished they could. At least then she would know what had killed them.

The surfaces gleamed, the smell of bleach and something darker underneath. She sipped her peppermint tea, her stomach rumbling, but she was too engrossed in what she was doing to think about food.

She was rereading her preliminary notes on Adam Stanton. Bloody awful, the presence of his wife on Monday. But she had known Wildeve for a few years, had always liked and respected her, and had been reluctant to ask her to leave.

She had not been sure if Wildeve had turned up in her capacity as wife or investigating officer. A grey area, but one she was not about to challenge, even though she was almost certain the required permission from the coroner for next of kin to attend had not been sought. There was no way she'd be able to watch Jonathan's post-mortem, though. Or those of their children. She had always treated the dead with the respect they were due, but she was too well acquainted with what went on to witness the taking apart of her own family.

Christ, she was tired. She would have to call it a night

soon. But she did not want to leave, the weight of failure on her shoulders, the taste of self-recrimination on her lips.

The printed letters blurred. She lingered over them, reading the same passage over and over again.

GASTROINTESTINAL SYSTEM: Approximately 213ml of partially digested semi-solid food is found in the stomach.

Nothing untoward about that. Most people had eaten something in the hours before their death. She rarely paid much attention to stomach contents. Most of the pathologists she knew – in the south-east, at least – were the same, and almost always relied on the blood and urine results.

Given the absence of external or internal injuries – aside from the eyes which had been removed after death – she and DCI Clive Mackie had discussed at length other methods of murder: the use of nerve agents, gases or poisons. Even fear. She'd once performed a post-mortem on a woman who had died of a heart attack during a botched robbery. It was certainly possible to be scared to death. But that had happened once in seventeen years. This was not the case here.

As for the toxicology tests – the ones that had come back, at least – they had so far been inconclusive. And if she didn't know what she was looking for, how could she begin to find it?

No signs of toxins in the lungs. And she had invested many, many hours scouring the skin of the dead for a needle's telltale pinprick. If any of them had been injected intramuscularly, she would need to harvest the tissues around the entry point. Intravenously, and it would show up in the bloods. But she could find no evidence of injections and nothing had flagged in the test results.

As for the contents of the stomach, she had erred on the side of caution and sent them to be tested, but, again, the results were either inconclusive or still outstanding.

213ml of partially digested semi-solid food.

A distant bell rang in her mind.

Partially digested.

Most food took a couple of hours to digest, which meant that Adam Stanton had eaten something in the two hours before his death.

She reached for the rest of the reports, flicking through them, a rolling drum picking up pace in her chest.

Natalie Tiernan.
GASTROINTESTINAL SYSTEM: Approximately 183ml of partially digested semi-solid food is found in the stomach.

Elijah Outhwaite.
GASTROINTESTINAL SYSTEM: Approximately 252ml of partially digested semi-solid food is found in the stomach.

Esther Farnworth.
GASTROINTESTINAL SYSTEM: Approximately 191ml of partially digested semi-solid food is found in the stomach.

Will Proudfoot.
GASTROINTESTINAL SYSTEM: Approximately 265ml of partially digested semi-solid food is found in the stomach.

All of them had eaten *something* in the two-hour window before their deaths.

Coincidence or something more sinister? She had been able to establish that the bodies had been killed at different times and had been dead for varying periods before they were discovered.

But what if something they had *all* eaten had triggered cardiac failure?

She blew out an impatient breath. She was being stupid. *Of course* they would have eaten something. Breakfast, lunch, whatever. But her instinct was nudging at her, urging her not to ignore this. That it might be a waste of time, but it was worth a closer look.

She put down the reports and checked her watch. Technically, this could wait until morning but she knew she wouldn't sleep. It would whirl about in her head until she had satisfied herself that she was dancing up a blind alley.

Mathilda put on a plastic apron and a pair of gloves and headed for the refrigeration units, where she pulled out the metal tray containing the remains of Adam Stanton.

She tried not to look at his sightless eye sockets, the greyness of his face, the patchwork brutality of her own doing.

With careful fingers, she prised open his lips and shone a slim torch that she kept in her handbag into his mouth.

At first, she thought she was being stupid, and that her instinct had been way off beam. The absence of his tongue had left a bloodied cavity that made goosebumps rise on her skin, she, the most hardened of them all.

And she had checked his mouth, hadn't she? But then she remembered that Wildeve Stanton had arrived and she'd been distracted, and now she thought about it, she couldn't remember anything about Adam Stanton's teeth at all.

And what about the other victims? Clarity and focus were important parts of her job. But it was difficult to maintain 100 per cent concentration at all times. Her focus had been on the heart and its surrounding muscles, the lungs and the oxygen levels in the blood. She had been so busy establishing a cause of death, looking in one direction for supporting evidence, that she had forgotten the basic mantra of her mentor, Dr Sedrowski.

Think outside the box, Mathilda. Dig a little deeper and instead of stones, you might uncover diamonds.

She shone her torch onto the roof of his mouth, across the upper and lower jaw. At the back of his mouth, buried in his left molar, was a brownish speck. Using a pair of tweezers, she removed it from his tooth and placed it in a sterile plastic bag.

In the morning, she would order checks on the remaining bodies and their teeth, and closer analysis of the stomach contents.

She pushed the metal tray holding Adam Stanton back into place. Her sharp ears caught a tiny sound, almost like an escaping sigh, and if she had been a fanciful woman, she might have said that Adam was breathing out his relief that at last she was on the right path.

But she wasn't a fanciful woman, she was a rational one. Her only concern was whether she could find the answer before the killer claimed another life.

80

The Avenue – 2.25 a.m.

The postman had stopped going home.

She was there when he lay in the darkness of his bed-room, and when he sat at the kitchen table, his meal turning to cardboard in his mouth. And once, when he had gone upstairs to run a bath, she was lying in the tub with a scalpel sticking out of her eye.

He had taken to sleeping in the back of his van. A camping mattress and a pillow, and he could snatch a few hours' rest. But the truth was he couldn't escape her, even there. She haunted him. And so did his mistakes.

The postman had been dozing for a couple of hours when he sat up abruptly, his hair stuck to his forehead in the moist heat of the night. For a minute, he forgot where he was, and he was back in the basement of the club, the woman lying dead on the bloodstained concrete, the thump of the bass and the smell of sweat and testosterone. He lay back on the mattress, his hands behind his head.

Wide-eyed, alone, in the darkness.

81

25 The Avenue – 2.26 a.m.

Evan stood outside the back door, cloaked in the shadows of the night-time garden.

He had almost changed his mind when he'd crept past the lamplit sitting room and seen the top of his father's head rising above the armchair. He had paused, uncertain, and then his ears had picked out the steady rhythm of his father's breathing. The boy guessed he'd been waiting up all night for their mother to come home and had succumbed, briefly, to sleep. Another pang of sorrow lit his heart.

The heat was beginning to break up, and a freshening breeze shook the leaves until they danced. Evan didn't like it. The muttering of the dry leaves represented all the things he had come to fear; the whisper of ghosts, and the unseen. He smelled rain. The bushes rustled and his heart jumped.

The treehouse loomed at the distant end of the garden. For a boy of nine, it seemed a long way away. The copse behind it was a smudge on the horizon, a portal into the dark world of his imagination. Through the gloom, Evan was certain he saw shapes with stick arms marching onwards, an army of tree men. He almost turned back then. But he pressed on, his stubborn heart set on finding the answers to the mystery of the cassette.

82

Now

You did not believe me.

The children in the shop on the day of the Grand Re-opening – that date, Saturday, 20 July 1985, is scored into me even now – had allowed themselves to be fooled, but you were different. You pulled away from me when I reached for your hand, shrank into yourself as we walked home. Took yourself off to bed as soon as the door closed behind us.

You had taken one look at the watch on her wrist and known exactly who was in that forgotten chest in the store-room. You refused to speak to me. You could read the guilt on my face.

Now, when I look back on that last day, I wish I might have told you the things I tell you now.

That I love you. That regrets are a waste of energy. That the past may not be undone. It simply is. That life is a series of complex events, shaping us into the selves we are. For all its glorious colours, we are shades of grey. That we are driven to act the way we do by instincts we do not understand. That as some are drawn to the light, some of us are compelled by darkness, our strength coming from the hidden places within. That we can never truly know what lies beneath the flash of a smile, a kindly word. We all wear masks.

But what happened that night was because of my careless tongue.

'We need to get rid of it,' I said, my mouth pressed to the telephone receiver. Seven words that set the wheels in motion.

You must have been listening. You flew down the stairs.

'No,' you said. 'You have to call the police.'

You snatched up the handset from me, pressed down and cut the call. It was one of those old-style rotary telephones. I caught the dialling tone, the rotation of the finger wheel, the sound of the spring as the dial returned to its resting position.

Why did you do that? I wonder that, even now. Why did you not accept my half-truths and go to bed? In the morning it would have been an uncertain memory and in a year's time, a forgotten one. I loved you so much. But not as much as I loved my own life.

You were quick. You had already dialled the second nine by the time I reacted. I pulled the wire from the wall. I wanted to talk to you, to explain everything, but you would not listen.

You ran from me, through the back door and into the garden. The heat of that summer as hot as this one, hotter perhaps, and burned into my memory.

I followed you, but you were scrambling over the fence and into the garden of the house next door. I watched you, climbing up the ladder – not rotten then – and into the treehouse you had been given permission to use whenever you liked.

Shadows had fallen across the garden. The neighbours – a young childless couple whose names I've long since forgotten – were on a round-the-world trip.

I took my time, enjoying the scent of the jasmine. My love wasn't home. It was just you and me.

You were muttering, talking to someone who wasn't there. But you stopped when you heard me coming. You were lying on your stomach on the treehouse floor, your hair sticking up in tufts. As I stood over you, I considered giving you the benefit of the doubt. But you were always one to keep your word, even at the age of ten.

You started to scream.

I only wanted you to be quiet.

83

Wednesday, 1 August 2018

25 The Avenue — 2.31 a.m.

Up high, in the heart of the tree, the wind in the leaves was as loud as rushing water. Evan was cold and wished he'd worn his dressing gown. A twig caught his cheek, tearing the skin. His fingers touched blood. The branches grasped at his hair and his pyjamas, and he struggled to free himself, his arms flailing, panic on his lips.

He was crying by the time he collapsed onto the hard boards of the treehouse floor, his torch casting shadows, startling him at every turn.

A plum fell onto the metal roof and the thump made him cry out, and he wanted nothing more than to be back in the safety of his bed, his mother and father bickering downstairs, the music blaring from his sister's room, and the security of his family unit, everything as it should be.

He took several deep breaths, fighting to calm himself. In his head, he kept hearing the sound of the scream, and he didn't want to think about it, but there it was, right at the front of his brain, and it made him think about all the dead

319

people in the woods across the road, and he was scared, properly scared.

The wind was rising, the clouds scudding across the sky, speeded-up like when Aster fast-forwarded the television, and the moon was flashing on and off, like his torch, and he stood up, ready to leave, ready to forget everything he had come here to do, a powerful urge to crawl onto his daddy's lap. Across the gardens, all he could see was the glint of silver light against the glass of the greenhouse next door.

The first faint spots of rain began to drum against the corrugated iron, and the wind was moaning and moaning, and the ladder was shaking as he began to climb down. A splinter of wood buried itself in the bulb of his thumb, and it made him think of the children's collection of Shakespeare stories his mother had bought him.

By the pricking of my thumbs, something wicked this way comes.

Evan's face was a pale daub in the darkness, one slipper resting on the third-from-top rung, his hand gripping the one above, torch stuffed down the band of his pyjama bottoms.

The wind was still moaning.

Except it didn't sound like the wind anymore.

It sounded human.

Evan squeezed his eyes shut, and the speed of his heart was the echo of his childhood; the beat of a wooden spoon against a tub, the pound of a toy drum, the banging of his fists against a saucepan.

He wondered if the killer was coming for him and a sob rose in him. The police lady had said she was going to wait one more day until she started looking for his mother. He wondered if they always took that long. If the killer was in his garden, it would be too late for him. He would be dead by then.

But then he remembered that his mother had taught him to stand up to bullies, to find his courage and to use it, and he made himself open his eyes.

Evan peered over the edge of the ladder, in the direction of the sound. It was coming from the copse, but all he could see was a bank of trees, and the fence that ran across the length of the bottom of his garden.

He reached for his torch and switched it on, sweeping it across the copse, illuminating the claws of the trees, and they were reaching for him, and so he swung the torch lower until it ran across the inside of a deep drainage ditch that he had barely even noticed before.

His torch spotlit pockets of toadstools and dried mud, fallen leaves and ferns and weeds. He saw a flicker of movement, a mouse scrambling out of the way of the beam, and a sandal.

His mother's sandal.

And lying in that ditch was a familiar shape in a poppy-red dressing gown.

84

The copse – 2.33 a.m.

Despite her family's fears, Olivia Lockwood was not missing, nor was she dead. She was lying face down, dirt in her mouth and nose, leaves tangled in her hair, disoriented and dizzy, but very much alive.

Twisted beneath her was the leg that had broken in three places when she had stumbled into the ditch during the darkness of the previous night. Her wrist had snapped when she had thrust it outwards to break her fall. A large bruise was beginning to form near the top of her forehead. Although she did not know it yet, Olivia had suffered a linear fracture of her skull when she had smacked it against the corner of a wooden crate that had, in the extreme heat, worked its way to the surface of the dried-out and shrunken soil.

She had been unconscious for three or four hours after the fall, although she couldn't remember the precise details of waking up, apart from an overwhelming sense of nausea. All she knew was the pain in her broken limbs had been so extreme that she had spent much of the last day in a semi-conscious state, drifting in and out of a patchy sort of greyness, unable even to muster the energy to call out.

The fence, trees, plant detritus and the deep sides of the ditch that had hidden her from the house had also largely shielded her from the fierce gaze of the sun, although one of her legs had been exposed and sunburn blistered her calf.

Her tongue was swollen and rough, and had stuck to the roof of her mouth. Her breath came in rapid gasps. She was badly dehydrated. As the rain fell onto her face, she tried to lift her head and wet her lips, but even that felt like too much effort, triggering another bout of dizziness.

She shifted in the dirt, trying to clear her vision, and experienced another landslip of pain. Olivia moaned, and in her half-there state, she thought she heard one of her children calling to her. She knew, with certainty, that she had a son, although she couldn't remember his name, couldn't form a memory of him.

Nor could she remember returning from the car and catching the flicker of a torch at the bottom of the garden or stumbling into the ditch as she had gone to investigate.

Her mobile phone was lying amongst the leaves and insects a couple of metres beyond where she lay, its battery long dead. The sound of rustling leaves filled up the spaces in her head, and she thought that she might like to sleep for a very long time.

'Mummy.' Hands stroked her hair from her face, and she tried to smile, but the muscles of her cheeks could not seem to move. 'Mummy, wake up.'

The boy was shaking her, and it was making her head hurt and shooting pain down her shoulder, towards her broken wrist. She couldn't form the words to ask him to stop, but he must have guessed because he said, 'Don't move, Mum. I'm going to get Dad.' And she heard that rustle of leaves again, the sound of small hands and feet scrambling through brambles, trying to clamber up the sides of the ditch, and her eyes did not want to open, but she became aware again of the absence of light and the dark mouth of the night.

She could not say how many minutes had passed, only that she was drifting and floating, and then she heard loud voices and lights, and strangers were speaking to her in calm voices, and sliding her onto a spinal board and she could not remember how she had got there or what had happened.

'Thank God,' said a man's voice, and his lips were warm against her cheek. He said things like 'I love you' and 'I'm sorry for being such a dick' and 'Things are going to be much better from now on, I promise.'

Her eyes flickered open and closed, and the skeletons of the trees above bowed to her, and the moon was cold and she saw snapshots of black and silver, and felt the rain on her face, and she thought, *Is this what it is to die?*

She wanted to scream at them to leave her where she was because the moving of her body had triggered a wave of agony, but the monochrome landscape blurred until all the colours were washed out, and her world collapsed in on itself.

85

27 The Avenue – 2.41 a.m.

The walls were talking to her.

Audrina could hear the cry of a child, like the slash of a knife across the peace, disembowelling it. Unexplained noises. A thump. Footsteps running across carpet. The register of a boy's voice, high and clear. For the briefest of moments, she mistook him for another boy from another time.

She floated up through sleep, throwing it off, eyes wide open, heart buzzing, hands reaching for a ghost.

The blue wash of sirens lit her bedroom. A man's voice, low and serious, was talking beneath her window. At the slamming of a van door, she pulled herself up in bed, fear in her eyes, fingers plucking at the cotton tie of her nightie.

'Surely not another one?' When he didn't answer, she felt the first stirrings of panic, as if something important had changed. 'Cooper? *Cooper?*'

Cooper was at the window, peering down on the street

below. His white hair looked yellowish. He shook his head. 'No. But it's something.'

'Come back to bed,' she said.

But he didn't move.

Audrina could feel the foundations beneath her start to tip. She looked at the man she had married all those years ago, could hear the echoes of everything she had lost, and the knowledge that had weighed upon her. Upon them both.

'Cooper,' she said again, and her voice cracked. He turned towards her then, as he had always done. As he always would do. He crossed the room, and the heft of his body on the edge of the mattress tipped her towards him.

His fingers were tender as he stroked her face. She rested her cheek against his hand, closed her own fingers around his.

'I love you,' he said. 'Fifty-two years, and that has never changed. That will never change.'

'I'm scared.'

'You have nothing to be scared of.' He sounded warm, reassuring. Kindly. 'I will look after you. Like I've always done. Like I always will do.'

'Cooper, I—'

'Hush now, don't say anything,' he said, and pressed a finger to her lips to silence her. 'Do you understand?'

He was smiling at her, and there was so much love in his eyes, and she wanted to tell him that everything would pass. That they would ride this storm, as they had ridden countless others. But instead, she nodded and he said, 'Good girl.'

And then he pulled on his clothes and went downstairs.

86

25 The Avenue – 2.42 a.m.

Evan watched the rescue unfold from the edge of the ditch. The paramedics had administered pain relief and he saw his mother's face relax into unconsciousness.

His father pulled him into a hug, picked him up and swung him around. 'Well done, Evan,' he said. '*Well done.*' The paramedics were about to carry her up the garden to the waiting ambulance. They were moving with extreme caution. 'You might just have saved your mother's life.'

His father did not ask why Evan had been out of bed. The boy guessed that question was for another time. Or perhaps not at all. When he thought about what might have happened if he hadn't gone down to the treehouse, he felt odd and shaky.

'Go and wake Aster. I'm going to follow the ambulance in my car. I'll call your aunt, and she can drive down and mind you.' The relief in his father's face pushed Evan to the edge of tears.

* * *

Aster was not in her bedroom. She was not anywhere in the house at all.

Evan was trying to think of a way to share this worrying development with his father when a commotion by the front door stalled him. The boy sat on the staircase, his face pressed against the spindles.

His father was dangling his car keys in his hand, talking on his mobile phone. In another hour, the sky would begin to lighten, darkness diluting into a full-blown blue. Garrick shut down his call, opened the door, and there stood Aster with a crying boy who was dripping with red paint.

Evan was tired and he rubbed his eyes. When he looked again, the older boy was still there.

His father did not react in the way that Evan expected him to. At all. He took one look at Aster's face, and the boy clutching his arm, and he said, 'Let's get you sorted out,' in a voice that was gentler than Evan had heard in a long time. Aster's lip wobbled and she ran to her father, and Evan heard him murmur, 'It's OK, sweetheart, we've found Mum.'

The ambulance had already left with Olivia, and so Garrick loaded the boy into his car and instructed both of the children to go to bed. Their aunt would be there in the morning.

'You're in charge, Aster,' he said. 'I'm trusting you not to leave the house this time.' She nodded, a miserable expression on her face.

Her father gave her a rough hug. 'I'll call you with news as soon as I have it,' he said. Then he was gone.

* * *

Neither child was tired enough for bed, the residue of adrenaline from the night's events still spinning through their young bodies.

Aster made them both hot chocolate, but Evan couldn't bring himself to enjoy its cloying sweetness, fear for his mother like a lead weight in his stomach.

His sister was reluctant to talk about what had happened at the old man's shop, but Evan had been unable to contain his own adventure, the facts spilling from him like water from a well.

'She might have been able to shout for help if she hadn't banged her head,' he explained. 'They don't know yet. Or maybe she did call for help, but it was night-time and no one heard her. Or maybe the pain from her broken bones was too much to cope with and passing out was her body's defence mechanism.' He was parroting the conversations he had overheard between his father and the paramedics. But then he was back to being Evan. 'She hit her head on a box, Aster, and the bruise looked like a flower.'

'What type of a box?' It was an idle question from Aster. She was rinsing out their mugs, dark circles beneath her eyes like half-moons, yawning, not expecting much of an answer.

'I don't know,' said her brother. But it triggered something inside him, and all of a sudden, he burned to know what was inside that buried crate with its smear of blood on the edge where his mother had hit it when she'd fallen.

The first streaks of dawn were opening up the day when Evan ran down the garden, the grass still shiny from the rain. In his haste, he slipped over, muddying his knees, but then he was up and off again, through the gate in their fence and skidding down into the dip of the ditch.

The crate was in exactly the same place. Not on either of their properties, but roughly halfway between 25 and 27 The Avenue, and in the copse that lay beyond the fences at the bottom of their gardens.

It was about the size of the box that his parents' wine was delivered in at Christmas, twelve bottles all at once. But it had a lid, and there were nails in the wood, and one corner protruded from the ditch. Evan did not know this, but the hot weather had pushed it up through the shrinking, dried-out earth.

Evan tugged at it, but it was lodged in the dirt and it wouldn't shift. He stared at it, hands on his hips, when a shadow-shape in front of him said, 'Let me help you with that.'

Cooper Clifton, the man from next door, was standing by the section of ditch that ran behind his own garden fence. He shut his gate before Evan had a chance to protest.

In one hand he carried a spade, and its steel edge gleamed hard and sharp.

87

4 Hillside Crescent – 2.48 a.m.

Wildeve took a large mouthful of coffee and picked up her keys. Showered, dressed and ready to go in twenty minutes. *Not bad, Wild.*

Of all the phone calls she might have expected to receive at almost half past two in the morning, that had not been one of them.

'Hello?'

'*Wildeve, it's Roger Sampson.*'

The Detective Chief Inspector had sounded wary, as though he was uncertain of his reception.

'It's very late.'

'*Or early, depending on your point of view.*' He had grunted and she guessed he'd been dragged from his own bed, which meant something significant had happened.

She had stifled a yawn. 'What can I do for you, guv?'

'*It's Lovell. He wants to talk.*'

Wildeve bit back her natural instinct towards sarcasm. 'That's great.' But that didn't explain why Sampson was

331

calling her at this unsociable hour. 'I'm not sure what that's got to do with me.'

'*He wants to talk to you.*'

Wildeve had leaned back against the pillows of her bed, the photo album forgotten, electrified by his change of heart.

'Why me?'

'*Because of Adam.*'

'When?'

'*Now.*'

'Any chance it can wait until morning?'

'*'Fraid not. He says he knows who the killer is.*'

88

Now

The beginning of the end.

If only we could freeze that fragment of time when things begin to unspool, we might catch the end of the thread between our fingers, wind it back onto the reel and tie it off with a knot.

I could not begin to say when I realized that the comfortable shape of my life was drawing to a close. Perhaps it was that third time I took a life that did not belong to me. Or Adam Stanton's death. Or the day that the Lockwoods moved in. Perhaps it was Mr Lovell's discovery, his subsequent phone calls.

But if I had to choose, I believe it was in the uncertain light of the dawn when the ambulance came to The Avenue, and Evan Lockwood opened more than a can of worms.

89

Interview Room, Rayleigh Police Station – 3.27 a.m.

Trefor Lovell's eyes were dark holes in his face, and there were bristles on his chin. He smelled of sweat and dirty clothes.

A cup of coffee was on the table in front of him, but he did not touch it. When Wildeve entered the interview suite, he smiled up at her.

DCI Sampson was not usually present for interviews, but he had opted to sit in on this one. In truth, he was dubious about the sergeant's ability to conduct herself properly, but if this was the only way that Lovell would talk, he was prepared to take a gamble.

He had given her an up-to-date briefing on the phone. Tests had confirmed that the 'make-up' on the victims was a specialist kind of doll paint. His attitude was evident in the way he held himself, the aggressive forward slant of his body. He had seen what Lovell had done to DC French and he was certain the old man was guilty.

The harsh light blanched all lines from the faces in the

334

room. It was not a large space. A table. Two chairs either side of it. A machine to record their conversation.

Wildeve introduced herself, gestured at DCI Sampson and Trefor Lovell to do the same, recorded the time and date, and read the suspect his rights. She was ready to begin.

'You're entitled to legal representation, Mr Lovell. You may find it useful.'

He shook his head. 'I don't need it. The only thing I've done wrong is hurt that officer of yours, and I'm prepared to take responsibility for that, even though he provoked me.'

'There was a dead body in your house, Mr Lovell? Who was it?'

'Annie, my wife.'

'She'd been dead for a long time.'

His eyes filled with tears. 'Yes.' He cleared his throat. 'She had bone cancer and it spread. I didn't want to let her go.' His voice broke. 'I couldn't.'

Wildeve felt the heat of grief in the back of her own throat. Their eyes met and she read the sympathy in his, and so she busied herself by glancing through the paperwork in front of her. 'Your GP has confirmed her illness. We'll see what the post-mortem says.' In truth, the PM might not show much at all, given the state of her body, but she wasn't about to share that.

He shrugged. 'It won't show anything different.'

She changed tack. 'Mr Lovell, five bodies have been found in the woods that edge the place you live and work. Is there anything you would like to tell us about that?'

'Aye, it's awful. God rest their souls.'

'Did you know any of them?'

'No.'

'Don't you think it's a coincidence that you make dolls, and each of the victims was found with glass eyes in their sockets? That you have a talent for painting the faces of your dolls, and each face was skilfully made up with paint?'

A bitter laugh. 'Of course it's not a coincidence. Someone was trying to set me up.'

'Is that so?' DCI Sampson couldn't contain himself. Wildeve gritted her teeth, but Lovell only laughed again.

'Obvious, isn't it?'

'Not entirely.' Wildeve leaned forward. 'Do you have any idea who?'

'I have my suspicions.'

'Care to share them?'

He opened his mouth to answer, but the door to the interview suite opened, and PC Taylor stuck his head through the door, his cheeks reddening.

'Sorry to interrupt you. There's a call for you, Wildeve. Won't wait, apparently.'

Wildeve picked up the extension, irritated by the interruption.

'This is Wildeve Stanton.'

'*It's Mac.*'

She was surprised to hear from him. 'What's up, Mac? It's the middle of the night. And I'm interviewing a suspect. Is it urgent?'

'*Sampson call you in, did he? I guessed he might need you in the end. Is it Lovell?*'

She heard the blare of an ambulance siren. 'Are you at the hospital? Is everything OK?'

'*I've just had a call from an old nurse mate of mine who owes me a favour. He didn't realize I was off the case.*'

'Go on.'

'*Garrick Lockwood's wife's turned up.*'

In truth, Wildeve had forgotten all about her, distracted by events of the last couple of hours. 'That's great, Mac, but I'd better go. I think I'm getting somewhere with Lovell.'

'*Yes, but that's not all.*'

'Go on.'

'*He's just treated a kid with a gunshot wound in his arm.*'

'And?'

'*And the kid was breaking into a place in The Avenue when he was shot.*'

'Which house?'

'*It wasn't a house.*'

A pricking across the back of her neck. 'Where then?' she said, but she already knew what he was going to say.

'*That toy shop at the top of the road,*' he said. '*The one belonging to Trefor Lovell. And, Wildeve, you need to prepare yourself. Adam's ID was inside.*'

90

26 The Avenue – 3.39 a.m.

The dressing-gown belt was drawn so tightly around his hand that the bones of his knuckles were visible through his skin.

Dessie recognized it as the one belonging to the new woman opposite. She'd been wearing it a day or two ago as she'd hefted rubbish bags into her wheelie bin. The same woman was now missing, according to her husband, who'd knocked on Dessie's door earlier in the day, asking if she'd seen her. She swallowed and her mouth tasted sour.

'What were you doing?' Fletcher's voice was pleasant and even. That frightened her more than anything else. His gaze lingered on the camera by her feet and they both knew.

'I . . .' She didn't have the faintest idea what to say to him.

'You found it then,' he said. No question, just a statement of truth.

'You lied to me,' she said. She tried to keep her voice steady, but it broke on *lied*.

338

'What are you going to do?' He took a step towards her, and she flinched, pressing herself closer to the wall, trying to make herself disappear. 'Are you going to tell the police?'

'Fletch—' The police had to be told. It was the right thing to do. The only thing.

'They'll put me in prison this time, Dessie.'

She shook her head. 'No, no, I'm sure it won't be like that. You can explain that you didn't mean to take those pictures, and you need to get help—'

'And you think they'll believe that? This is a second offence, Dessie. A custodial sentence.'

'You'll think of something, Fletch.' Her eyes were pleading with him to make this easy for her, to accept his mistakes and to walk away without a fight.

His fingers bruised her arms. 'Two years, Dessie. Maximum sentence for voyeurism.'

She thought about lying to him, promising that she would not tell a soul about the photographs she had discovered on his camera, that she would keep his secrets buried in a place that she would never visit and would allow to grow over, covered in brambles. But she could not bring herself to say that. Because it was not true.

He was looking at her, and she stared back at him, a challenge. She thought she saw love in his eyes, and a tentative plea for clemency. But she could not bring herself to offer him the reassurance of even a half-smile.

A siren wailed in the street outside.

'Why have you got that belt? It belongs to that woman across the road.' She swallowed again. 'The missing one.'

'I saw her last night,' he said. 'She lost it.'

She flinched again and his grip loosened, his hands

falling away. She wrapped her arms across her chest, rubbing at her violated skin. The expression on his face had changed to sorrow.

The camera was still lying on the floor. She calculated it would take less than three seconds to grab it. Around six seconds to make it to the end of the hallway, open the front door and run into the street. Another couple of minutes to alert the police. Or perhaps she could run to the end of the road. See if those officers were still waiting in their car outside number thirty-two.

Fletcher was unspooling the dressing-gown cord he had wrapped around his knuckles. The skin on his hand was marked, indented. He smoothed out the belt, its silk creased and spoiled now.

He stepped towards her, hands reaching for her.

Dessie kneeled forward, her limbs loose and liquid, and for a tantalizing moment, it looked as though she was moving towards Fletcher, to immerse herself in the warmth of their love.

But his girlfriend snatched up the camera and bolted for the front door.

Fletcher watched the woman he loved run from him. But he did not call after her. He let her go.

The mess of his life was nothing more than a dirty scribble on the page. No way to erase it. No way to start again now. Even if he tore it into a dozen pieces, the stain would still be there.

The boxes of tablets were spilled across the hallway floor. He did not bother to pick them up. Soon the police would come. He would lose his job again. He had already lost the love of his life.

They might try to pin those murders on him.

And there was an ambulance outside number twenty-five. Was Mrs Lockwood hurt? She'd been upset but she hadn't wanted to talk to him. Who would believe him when he said he'd found the belt snagged on the bushes *after* she'd left? That he'd intended no harm, but had wanted it as a keepsake, a coveted treasure to hide amongst his photographs. To stroke and press against his skin. With his track record, not even Dessie.

The fear of prison – of what might happen to him while the guards looked away – was swallowing him up, threatening to drown him. He could run. He could grab his clothes and his wallet, and he could hide himself from the world until it was safe to live again. He'd done that before. He could do it again.

But he remembered how that had felt. The scour of anxiety in the pit of his stomach at every job interview, every new friendship. That was no life. And if that was his future, that was not a future at all.

The ribbon of silk had entwined itself around his fingers. He trudged upstairs, the weight of his body making every step creak.

Marriage. A family. Once upon a time, he had longed for those prizes, but they were not for the likes of him. He could not resist his impulses, not even when every fibre of himself fought to look away. Caught in the pull of a magnet, he found himself helpless. Weakened. No woman would accept that. And the cycle of secrecy and discovery would roll on until he was wrung dry of all hope and feeling, and he would find himself right back in this dark place again.

The spare room was how he had left it, telescope pointing to the sky.

The rain had rolled in and the clouds were gathering. *Nimbostratus. Cumulonimbus.* He repeated their names over and over until he stopped crying and his breathing had calmed.

From his vantage point at the window, a barefoot Dessie was half running down the street towards the parked police car outside Trefor Lovell's house. Not much time. Five minutes. Ten, at the most.

Fletcher opened the wardrobe door and dragged free the stepladder they used to access the loft. Its metal feet scraped his shin, an ugly burst of pain, but he did not feel it. He was somewhere else now, at peace with himself, a decision made.

He positioned the ladder beneath the opening of the loft, climbed up, pushed against the hatch, and heaved himself through until he was sitting on its edge, feet dangling below him. Leaning across, he looped the silk dressing-gown belt around the floor joist, tying it off. He tugged on it as hard as he could. It held. With the tip of his toe, he kicked away the ladder.

His fingers worked the rest of the length of fabric, deft and sure, the memory of his father's voice as fresh as yesterday. The reef knot. Clove hitch. Figure of eight. Sheet bend. Bowline. *Come on, Benji. Make sure it's nice and tight. Don't want it to unravel at a crucial moment, son. Your life might depend on it.*

Yes, Daddy.

THE NEIGHBOUR

And the knot hadn't unravelled, had it? Not twenty-five years ago when the path of Benjamin Turner's young life, bordered by farm animals and meadows and sweet-smelling flowers, had taken him off the edge of the cliff.

For a moment, he was back there again, right on the precipice. He remembered his own breath, coming faster and faster, a band of pain across his chest, tightening with each footstep, and the feel of wheat brushing against his calves as he pounded through the long grasses. *Daddy, where are you? Dinner's on the table. Daddy. Daddy.*

He had only stopped by the barn in the top field because he had noticed his father's cap hanging on a nail where they kept an old bucket.

Daddy, are you in there?

He had called again for his father, excited to have found him, and hungry for his own meal. Pushed against the barn door, anticipation written into the innocence of his face, words of entreaty rising to his lips. *Come on, Daddy, hurry up. It's spaghetti bolognese.*

Three memories had remained with him from that Thursday teatime on a sunny afternoon all those years ago.

The stink of hours-old urine.

A bucket on its side amidst the hay and dirt.

And his father's body swinging from the rafters, a puppet on a string.

Fletcher blinked. Those photographs of the past – brought to life by the events of these final hours – were taking shape into something more concrete, drawing out the silver halides, sealing the negative in place. Black and white. Right and wrong. Life or death.

His fingers traced the silk cord he'd fashioned into a hangman's knot.

Fletcher placed the ligature around his neck.

The film of his life – all those mistakes, the hurt and the highs, the love and the terrible, terrible lows – began to play. But each memory was a spike of glass.

Fletcher closed his eyes to shut off the images. He thought about the rarest of cloud formations he dreamed he would one day witness. The UFO-shaped *lenticularis*, the iridescent beauty of *nacreous*, the magnificent power of a *supercell* storm.

Lenticularis. Nacreous. Supercell.

He murmured them over and over again, as if the rolling rumble of the words would ward off the fear in his heart.

And then Fletcher Parnell – once a young boy filled with hope named Benjamin Turner – tipped forward and let himself fall.

91

Interview Room, Rayleigh Police Station – 3.40 a.m.

Wildeve could feel a fire within her grow.

'Mr Lovell, that was a colleague on the phone. A sixteen-year-old boy has been shot with a gun that discharged in your shop.' She slammed her hand on the table. 'It was a deliberate set-up, apparently. A trap. What the hell is going on?'

DCI Sampson's head jerked up in surprise. Lovell let out a moan.

'Did it – is he—?'

'You're lucky he isn't dead.'

Lovell seemed to shrink, as if the air was being sucked out of him. Wildeve moved her chair a little closer.

Her voice was ice. 'That's not the only thing in your shop. Perhaps you would care to explain how Detective Inspector Adam Stanton's warrant card found its way there too.'

Lovell's mouth sagged open.

'This isn't looking good for you,' she said. She counted

off on her fingers. 'The dead body of your wife, the doll's eyes, the paint on the bodies of the victims, the identification of a murdered police officer you spoke to on the day of his death found on your property, and now a kid with a gunshot wound. Concealing a body. Possession of unlawful ammunition and an unlicensed firearm. You'll be going to prison for a very long time.'

'I didn't do anything,' he said.

'It will be better for you in court if you tell us the truth now,' she said.

'I didn't do anything.' He was insistent and his gaze was steady. No shifting eye contact or overconfident *No comment*. No body language to indicate he was telling her anything but the truth. To hide her confusion, she took a sip of water.

'Mr Lovell, why would you have a gun in your shop?'

'It's not a real gun. It's home-made. It fires newspaper pellets. Mix them with sodium chlorate and charcoal and sulphur and they pack a heck of a punch.'

'But it was aimed at the door, ready to—'

'It was suspended from the ceiling of the shop and connected to a battery-powered tripwire. It was aimed at the door to deter intruders.'

'And you get a lot of those, do you? Reported them to the police yet?'

'No,' he said softly. 'Except those damn kids. Didn't expect *them* to break in, though, did I? I go in the back way and disable it in the morning when I go into work. I—'

'But you think that someone is regularly coming into your shop?'

'I know they are.'

She raised her eyebrows to express her disbelief.

She changed tack. 'How long have you owned the Doll & Fancy Dress Emporium, Mr Lovell?'

An expression of startled surprise lit his face.

'I don't own it,' he said. 'I'm just a tenant.' He looked at them both. 'I thought you knew that.'

Wildeve was aware of Sampson pulling himself up a little straighter. Her own breath caught at the back of her throat. Lovell picked at a spot of dried paint on his trousers and carried on talking.

'They've got a key, see? Let themselves in as often as they like. Muddling around. Taking things that don't belong to them. My paints. The eyes. *That's* why I set the trap.'

'Who owns the shop?'

The question fell from her lips, a stone disturbing the stillness of the room. She imagined it rippling across the surface, setting off a chain of events that would allow those five lost souls to find their way home. Four words that might hold the key to this investigation.

To her husband's murder.

'The old couple at number twenty-seven. Cooper and Audrina Clifton.'

92

The copse – 5.11 a.m.

Evan was thinking about Lucas Naylor. An in-and-out friend. He called him that because sometimes he was fun to be around and sometimes he was cruel. Mostly cruel.

But he'd do anything to have Lucas Naylor by his side right now.

Cooper Clifton was burying the spade in the soil and each strike of the earth caused Evan to flinch. Although the heat had broken, most of the rain had run off the land and the mud was solid, difficult to split apart.

The edge of the blade hit the crate and the wood splintered. Cooper swore softly under his breath and Evan watched with wide-open eyes. The old man slid his spade down the side of the crate, into the dirt, and leaned on the handle, using his weight to lever it free.

The box loosened and lifted from its grave.

Cooper smiled at Evan.

'Give me a hand, will you?'

Evan was used to obeying the command of an adult.

Although some children might have refused, he was young for his age and not yet confident enough to challenge Mr Clifton's authority. But he was stubborn too, with a keen sense of justice. As far as he was concerned, the box was his. He leaned forward and picked up two corners of the crate, Mr Clifton on the other side.

'I'll come back for my spade,' the old man said.

Evan wanted to explain to Mr Clifton that the box belonged to him because his mother had found it, and he wanted to see if there was treasure inside. Everyone knew it was finders keepers. But the old man was edging towards the gate of his own house, a determined look on his face, and Evan had no choice but to follow him.

Despite the rain, the air was still warm and Evan could smell the waking up of the day, the freshness of the grass, the slow opening of the flowers. The sky was beginning to lighten. He rubbed his eyes and wondered how his mother was faring.

Mr Clifton dumped the crate on the kitchen table. Clods of dirt scarred the tablecloth but the old man didn't seem to care.

Evan stood awkwardly, not wanting to be there but not willing to relinquish a prize he believed to be his.

'Shall we open it?' he said.

'I don't think so,' the old man said.

'But it's mine.' Evan's voice was hot with injustice.

Mr Clifton laughed. 'Actually, it's mine. And I don't want it getting into the wrong hands.'

If he had walked out of the kitchen then, Evan Lockwood might have been allowed to leave, to eat breakfast with his sister and speak on the telephone to his father, who would ring home in exactly six minutes' time to tell them that their mother was in pain but expected to make a full recovery. But the fates conspired against him.

Whether weakened by rot from the years underground, or the force of Cooper's spade, or the pressure of movement from earth to air, one side of the box fell open, dirt flying as it thudded against the tablecloth.

Two sets of eyes stared at its contents.

Evan did not know what he was seeing. He stared at it, trying to process it. A museum exhibit, perhaps. Or a piece of artwork.

He took a step towards it, leaned in for a closer look. And let out a cry.

Inside the box was a human skull, no bigger than his own.

93

Interview Room, Rayleigh Police Station – 4.32 a.m.

The floodgates had opened.

Trefor Lovell could not stop talking. He had taken over the shop almost thirty-one years ago, a few years after he had moved into the street with his wife, Annie. They had become friends with the Cliftons and their young son, Joby. A friendly place, full of community spirit.

But things had changed after Joby ran away. The Cliftons no longer socialized. They withdrew into themselves.

'Wait,' said Wildeve. 'Their son disappeared?'

Lovell nodded. 'They didn't talk about it. Told most folk he'd been sent away to relatives because they couldn't bear to go over every tiny detail. Agonizing, it must have been. But we saw Mr and Mrs Clifton the morning after he took off, and she was white as a sheet, trembling, she was. She had his Walkman in one hand, and Cooper had a bucket of cleaning stuff in the other. He'd been tidying up that tree-house before their neighbours got back. Audrina told me herself that Joby had run away, and Cooper shouted at her.'

'So the police were involved?'

'I suppose so. But we never saw them. We guessed the Cliftons had their reasons for acting like they did.'

'And when was this?'

Lovell scratched his head. 'It must have been the summer of 1985.'

'Did he ever come home?'

'Not that I know of.'

DCI Sampson was watching Lovell intently. Wildeve wiped her palms on her trousers. The time had come to bring up the contents of Adam's documents, but she didn't know how Sampson would react to having been kept in the dark.

'According to some statements from old police files I've – um – obtained, it appears that a former owner of the shop you now rent – Bridget Sawyer – also disappeared. Around September 1966.' Her cheeks reddened under Sampson's gaze.

Lovell nodded, eyes downcast.

'Aye, your husband was investigating that.' He met her eyes. 'He was getting close. I'm sorry about what happened to him.'

A heat again at the back of her throat. She nodded, an acknowledgement.

'He was asking after Joby, too. About when he had gone missing.'

'He knew about him?' Her voice lifted in surprise.

Lovell shrugged. 'I guess so.'

'Do you know how?'

He shook his head, and she saw a drift of dandruff settle on his shoulders.

'What about Bridget Sawyer? What do you know about her?'

The smallest of shrugs, almost imperceptible. 'More than you, by the sounds of things. I'm sorry I didn't tell you sooner.'

She fought to keep the anger from her voice. 'Mr Lovell, you need to stop playing games and tell us everything you know before someone else is killed.'

So he did.

94

Major Incident Room, Rayleigh Police Station – 5.53 a.m.

DCI Sampson called an emergency briefing.

He was short and to the point.

New information had come to light in the past half an hour. It gave them grounds to suspect Cooper Clifton of 27 The Avenue of multiple murders, dating back to 1966.

They were going to bring him in.

And they were going to do it now.

354

95

Between Rayleigh Police Station and The Avenue – 6.15 a.m.

DS Wildeve Stanton was a passenger in her own car, Mac at the wheel.

The older man had come straight from the hospital to the police station. He deserved to be a part of this, even if he had been kicked off the case. 'As long as he stays out of the way,' Sampson had growled.

But it was all as clear as mud.

The police had not had time to verify Lovell's latest revelations, but his story had the ring of truth about it. They would find out soon enough. He was still in custody, they weren't that stupid. But she believed him. She believed every word he had told her.

But she was still puzzled about how Adam had known about Joby Clifton's disappearance.

She watched the streets blur, and imagined her husband's last day on earth. Talking to the neighbours on The Avenue, piecing it all together, a gradual dawning of the truth. The old police statements. The newspaper article. The missing school photograph from Adam's old album.

Croft Lane County Primary School.

If Lovell had been telling the truth, Joby Lockwood vanished in the summer of 1985, when he was ten.

Adam would have been ten then, too.

Another distant ringing in her brain.

She pulled out her mobile, looked up the phone number of the school and left a message for Mrs Hardcastle, the headteacher, urging her to call back as soon as possible.

96

27 The Avenue – 6.17 a.m.

Cooper glanced sadly between the boy and the skull in its wooden crate.

'Now, looky here. That's a crying shame.'

He took a step towards Evan, but there was something in the shape of him that made the child edge away.

'I've been here ages. My dad will be wondering where I am.'

'*Thou shalt not bear false witness against thy neighbour.*' Cooper wagged his finger. 'I saw him get into the car and follow the ambulance with your mother inside. A lie will always be found out, young man.'

Evan bit his lip.

'I really did think things had gone far enough.' Cooper's sigh was full of regrets. He brushed the dirt off the cloth and into the palm of his hand. Lifted down the box and placed it, out of sight, under the table. Then he walked over to the door and called upstairs. 'Audrina? Please come down here.'

He turned back to the boy, full of bonhomie. 'I don't think it's too early for breakfast, do you? Sit down.'

Evan hesitated, his gaze straying towards the back door.

'Sit down,' said Cooper again, grin slipping, iron in his voice.

Evan sat.

'Right,' said Cooper. 'Orange juice.'

He poured the child a glass.

'Now,' he said. 'Breakfast.'

Evan had his back to the kitchen door and when Audrina entered she gave a little scream at the sight of his dark hair and pyjamas, her hand to her mouth.

'What's going on? What's *he* doing here?'

'This lad needs something to eat.'

Something unspoken passed between Cooper and Audrina. She bent over the boy who reminded her so much of her son.

'A muffin?' she said, a warm smile spreading across her face. 'Or cereal with a sprinkling of dried fruit?'

97

Wednesday, 1 August 2018

The Avenue – 6.18 a.m.

Morning had officially broken on The Avenue, the sun drying the earlier rain.

The postman drove his van down the road and parked outside number thirty-two. Mr Lovell's house. The police car was still there, but there was less activity than yesterday. He wondered what had happened to the old man, but knew he would find out soon enough. He trusted his instincts, though. Lovell was harmless.

He swigged some water from a bottle. He had a horrible taste in his mouth, but he had left his toothbrush at home and didn't have time to go back now. Something was worrying him. Nothing more than a niggle, but he had learned over time to trust himself. He had never been wrong.

Except about her.

He shut down the voice in his head. He was not going to fuck this up.

Mrs Clifton had seemed a little agitated this morning. He'd waved to her as she'd collected milk bottles from her

359

doorstep. She always waved back. Always. But not today. Instead she had turned away and shut the door, more distracted than usual.

This concerned the postman a great deal.

He got out and opened the double doors at the back. One small sack of mail. A trolley. His makeshift bed. At the delivery office, he'd bumped into Arthur, who sometimes shared this van. Arthur had given him a strange look when he'd clocked the size of the mailbag and his pillow, but the postman had glossed over it. 'Light load today, mate,' he'd said, but Arthur had seemed unconvinced. He would leave it, he decided. *Don't draw attention to yourself.*

But he was fed up with waiting. He had to do *something.*

The postman rummaged through the letters and parcels until he found the bundle he was looking for, sending up a prayer. He breathed out his relief. *Mr and Mrs Clifton.* Two letters. That was a stroke of luck.

He'd persuade Mrs Clifton to let him in for a cuppa. That should do it.

He shouldered the mail pouch and walked up the garden path.

98

Rayleigh Police Station – 6.20 a.m.

Trefor Lovell's only regret was that he should have shared his suspicions with the police months ago.

The Cliftons had been friends once, but that Cooper was a cold fish. Slippery, too. It had taken Trefor weeks and weeks to notice the dolls' eyes had gone missing, because he preferred to paint them on his creations. But a few days ago, when one of his regular clients had requested a bespoke doll with glass eyes and hair, he had checked his accessories box and been puzzled to discover his supplies were so low. As for the paint, for a long time he assumed he'd been careless, blaming himself for misplacing the specialist pots of *Peach Lip*, *Rosey Blush* and *Soft Lash*. But now he knew.

That bastard Cooper Clifton had set him up.

Lovell shifted on the hard bench of the cell in the custody suite. Their ridiculous game of cat and mouse had finally come to an end.

The old man had found himself in an impossible situation. Eight months ago: that's when he should have gone to

361

the police. The night he'd asked his new neighbour Fletcher Parnell to take some photographs of his dolls for his website.

Fletch had come one evening after work, armed with two cameras and their fancy bits and pieces.

'Look,' he'd said proudly, showing it to Trefor. 'It can do all sorts.'

Trefor hadn't been listening. A basic website was the height of his technological know-how. But Fletch had snapped away happily, occasionally showing Trefor, painting at his workbench, what he had done.

When he had finished, he'd pulled out what looked to Trefor like a lens cap. Fletch had grinned. 'It's an external infrared filter.'

'What does that mean in plain English?'

'It means I can see things invisible to the human eye.'

'Aye. We'd learn a lot about folk if we all had one of those.'

Fletcher had begun to take pictures in Trefor's workroom. The dolls on their shelves. The paint pots, the real hair and eyes.

He had wandered off down the corridor, towards the front of the shop. Trefor hadn't paid him much heed. Fletcher was a friendly enough chap, but nervy and twitchy, as if his body was charged with electricity. He'd let him get on with it.

After a while, Trefor had washed his paintbrushes, wiped over his workbench. The usual end-of-the-day routines.

He was just about to turn out the light when Fletch came barrelling in.

'You have to see this,' he'd said, jerking his head in the direction he'd just come. 'This is seriously weird.'

Trefor had lumbered after him with low expectations.

A dim light was on. Fancy dress costumes lay in

haphazard piles. One clothing rail was pressed against the wall. When he'd agreed to rent the place all those years ago, Cooper Clifton had offered to redecorate. The smell of fresh paint had stayed with Trefor for days.

'Look,' Fletch had said, pointing towards the far wall. 'Can you see it?'

Trefor had looked at him as if he was mad.

'It's a wall.'

'Yes,' said Fletch, fumbling with his camera. 'Now, look at this.'

At first, Trefor could only see the magenta hue of the infrared images on the digital screen. Specks of dirt and lint and smudges that weren't apparent to the naked eye. But as he became accustomed to the peculiarities of the picture, he saw what Fletch was talking about.

Spatter.

He blinked several times. The spots were clustered together, as if something had sprayed against the wall. Beneath it were smears, but they were patchy, like negatives, as if someone had tried to wipe them clean with limited success.

Fletcher was explaining the science behind his discovery, how infrared has longer wavelengths than visible light. But Trefor was not interested. The facts were simple. The camera had cut through multiple layers of paint to reveal this secret.

'What do you think it is?' said Trefor. But he had known.

During the early years, when he'd been young and hungry for action, when he had left the Royal Marines and taken a job abroad in security for an oil company, before he had realized the cost of killing, he had stabbed a thief. The blood had sprayed the wall in exactly the same way.

Someone had died here.

And then he remembered the jokes amongst the other shopkeepers on the parade when he'd taken it over, the mysterious disappearance of Bridget Sawyer and her relationship to Cooper Clifton. And what about Joby Clifton? Losing one family member was careless, but two was surely more than coincidence.

His first instinct had been to call the police. But Fletch was resistant. *No, no, it's none of our business. What if they decide to close you down? Let's not get involved. Whatever happened here, it was a long time ago.* And then Annie had become so ill he had allowed it to slip from his memory.

Until she died and everything had spiralled from his control.

One winter's evening, gone midnight, he'd brought her body in from the garage, but in a rare lapse of judgement, had forgotten to draw the curtains.

A shadow at his window. The white hair of Cooper Clifton.

Trefor had never breathed a word about the disappearance of Cooper's son, Joby. He'd maintained the Cliftons' pretence to protect their feelings. Because of this, he assumed they'd have an understanding, a gentleman's agreement. Each to their own. Live and let live.

A few days later he had bumped into Cooper. His old friend hadn't said it outright, but he had hinted that he knew. That he'd seen Trefor moving his dead wife's body. That he could make life *uncomfortable*. Perhaps raise the rent.

Incensed, Trefor had got his own back.

Anonymous calls to the Cliftons, hinting at his own suspicions about Birdie Sawyer and Joby.

Tit for tat.

But when things began to disappear from his shop, and

the bodies appeared in Blatches Woods, Trefor started to panic. If he contacted the police, he would have to tell them about Annie, and he wasn't ready to do that. If he said nothing, others might die.

What Trefor had not yet been able to puzzle out was how Cooper had known it was him on the end of the phone.

Trefor conjured up the image of a ten-pence piece.

Heads.

Tails.

If he did nothing, he would never speak to Cooper Clifton again. But he wanted that murdering bastard to know exactly who had led the police to him.

He banged on the door of his cell. Minutes passed. He banged again, loud and urgent.

Eventually, an officer appeared. 'I'd like to make a phone call,' said Lovell.

The request was relayed to the duty inspector. Luck was on Trefor's side. The duty inspector wanted to eat his sausage and egg sandwich while it was still hot and grunted his assent.

There were six rings before he heard the click of a receiver being picked up.

'*Hello?*'

'I want to speak to Cooper.'

She sounded wary. '*Who is this?*'

'Just put him on the phone.'

'*He's busy, I'm afraid.*'

'It's Trefor Lovell.' He paused, trying to find a way to frame the words, to let her know that Cooper's attempts to set him up were nothing but dust now.

'I've told the police everything. Your husband is going to die in prison for what he has done.'

99

Now

The police are almost here. The neighbours will gather in tangles on the corner or peer from behind their curtains, ashamed of their prurience but too hungry to deny it.

They will shout at the journalists with their cameras and intrusive questions. They will shake their heads and tut at the spectacle of their street on national television again. They will breathe out their shock at the discovery of a killer in their midst.

Tomorrow morning, these hypocrites will hurry up the street with a newspaper tucked under their arm.

It fascinates me, the way we pretend to be something we're not. The face we show to the world hides a darkness.

Mother. You. Natalie Tiernan, Esther Farnworth, Will Proudfoot, Elijah Outhwaite, Adam Stanton.

A roll call of the dead.

My dead.

But not quite all of them.

Time is almost up. I must say goodbye to my garden in

THE NEIGHBOUR

case I do not see it again. I must walk the corridors of this house.

It's the end of the road.

I am ready.

I will submit.

100

27 The Avenue – 6.27 a.m.

Audrina poured granola into Evan's bowl and sprinkled on an extra handful of raisins from a tub in the cupboard.

'Honey?' she said, already drizzling a spoonful, thick and sweet, across his cereal.

Evan stared at his breakfast, shoulders hunched, head bent. He did not look at either of the adults.

'Eat up,' she said. Kind. Full of encouragement.

Cooper stood by the back door. He was wearing his gardening clothes, and he was holding a small and neatly labelled envelope of seeds he had harvested himself, ready for planting. An ordinary scene in the life of an ordinary family. Except Evan didn't belong to this family and there was a plywood box containing a child's skull under the kitchen table, although Audrina didn't know that.

Audrina's heart broke for herself. For her husband. Fresh lines marked his face. He was old now. Defeated by circumstance. But they would get through this. As they had done before. As they would do now.

'Who was on the phone?' Cooper sounded steady but she had known him for enough years to detect the break in his voice.

She flicked a look at Evan and back again to her husband. Cleared her throat. Started towards him, to soften the blow of her words with touch. 'That Trefor Lovell. He says the pol—'

The sound of sirens filled the kitchen. Their family home. The place where love had found its way through the weeds that might have choked weaker marriages. Cooper's head snapped up. Their eyes met. He held open his arms and she stepped into them. The comfort of the familiar was an undervalued gift.

Through the wall of his chest, Audrina could hear his heartbeat. Constant. Steady. Unwavering. She closed her eyes, breathing in the smell of him. Soap and the earthy scent of geraniums.

'Remember what I told you?' He chucked her lightly under the chin. In some marriages, this might have seemed dismissive or patronising. But not here. This was a gesture of affection. A tender goodbye.

'I love you, Audrina.'

She shook her head, a violent denial. 'No, Cooper. I—'

He placed his finger on her lips. 'Hush now, my love. You've been a good wife. I've been happy. Haven't you?'

'Yes, but—'

'No buts, my love. Promise me you'll do as I ask.'

'Cooper . . .'

'Promise me.'

'I promise.'

He kissed her. To a casual observer, it may have seemed

chaste. His lips grazed hers, barely touching. But every ounce of love he felt for her was in that kiss, his desire to protect and cherish and honour as undiminished as the day he met her.

The back door slammed. The sound of running foot-steps.

Cooper and Audrina spun around in unison. A spoon lay on the floor, two or three droplets of milk marking the lino-leum. The boy had gone.

And so had the crate.

Cooper's lips pressed together until they went white around the edges. His shoulders slumped, the balloon of his hope pricked. Audrina brought her handkerchief to her mouth. Their hands sought and found each other, fingers entwined like vines.

Time slowed and stilled. Blue lights moved against the walls in a hypnotic dance. The clock in the hallway counted down. Neither moved, savouring this pause in breath before their lives were split apart.

The sound of loud voices and heavy hammering at the door.

'"*Those who have courage and faith shall never perish in misery.*"' Cooper was trying to smile, and Audrina had a pain inside her, flavoured with regret and a quiet sort of anger that was filling her up, setting her alight.

'I can't live without you,' she said, and there was so much truth in those words that she did not know where to put it, how to shape it.

'You can,' he said, and his anger had teeth. 'You must.'

And she nodded at him, slow and sad. Resigned to this hand of cards.

THE NEIGHBOUR

Cooper discarded Evan's uneaten cereal in the dustbin and put the packet of seeds on the table. The envelope was open and a handful spilled across the cloth. He moved towards her, and they lost themselves in one last kiss, a slow-falling stepping off a cliff. Fifty-two years of shared history. A promise, then, to protect their past, to steady their present and light their future.

'I'm sorry,' he said.

And then Cooper Clifton opened the door to meet his fate.

101

27 The Avenue – 6.28 a.m.

In the beginning, it was never about the killings. That came much later, when too much water had passed under the bridge and going back would be like rubbing himself out.

There had been no intent, not at first. But falling in love had triggered a rare kind of alchemy, and by the time Cooper had recognized the threat of it all, he was in too deep to find his way home.

Not that he had wanted to.

The sense of power had been unexpected. It had started with the old woman, years and years ago. Bridget. Always going on, she was. *Do this. Do that.* She had made Audrina scrub the shop floor, even though she was eighteen and star-bright, sharper at accounting than most women twice her age. When he had protested, the bitch with the permed hair and crepe-paper hands had stared at him with scorn, eyeing the dirt beneath his nails, the stains on the knees of his trousers, his lack of *everything*.

His anger had ignited, white-hot, blinding him to

common sense and decency. His hands had been trembling when he turned the sign from OPEN to CLOSED. Drew the bolts across and pulled down the blind.

Credit where credit's due, mind. When he'd smacked her on the back of her skull with a wooden mallet, she had staggered, but she hadn't fallen over. She'd been stunned, though, and fracturing bone makes such a distinctive sound.

He'd hit her again and again, the powder flying from her made-up face like dust from a beaten rug, blood spattering the wall. But the child's hammer he'd snatched up from the miniature version of a carpenter's workbench lacked the heft to finish what he had begun. Weakened, yes, but she still had the strength to drag herself away from him, crawling like a baby amongst the teddy bears and building blocks.

He'd cast around, looking for a more effective weapon. The puppets watched him, unblinking. The wooden trains with their tiny passengers paused on their journeys to see what he would do next.

In the end, he'd settled on a spinning top. He'd smashed the metal casing against the wall until it dented and split, and a corkscrew-shaped spike lay in his hand.

He punctured her temple, burying it in her brain.

The blood flowed dark, the thinnest of trickles against the smudge of her face. Rat poison in her mouth to finish the job. Even then, the disorder of death made him uncomfortable.

Bridget Sawyer's body was slight enough to hide in one of the hand-carved chests decorated with the alphabet, all pastel flourishes and curls.

His wedding gift to Audrina, the woman he loved.

102

27 The Avenue – 6.28 a.m.

Cooper Clifton let go of his wife's hand and held out his wrists in submission, his fingers loosely curled into his palms.

'I know why you've come,' he said.

In all her years of policing, Detective Sergeant Wildeve Stanton had never heard a suspect say that.

As the police cars had pulled up outside 27 The Avenue, with its flower-filled garden and freshly painted brickwork, she had thought how it was always the same: that seam of darkness hemming the lives of ordinary folk. That so much of the ugliness of her job was found not in city alleyways or late-night street stabbings, but behind the mown lawns and washed cars and laundry on the line, the mundane and everyday.

Inside lives quietly lived.

She stared at his face. The white softness of his hair. The smile lines that fanned out from his eyes. The inoffensiveness of his ironed polo shirt.

The limp effort of his body.

This man had killed Adam.

The urge to fly at him surprised her. She dreamed of plucking out *his* eyes and dragging her nails down his face, of holding his wrist over the flame of the cooker's gas ring until the skin blistered.

She felt all these things, but she believed in the process of law. Instead she spat out his rights – *arrested on suspicion of murder* – and handcuffed him.

'What on earth's going on?' The older woman had stumbled into the hallway and collapsed into her wheelchair. She wore a look of perplexed mystery.

'Try not to worry, my love.' Mr Clifton attempted to pat his wife's hand, but the bite of the metal forbade it. 'Things will be as right as rain. I'll be home before you know it.'

Mrs Clifton's face crumpled and Wildeve felt a tug of sympathy for her.

'Someone will stay with you,' she said kindly. 'They'll explain what's happening.'

Officers were spreading out across the house, a thorough search already underway. In a minute, Wildeve and Mac would escort Cooper Clifton to the car parked outside. But both of them were distracted by Mrs Clifton, who was clutching at them, plucking at their clothes.

'Please, my husband wouldn't hurt a fly. There's been a terrible mistake. He's not capable of something like that.'

More officers were entering the house, the front door wide open. Noise and chaos. A sense of relief.

And Wildeve and Mac, delighted with their early morning's work, were lulled into a false sense of security by

Cooper Clifton's lack of resistance, his willingness to co-operate.

But Cooper's years of gardening had lent him a wiry strength and he had the element of surprise on his side. He shoulder-barged his way past the female officer coming through the door and found himself on the street outside. Empty.

He threw a glance to his right. His left. Straight ahead.

He took off in the direction of the woods, seeking the cover of trees.

Behind him, the shouts of police officers on his tail. He was a fit man, but they *would* catch him. Wildeve was running too. She was running as if her life depended on it. Because it did.

As she headed towards the mass of woodland, Wildeve threw a look over her shoulder at the house behind her. 27 The Avenue. Modest. Respectable.

Years later, when she was retiring from the police force, a life spent pressed up against the dark heart of human nature, she would still remember Audrina Clifton sitting in that doorway in her wheelchair, a hunted look on her face.

103

The Avenue – 6.37 a.m.

Across the street, the postman was pushing an envelope into a letterbox when a series of shouts ruptured the stillness of the early morning.

His head jerked upwards.

Five minutes earlier, he'd been halfway up the Cliftons' garden path when the scream of police sirens had forced him into the shadows, but he'd been on high alert, a familiar fizz in the pit of his stomach.

The tall hedge of number thirty obscured the postman from view, but his sharp ears caught the sound of footsteps. He stood up and looked over the hedge.

Cooper Clifton was running across The Avenue, towards the entrance of Blatches Woods. The old man was a hair's breadth away and had no idea the postman was there.

He dropped his mail pouch and took off after him.

His soles stung as they slapped against the pavement, but the postman was alive with the joy of the chase. Cooper swerved into the woodland and the postman followed him, light-footed and sure, way ahead of the police officers who were somewhere behind them. Clouds of aphids filled his mouth. Twigs and bracken and the mulch of the forest floor. The blood sang in his veins. The postman was closing the gap between them, but Cooper had the advantage of local knowledge. He knew the paths of this place like his own hand.

The heat of the day was making the postman sweat. It trickled into his eyes, stinging and blurring his vision. His mouth tasted of salt. The pump and flow of his blood roared in his ears. He swiped at his face, trying to clear his sight. And he couldn't see Clifton anymore.

A buzz of panic electrified him.

Alone amongst the trees, he turned on his axis, spinning around, looking for clues, failure taunting him, teasing him. He'd lost him.

But Cooper was twenty-six years older than the postman.

His own heart was thundering in his chest, his legs burning with lactic acid. He stumbled and tripped over the stump of a dead oak.

In the silence of the woods, the postman heard the thump of a body falling. *North-west*. He swung around to the left, following the path deeper into the shadows.

Last time, he had done nothing. He had stood there, and he had stayed silent, and he had let them kill her. The woman he'd persuaded to risk everything. The woman who'd betrayed her lover and turned informant. The woman who had, even at the brutal, bloody end, protected him, and kept his identity a secret from the drug-running gang he had covertly infiltrated.

But this time he was not going to stand by.

THE NEIGHBOUR

Cooper Clifton was lying on his side, his bound hands in front of him.

The postman straddled him, fumbled in his pocket for another pair of handcuffs.

Cooper stared at him, silent, eyes like saucers.

The postman cuffed his ankles, then flashed his warrant card, his own secret revealed.

104

Blatches Woods – 6.43 a.m.

Wildeve Stanton had a stitch in her side. She'd barely eaten over the last couple of days and the pain made her want to bend double, to fall to her knees, but she fought against it. She would not weaken now.

Despite the early hour, sunlight was dappling the leaves, streaming through the gaps between the trees. Woodlice crawled over the bark. The woods were waking up.

Mac was at her side. 'All right?' he said. She nodded, still catching her breath. He checked his phone. 'They're at the north-west corner. Fifty metres or so.' He took in a lungful of air. 'I'm sorry I couldn't tell you.'

She understood. An undercover police officer deserved the protection of his senior officers, no matter what. Mac – a former head of Essex Police's specialist undercover unit – had personally requested him for the job. Adam had known about the operation, too, but not the mechanics of the surveillance or the officer's name. And later, Roger Sampson was also made aware. But the 'postman's' loyalty had remained with his guv'nor, even if he had been forced out. That's why Sampson and his team were still lumbering through the woodland. Old habits die hard and he'd tipped off Mac first.

When Wildeve reached them, Cooper Clifton was sitting up, leaning against the trunk of a hawthorn tree, his hands and ankles cuffed. The undercover officer nodded at her, laid a hand on her shoulder.

'For Adam, eh?'

For Adam.

Adam's investigations into the disappearance of Joby Clifton had pointed the finger of suspicion at the boy's father, Cooper, who had recently been placed under surveillance. In a bid to maintain his cover, and because Royal Mail did not deliver on Sundays, the postman had been absent on the morning that Adam disappeared. A fuck-up with rotas, a lack of bodies, meant no one had filled that gap.

She kneeled beside the old man. His face was grey, patches of sweat in semi-circles beneath his armpits. His right hand was curled into a protective fist.

One word on her lips. 'Why?'

Cooper shrugged, his eyes sliding away. But there was something in his expression. Resignation, yes. But more than that. Acceptance.

She gripped his shoulder. 'Tell me.'

'Greater love has no man than this: to lay down one's life . . .' He was mumbling now, the words spilling from him. He closed his eyes and smiled, as if staring into the face of God himself.

'What do you mean?' She was shaking him now, and he was unresisting, his head flopping back and forth. '*Tell me.*'

A scream was rising in her, a fury so bright and blinding that she did not know if it would ever dim. In her heart, she knew what he had done. Guilty. Plain as day. Written in the slump of his shoulders and the coy smile and the infuriating refusal to explain himself.

Mac pulled her away and she struggled against him, resisting. 'Let me go,' she said, tugging at his arms. 'Get off.'

'Stop it then,' he said. 'Don't give Sampson the satisfaction.'

She threw him off and stalked towards the tree, circled around and back again. Crouched next to Cooper Clifton with fire in her eyes and her heart.

'If you won't tell me why, then tell me how.'

The old man raised his eyes to meet hers. A watery blue sea surrounded by yellowing sclera. His pupils were dilated in the murk of the trees. Tiny red capillaries. Witness to so many horrors.

The wood seemed to still. Time did not march on, but paused, to see what would happen next. The other officers burst into the clearing. DCI Roger Sampson. A couple of uniforms. Five seconds from justice. That was all. The time it took for Cooper Clifton to execute the plan he had so carefully conceived.

In a graceful movement, he lifted his restrained hands to his mouth and funnelled in the contents of his tingling palm.

Four.

Five.

Six of them.

One missed his mouth, and it rolled down the front of his polo shirt and came to rest in his lap.

A small, dark seed. Innocuous. Like the brown button eye of a bird. Or the pupil of a porcelain doll.

Cooper's face twisted at the bitterness, but he forced himself to swallow them, fighting an instinct to spit them out.

The toxins began to work almost immediately, numbing his face and his mouth, slowing the muscles of his heart, triggering respiratory paralysis. He slid down the tree, his breathing laboured, and closed his eyes.

A cry leaked from Wildeve.

She threw herself at him, pumping his chest, willing him to live, the anguish splitting her face almost too painful for her colleagues to witness.

On her hands and knees, she leaned into him, so desperate for him to survive that her judgement was clouded, but Mac was by her side, wrestling her off. 'Don't be stupid, Wildeve,' he said. 'Not mouth to mouth.'

By the time the paramedics arrived, Cooper Clifton was dead.

105

Southside Hospital, Essex – 11.31 a.m.

'*Aconitum napellus* or Monkshood, also known as Devil's Helmet, Wolfsbane and the Queen of Poisons,' said Mathilda Hudson.

The pathologist looked over her glasses at DS Wildeve Stanton and DCI Roger Sampson. 'Fun fact: its deadly toxins were once painted onto arrowheads and used to kill wolves. All parts of the plant are poisonous, especially the seeds and root. Principal toxic alkaloid is aconitine. Causes a numb, burning mouth, hypotension, cardiac arrhythmia and muscle paralysis, although –' she grimaced – 'the brain is still conscious at the end. Invisible in toxicology tests, unless you're looking for it.' She sighed. 'I'm not justifying myself, though. The signs were there. If only I'd known what they meant.'

Sampson cleared his throat. 'There's no blame here, Mathilda. We got the bastard. I'm just relieved he's not around to do it again.' He glanced at Wildeve. 'And we got a result for Adam.'

Wildeve tried to smile. But in truth, she felt cheated. Cooper Clifton was dead. No justice for her or the families. No court case. No victim impact statements. No prison sentence to darken the twilight of his life. No Adam. The future stretched ahead of her, an empty tunnel.

And still so many unanswered questions.

Cooper Clifton had been cultivating the plants in his greenhouse, using his expertise as a gardener. His poor wife had shown them the pots of seedlings, so toxic that even brushing against the leaves with a cut finger could cause harm, and the mature plants by the fence.

'I had no idea,' she said. 'I just thought they were pretty flowers.'

Poor Audrina Clifton. As well as his suicide, she'd had to cope with the knowledge that her mild-mannered and loving husband was a serial killer who had beaten their son and the boy's grandmother to death.

The police had found a handwritten note in his trouser pocket, confessing to seven murders: Bridget Sawyer; Joby Clifton; Natalie Tiernan; Esther Farnworth; Will Proudfoot; Elijah Outhwaite and Adam Stanton.

Adam had been killed because his suspicions about the disappearances of Joby Clifton and Bridget Sawyer had led him to Cooper.

But it was still unclear as to why the other victims had been targeted. Thanks to Cooper's revelations, they had studied the newspaper caption in Adam's belongings, and confirmed that the five children in the photograph, which included Joby Clifton, were at the Doll & Fancy Dress Emporium on the day of the Grand Reopening in 1985. Cooper had killed them all.

Confused and elderly, his wife was less help than they'd hoped. Apart from her family, she was unfamiliar with the names of his victims, except for Adam, and even then, she had only recognized him because he was a police officer who had been working on the case.

As Audrina Clifton explained, she had no idea how Cooper had poisoned his victims, or when or where, or even why. Life had continued as normal, she had explained to them. There had been no signs. None at all.

Wildeve did not think she would ever forget the look on Mrs Clifton's face when she had explained, so gently, about the discovery of the child's bones in the crate after Olivia Lockwood had banged her head.

'We can't be sure,' she told the old woman. 'But the size of the skull is consistent with a child aged around ten.' She had left the rest of the sentence unspoken.

'You think – could it – might it be Joby?'

'It's highly likely,' she said. 'I think you need to prepare yourself for that eventuality.' She had explained to Mrs Clifton that if it had not been for Olivia Lockwood, her son's fate may have remained a mystery. That the tape recording handed in by the Lockwood children was evidence that Joby had been beaten before his death. That Olivia Lockwood's fall in the garden had triggered a chain of events that had led the police back here. To Cooper.

And the skull of her missing son was a key piece of evidence.

Then there was Bridget Sawyer.

Trefor Lovell had shared with them what he and Fletcher Parnell had uncovered on the walls of the shop. Advances in DNA techniques meant they would be able to confirm it. It seemed Cooper had been trying to frame Trefor and tie up loose ends.

Lovell had been bailed but he was due in court next month to face a charge of possessing a firearm with intent to endanger life and grievous bodily harm. He had accepted a caution for failing to register a death.

As for Fletcher Parnell, his suicide had been unfortunate. He had been trapped in the noose of his own guilt and fear.

He, too, was unconnected to these murders.

But something still bothered Wildeve. Cooper had been a calculated and methodical man. Why had he run? She would never know the answer, but she guessed it was for two reasons – because he knew he would be searched before getting into the police car, and he would not defile Audrina's memories of their happy home by killing himself inside it.

DCI Sampson was jubilant at the triumph of Essex Police in tracing a serial killer. He had been garlanded in the press. He had apologized to Mac, who had shaken his hand, and decided that retirement suited him after all. DC French was on extended sick leave. The case was closed. The dizzying whirl of long hours and no sleep and little food was over. All that was left for DS Wildeve Stanton was to fall apart and begin the long road of grieving the death of her husband.

106

25 The Avenue – 2.17 p.m.

It was nearing the end of the holidays, one of those afternoons when the dog days of summer were packed up and put away, when the season was beginning to turn and autumn was a promise in the smell of the air and the lifting leaves. The start of the new school term was a few days away.

A FOR SALE sign stood on the front lawn of 25 The Avenue.

Garrick Lockwood pushed his wife Olivia's wheelchair into the sitting room, which overlooked the garden. He tucked a blanket around her legs, careful not to knock the plaster cast. Her head was healing, but she would have a scar.

'Are you sure you're going to be OK?'

She smiled up at him. 'I'll be fine. I'm going to read and watch the trees and enjoy the peace and quiet.'

He checked his watch. 'Your sister will be here around six. I'm going to get on the road. We'll be back in a couple of days, once I've seen my mother and shown the children the new house. Make sure you rest, Liv. Enjoy the breathing space.'

She grabbed his arm, surprised by her sudden reluctance to let him go. Instead she said, 'I'm glad we're giving this another try, Garrick.'

He kissed her forehead. 'Me too. But we love each other, don't we? That's got to be reason enough.'

Against all odds, Garrick had landed the job at the architect's firm in London. His salary would be enough to rent a small house on the other side of the city while they waited for 25 The Avenue to sell. They had found new schools for the children. Remaking their marriage, their lives. This time they were both determined it would work.

Aster was next to say her goodbyes. Mother and daughter had developed a new closeness in recent weeks. Aster had plaited her mother's hair and painted her nails. Now she kissed her cheek. 'Can't wait until you're well enough for us to go shopping again.' They had both laughed.

And, lastly, Evan. Her precious boy.

'Can't I stay with you, Mum?' His eyes filled with tears. 'I'll help look after you.'

'I know that, sweetheart. But Granny wants to see you, and Daddy wants to show you your new bedroom. You'll have fun and you'll be back before you know it.'

Olivia did not know if Evan understood the extent of their neighbour's killing spree, or how close to danger he'd been. She had not pressed him, and he had not volunteered much. But he had wet the bed a couple of times since he had dragged home the crate containing that young boy's remains. And every day she thanked a God she didn't believe in for sparing her son from Cooper Clifton.

The hallway filled with suitcases and shouted goodbyes. With silence.

Olivia watched the first sycamore seeds of the season spin in the wind, like tiny helicopters. She had not heard from Orson since the night of her accident and she had not contacted him. But her brush with death had opened her eyes. She loved her family, and she would fight for them. A part of her was uncertain, frightened by the future. But she felt lighter than she had done in a long time.

Half an hour later, the doorbell rang.

She grinned. She knew who it was.

'It's open,' she called.

Audrina Clifton bustled into the sitting room. Olivia had put on some music and the swell of the notes filled the room. The women had become closer over the last few weeks, bound together by their shared sense of loss. Olivia's affair was over and Audrina's husband was dead. Both widows, in their own ways.

Audrina hung her coat on the back of the chair and made sure that Olivia was comfortable.

'How about a nice cup of tea?' the older woman said.

When the neighbour returned to the sitting room, she was carrying a tray. Two teacups. A teapot. Milk jug and sugar bowl.

And a plate filled with thick slices of Dundee cake, bulging with raisins.

107

M25 motorway – 2.37 p.m.

In the car, Garrick and Aster Lockwood were singing along to the radio.

His father had not been this happy in months and it gave Evan a warm feeling inside.

He dug around inside his rucksack until he found what he was looking for. He'd promised his cousin he would bring it with him for her to play with, but the truth was, he'd come to rely on its predictions.

Although his mum was out of hospital, he couldn't help but worry about her. But with the countryside speeding past, the exuberant sounds of his family and the knowledge that his aunt was on her way to look after his mother, the boy felt himself begin to relax.

He gave the Magic 8 Ball an enthusiastic shake.

Is everything going to be OK now?

He crossed his fingers, but when he saw its answer, his heart crashed against his ribs.

My reply is no.

108

Sutton Road Crematorium and Cemetery – 2.37 p.m.

Clots of friends and family dressed in black moved across the cemetery like scattered fragments of darkness.

For appearance's sake, Wildeve Stanton stared at the messages tucked into the carpet of flowers until most of the mourners had left, but she did not read them. That was for another time. Instead, she was counting her breaths.

A breath in.. *One.* A breath out. *Two.* A breath in. *Three.* A breath out. *Four.*

A rock to cling to in a sea of desperation.

Grief was a complex emotion. Possible to laugh, she had discovered, to go to work, to eat at the same time as waves crashed against her, threatening to dash her against the cliffs and overwhelm her.

When Wildeve was certain that everyone had left for the pub down the road, she glanced at the order of service. A black and white image of her husband. The dates of his birth and death, stark and irrefutable.

'I'm sorry this had to happen to you.' She traced her finger across his photograph. 'To us.'

Now that Adam's killer had been caught, she had agreed with Roger Sampson to take some leave from work. An old friend owned a lighthouse on Skye and she would spend a couple of weeks there, walking amongst the salt marshes and the sedge.

Her mobile phone vibrated in her pocket.

Ahead of her, she could see Simon and Emily Quick, Mac and his wife Peggy, Adam's university friends, Sampson, even DC French. She raised a hand to show them she was coming. Her phone vibrated again.

She might have ignored it. Most widows saying goodbye to their husbands would have done so. But it occurred to Wildeve that everyone she knew was at the funeral so it was either extremely important or not important at all. Either way, she would decide.

The number was familiar, a vague memory tugged at her.

'Hello?'

'Is that Sergeant Stanton? It's Mrs Hardcastle. I'm so sorry it's taken me a while to call you back, but it's the summer holidays and I've been in France. Today's the first time I've been back in school to pick up messages.'

It took a moment to register. Mrs Hardcastle. Headteacher of Croft Lane County Primary School. She considered explaining about her husband's funeral and the death of Cooper Clifton, but instead she said, 'Thank you for calling me back.'

'That's quite all right,' said Mrs Hardcastle. *'Now, you were*

asking about the admission records for Adam Stanton, is that correct?'

'Yes,' said Wildeve, although she was already tuning out because it no longer mattered.

The headteacher lowered her voice. *'Strictly speaking, under data protection rules, we're not supposed to hold any such records.'*

'I won't tell if you won't,' said Wildeve.

'In which case,' said Mrs Hardcastle, sounding relieved, *'we do appear to have some old files that I've found in storage. Your hunch was right. Adam Stanton did join our school in 1980.'*

'Thank you,' said Wildeve, although she could no longer remember why it had seemed so important to confirm the dates her husband had attended primary school.

The headteacher sounded uncomfortable. *'I'm so sorry to hear what happened to him. I wasn't here when he was a pupil, of course. But my mother's brother-in-law was headmaster at the time and followed his police career closely. We were proud of him.'*

'Thank you.' Wildeve could see the others beckoning to her, the door to the pub opening, animated faces, glasses in hand, filled with all the friends and colleagues whose lives Adam had brushed up against. Drinking and laughing. Remembering.

'Of course, it's such a tragedy, isn't it? Two boys from the same class and both killed by the same man.'

'Excuse me?' said Wildeve, her senses sharpening.

'Adam and his friend Joby Clifton.'

Wildeve frowned, trying to absorb this revelation. Trying to fit the puzzle together, to work out what the pieces meant.

'They were at school together?'

'*That's right. Thick as thieves, my mother's brother-in-law said. He remembers them because they both wanted to be policemen. Knocked at his office after school one afternoon, asking if they were too young to sign up, wanting to right the wrongs of the world.*' An indulgent chuckle. '*Joby left soon afterwards. That was the last the school heard of him until now.*'

Two ten-year-old boys, trying to make a teacher notice them. Trying to make themselves heard.

I'd like to connect with old friends, Wild. That's what Adam had said. That's why he'd gone back to The Avenue. Trying to trace his old friend, Joby. Trying to find out where he was now. He just hadn't mentioned his name.

When Joby had failed to materialize at the school reunion, Adam had searched the electoral roll and run credit checks, but Joby had disappeared off the face of the earth. And when the trail went cold, where else would he try but Joby's family home, his last known address?

Adam must have remembered that his friend's parents had run that toy shop. The disappearances of Joby and Bridget Sawyer had triggered his suspicion of Cooper Clifton.

Across the road, Mac loosened his black tie. She watched him say something to Peggy, and start back towards her.

Something was niggling at her.

What had Audrina Clifton said? That she had recognized Adam Stanton only because he had been investigating the murders in the woods.

But if Joby and Adam had been best friends, she *should* have known exactly who he was.

She *would* have known.

But why bother to keep the boys' shared history a secret? Why not mention it? Wildeve stilled, phone in her hand. Perhaps the old lady thought it didn't matter. Perhaps it didn't.

Unless she had a secret of her own to hide.

Adam's voice was a whisper in her mind, and his logic chilled her.

And then Mathilda Hudson's number was flashing up, her words tumbling down the phone. Wildeve's mouth dried, and she was shouting to Mac, running across cemetery grass, the smell of freshly turned earth in the air and the breath of a ghost on her neck.

109

Bonchurch Park, Essex – 2.37 p.m.

Mathilda Hudson had been pushing her two-year-old daughter on the swings in the park near her home when her mobile phone had pinged with an email.

The pathologist had ignored it. She was on a rare day off and had promised herself that work could wait until tomorrow. But when she'd sneaked a glance, she had noticed it was about the Doll Maker case. Childcare issues had meant she'd been unable to go to Adam Stanton's funeral, but she could honour him in this way instead.

She had settled her daughter at the cafe table with an ice cream and opened the attachment. It was the long-awaited toxicology report on the samples of the stomach contents, and the brown speck from Adam's tooth she had sent off a few weeks ago. Specialist testing often took months, so the quick turnaround was a stroke of luck, even if she already knew what it was going to say.

But as her eyes scanned the report, a bucket of ice water drenched her.

The stomach contents of the five most recent victims had been analysed. As expected, each contained the alkaloid aconitine, a neurotoxin. But it had not come from the seeds of the Monkshood plant, as she had anticipated. There were no signs of seeds at all.

The toxin had come from the root of the plant. It had been ground down and used to cook with.

The conclusion of the report had been simple. Every one of the victims' stomachs had contained a slice of home-made fruit cake, its raisins laced with a promise of death.

110

Now

Here comes a candle to light you to bed, here comes a chopper to chop off your head, chip chop, chip chop, the last one's dead.

My name is Audrina May Clifton.

I was a daughter and a wife and mother.

I am a killer.

But you know that already, don't you?

The sound of your screaming still plays in my dreams, Joby. Sometimes, when I'm on the cusp of sleep, I hear you calling for me, reaching out with your hands, tugging at my clothing the way Cooper tugged your dead body from the treehouse when I told him what I had done. But I do not fold your cold fingers into my own warmth. I stamp on them until you cry out and the accusation in your eyes haunts me.

You haunt me.

I hear your voice in the whisper of the wind and the cry of the migrating birds and the sucking earth of your home-made grave. I see your eyes in the eyes of the young boy from next door, your hair curling at his neck. It's you. I know it is. You've come back to me. For years, I've been waiting for my punishment. The moment of reckoning. And it is now.

I have lied and lied again to protect myself, but it is time to lay out the truth.

On our wedding day, your father made a vow to love and protect me. *Forsaking all others*. He kept that promise all his life. And at the end, when the police found their way to us, he urged me to feign ignorance and sacrificed his freedom to preserve mine.

He was a loyal and honourable man.

Birdie was killed because *I* had begged him to kill her. The scars on my wrist and between my shoulder blades were enough to convince him. But she was still alive as my fingers pushed pellets of rat poison between her lips. Mine was the last face she saw.

We were certain we could forget about what we had done, that we could parcel it up and put it behind us. That hiding her in plain sight was a way to maintain our control.

But you were more observant than I'd realized. On the day of the Grand Reopening, when Natalie Tiernan discovered Birdie's body in the shop, *you* discovered the truth about my mother. You had walked past her photograph in our hallway a thousand times and you recognized the watch on her withered wrist.

Do you have questions, my love? I will do my best to answer them. Forgive me for what you are about to hear.

You begged us to go to the police, but how could we do that? I was forced to make a choice. Sacrifice my husband or my son? I chose to save Cooper. Turns out I was more like Birdie than I had realized.

THE NEIGHBOUR

The sirens are crying. They are closing in now, pulling into the driveway. Three cars. Four of them. When I open the door, the police will be here.

Our future was promised. The simple pleasures of our garden and the sun warming our old skins. But Mr Lovell began to threaten us, bombarding us with telephone calls. He told us we had blood on our hands. We knew it was him, though. The distinctive rhythm of the old ceiling fan in the shop gave him away.

We dared not kill him because we could not be certain who he might have told. Because we had lost the element of surprise. Because he had a gun.

But it forced us to think. If he did tell the police about the blood on the walls, they might follow the trail back to the day of the puppet show. To the discovery of Birdie's body.

But there would be no trail if no one was left to remember.

And who better to frame than a loner who makes dolls, an old man with a skeleton in his closet who we wanted out of our lives?

Cooper had spent his life surrounded by plants and flowers, and I absorbed this knowledge without trying to. *The Poison Garden*, it was called. A book with photographs so glossy they might have been painted.

Page 311. A plant with the most beautiful purple flowers I had ever seen, like the cowl of a monk's hood. The most toxic plant in the garden.

The Northumberland estate where Cooper had worked the summer we got married had a wall of these plants at the far end by the manor house. I was curious about the way their helmets danced in the breeze, the disconnect between beauty and brutality.

When we returned home, I read everything I could. That knowledge stayed with me all my life.

The trick was to overcome the bitterness and disguise the taste. To experiment. Last year, I bought a kitten, ground the root into her meat and jelly, and she ate the lot. When I found her in the laundry basket, hidden amongst the tumble of dirty clothes, she was dead.

Cooper grew the plants and I used them in the cakes that I prepared. Depressed a syringe filled with poison into the raisins. Sugar to sweeten the taste. As a Neighbourhood Watch coordinator, he had a ready-made alibi. Once we had traced our victims and established they were at home by themselves, we posed as fundraisers selling Dundee cakes for charity. Who could refuse an old lady in a wheelchair? On the doorstep, I faked a dizzy spell and we were invited in. If they declined the cake, we forced it into them. The paralysis that followed allowed us to lift their bodies into my wheelchair, heads slumped, tucked under a blanket. By the time we got home, they were usually dead. We removed the eyes, painted the face and later, when the dark came, Cooper pushed my wheelchair into the woods, except it wasn't me sitting in it.

And we were almost finished. We would have been free to live out the rest of our lives in peace. Until the Lockwoods moved in. I was worried about what their diggers might unearth. Cooper tried to find you in the dead of the night, but the earth had shifted and so had his memory. He couldn't remember where he had buried you.

And then Olivia Lockwood, searching for the source of

the torchlight in the copse, hit her head on the box containing your remains and damned us all.

The telephone is ringing, over and over, but I do not let her answer it.

She is closing her eyes now, tears on her cheeks. I press the cake to her mouth, but her lips are flattened into a tight line and she refuses to swallow my gift.

Your old stuffed frog is in my pocket, Joby. I have sewn up the seam for you. I'm sorry I split it open with my knitting needle. Anger has always been my flaw.

And now, there is this.

The scratch of a key in a lock. The thunder of footsteps. A shout. 'Liv, it's me. Are you OK? Evan insisted on coming back to check on you.'

It is time.

Every death has a taste of its own. I expect you know that by now. Cooper is waiting for me. And so, I hope, are you, my boy. Joy and acceptance are my seasonings.

I take a sip of tea. I listen to the ticking of the clock, the slamming of car doors. The shouts of Garrick Lockwood and the police. And for everything I have done, I am still that girl of eleven, standing in the shadow of the woods, poisoned birds laid out at my feet in sacrifice, glorifying in my power over living things.

The crumbs spill across the plate. Sweet with an underwash of bitterness. I touch them to my lips. I break off a piece of the cake and swallow it down. A mouthful. And another.

And I wait.

ACKNOWLEDGEMENTS

In *The Neighbour*, Adam Stanton writes a love letter to his wife, Wildeve. The act of writing that scene made me think about what I might include in such a letter of my own.

For those of you who have read *Rattle* or *The Collector*, you will know my acknowledgements have become a place for me to write about the book's dedication, to offer my own love letter, of sorts. This time, it's the turn of my parents.

And then, as I began to write this, I realized that in some ways, each of the books I've written has been a love letter to them.

To my mum, Ann, who instilled in me a love of reading and writing. Regular trips to the library where I was encouraged to choose as many books as I could carry; word games at the kitchen table every night after dinner; pinning a poem I'd written to her computer at work; believing that I had it in me to reach for this dream and looking after the children while I tried. Thank you, Mum, for everything.

As a dyslexic with little support at school, my dad, Chris, never learned to read and write. He gifted me something very different but equally worthwhile: tenacity; the will to work and the importance of a job well done. Dad, who grew up with nothing but made sure his children had everything, showed me that anything is possible. Thank you.

Books are never written alone. Grateful thanks, as always, to my wonderful agent Sophie Lambert, who is so full of wisdom, and the team at C+W, especially Emma Finn and Alexander Cochran, and to Kari Stuart at ICM.

Being published by Pan Macmillan continues to be a joy and that is largely down to my editor Trish Jackson, a committed, passionate and dedicated champion of my writing. Thanks also to Rosie Wilson, Jayne Osborne, Neil Lang, Fraser Crichton and the sales and marketing teams who work so hard on behalf of not just me, but all authors.

It's important to me to ensure my books are as accurate as I can make them, but I couldn't do this without the industry experts who share their time and expertise so willingly. Thank you to forensic pathologist Dr Benjamin Swift, who has proved to be so generous and tolerant of my stupidity; Joss Hawthorn, Steve Bliss and Rebecca Bradley for such intelligent insights into police matters, and Anya Lipska for her brilliant post-mortem anecdotes. Any mistakes are my own.

When I write, it's mostly at a table in the dining room, on my own. But I'm never *alone*. Thank you to all my writing friends for their endless support, especially the Ladykillers (you know who you are), and to the bloggers and reviewers who take the time to read and review my books. I haven't named you all because I'm worried I'll miss someone out, but I appreciate every review and shout-out. A huge thank you to all the librarians and booksellers who champion and hand-sell my books, especially Fiona Sharp, Rebecca Choudhury and Gemma Allan, and to the readers who listen to them.

Love, as always, to my family. Especially you, Isaac and Alice, my reasons for everything. And to Jason, my husband, who knows me better than anybody else. On my birthday, there were no handbags or spa days, perfume or flowers. Instead, he tracked down a ridiculously expensive forensic investigators' textbook filled with real-life case studies of murders and how they were solved.

I don't think I've ever loved him more.